# MURDER AND THE MAÎTRE D'

# MURDER AND THE MAÎTRE D'

## ALEX COOMBS

NO EXIT PRESS

First published in the UK in 2025 by No Exit Press,
an imprint of Bedford Square Publishers Ltd,
London, UK

noexit.co.uk
@noexitpress

ISBN
978-1-83501-119-5 (Paperback)
978-1-83501-120-1 (eBook)

2 4 6 8 10 9 7 5 3 1

Typeset by Palimpsest Book Production Limited, Falkirk, Stirlingshire

Printed in Great Britain by CPI Group (UK) Ltd, Croydon CR0 4YY

The manufacturer's authorised representative in the EU for
product safety is Easy Access System Europe, Mustamäe tee 50,
10621 Tallinn, Estonia

gpsr.requests@easproject.com

*To Mike W. Miss you every day, old friend.*

# Prologue

*And you were there with Mummy, down by the lake. Of course, the locals didn't call it a lake, they had their own word for it. You still remember it well that August, brilliantly blue, the white shapes of boats seen from afar on it. You recall the details, that's not surprising, how could you ever forget? That summer's day, she had been lovely to you at first, this was Nice Mummy. You knew that there were two of her, Nice Mummy and Nasty Mummy, in that pretty, oval face of hers with the soulful brown eyes. If only, you used to think, you could tell what was going on inside that head of hers, you wanted to be able to see what she was thinking, maybe change it. Maybe one day you would study how people think. Because now Nice Mummy had changed into Nasty Mummy. It was hard to know when it was going to happen, you had some ideas by now... she didn't like other women around her, especially pretty ones. That brought out Nasty Mummy.*

*Right now there was no room for thought about these things. She was lying on the grass, her eyes open, unmoving, unblinking. A crow cawed and then the harsh sound stopped, disappearing into the blue sky with its decorative, puffy white clouds. The enormity of your act had stunned you, but the world didn't seem* to notice. *The birds were fine, the earth revolved, the breeze blew and you looked at her lying there, motionless. And you smiled, you felt as if a rock had been lifted from your shoulders. She couldn't hurt you anymore, that venomous tongue, her speech that was always alive to all your faults and none of your virtues, was now silent. Silent as the vanished crow.*

*You took a couple of breaths, tried and failed, for a tear to come, appearances are important. You looked at the lake far in the distance, the scene was unchanged. You realised then that despite the enormity of your act, the world still turned. You knew you would be unscathed by what you had done. Then you turned towards the big white house.*

*'Dad, Dad…' you shouted, 'there's been an accident.'*

# Chapter One

That gloriously sunny morning was May Day. I was prepping rhubarb in my kitchen and listening to Beech Tree FM, the local radio station, playing undemanding background music while I trimmed the stalks. It was a Wednesday, not usually a busy day of the week, and I was looking forward to a relatively relaxed lunch and dinner time service.

Gloria Gaynor was on the Golden Oldie Hour and I sang 'I Will Survive', along with her, a timeless classic musically, just like Steak Diane, Tournedos Rossini or Hollandaise sauce were classics of the kitchen. However, Gloria's eternal feminine wisdom was wasted on my co-worker. Not that he objected to the message she conveyed, who wouldn't have changed that stupid lock and thrown away the key? It was just the medium he didn't like, that is pop music.

'Can we turn this pish off please,' he complained. Murdo, my Scottish sous, a metal fan, strongly disliked any other genre of music. Particularly pop music. Pop music of any description, and he wasn't age discriminatory. Gloria Gaynor, Taylor Swift, baby-boomer pop like ABBA or Charli XCX, to his ears they were all equally unacceptable. Such is the cross I have to bear. But I was deeply fond of him and I uncomplainingly put up with the godawful racket he called music. Youngsters are famously intolerant, and Murdo was only twenty-one but with five years' top quality kitchen experience behind him.

'In a moment, Murdo,' I promised, 'after this song finishes.'

He muttered something inaudible and went on making the timbales for the vegetarian section of my menu. A timbale is a dish cooked in a mould. Mine had layers of aubergine and a filling of chopped sweated veg, herbs, capers and goat's cheese. Then, once cooked through, they were inverted onto the plate and were served with hassel-back potatoes and dressed curly endive. If you wanted, you could have them paired with a sous-vided chicken breast. It was a very popular dish.

'That okay, Chef?'

I walked over to the prep table and glanced down at what he'd done. Twenty dariole moulds full to the brim; they looked good, I knew they would be. Murdo had a great pedigree, a Michelin-starred background from one of Edinburgh's best restaurants. Not so shabby.

'They are great, Murdo.'

The track we'd been listening to ended and then, what had previously been drowned out by the music and the din of the kitchen extractor fans became audible. Floating through the open door of the kitchen we could hear the distant sound of sirens. Murdo and I looked at each other questioningly and then I shrugged and we got back on with our respective jobs. So that's how I was able to pin-point the time when I first heard the ambulance and the police cars that were the first signs that something terrible had happened, bookmarked in my memory between the rhubarb and the aubergine timbales.

Francis, my kp, looked up from scrubbing plates before stacking them in the large, Hobart dishwasher, his face red and sweaty through the steam, and wondered aloud. 'Seems to be a bit of a thing going on in the woods, I saw three police cars there on my way over.'

'Hope it's the police cracking down on the fly-tippers,' I grumbled. 'The council have been promising to get tough for weeks now.'

'Bet it's not,' Francis said, 'they're as much use as an ashtray on a motorbike.'

I was wrong about it being a quiet day. We only had a few bookings but we had a surprising number of walk-ins, and ended up having a ferociously busy lunch service and no time to think or speak until we started clearing down at half two. By then we'd forgotten about the police and the sirens, all external thoughts driven out by the volume of work.

Later I found out it wasn't fly-tippers. It was something much more serious.

It was 3 o'clock and I was sitting in my now empty restaurant with Jess, my manager, relaxing over a pot of tea when there was a knock on my door. I looked up in surprise and saw a familiar face peering at me through the window. It was the police, in the form of DI Slattery.

'Wonder what he wants?' I muttered as I stood up to go

and let him in. Jess caught my eye and grinned. She had a theory that the policeman had a thing for me.

Slattery and I had a somewhat complicated relationship. Initially, when I had first come to the village a couple of years ago now, he had been extremely hostile. He had suspected me of involvement in a sausage theft. That sounds like some kind of stupid joke; it wasn't. The robbery had been from a local pig-farmer. Someone had broken into his refrigerated shed and stolen several thousand pounds' worth of meat.

Then he had made me his lead suspect in a murder investigation, but since that terrible start, our relationship, initially so frosty, had thawed. Now we were friends. He lived just across the common from me, you could see his bedroom window 500 metres or so from mine. I knew he had a thing for me. I sometimes imagined him standing there late at night, forlornly looking out at the restaurant opposite and my lit bedroom windows, hoping.

He was a hard bastard, tough and uncompromising. I liked him a lot.

'Hello, Charlie.' His presence filled the room. He was six three, powerfully built and exuded an aura of command that made him seem even larger than he was. He looked like he wouldn't need one of those sledgehammers that the police have to knock down doors, he could just run through it. He was also good-looking, if you like your men slightly rough around the edges. A kind of home counties Heathcliff. The trouble for DI Slattery though was that I wasn't Cathy.

'DI Slattery,' I remarked. 'Always a pleasure. Coffee?'

Slattery ran on coffee it seemed. Jess pulled a chair out for him and he sat down.

'Please.'

I switched on the machine and ground the beans for his espresso. I looked at him expectantly, eyebrow raised, waiting for him to tell me why he was here.

'Have you heard about what happened in Potter's Wood earlier today?' he asked.

I shook my head as I finished making the espresso and brought it over to him, sitting down opposite. 'No, I've been in the kitchen all day, only just finished.'

'I'm surprised no one noticed.'

'Look, we were so busy we wouldn't have noticed if World War Three had broken out,' I said.

Jess frowned. 'Is it anything serious?'

'Very serious.' He sighed. 'It's rather bad news, I'm afraid...'

Not the words you want to hear from anyone, least of all a policeman. I hoped it didn't involve anyone that I knew. Slattery took a sip of coffee, nodded in approval and said quietly, 'John Mayhew was attacked and killed there earlier this morning.'

I stared at him in disbelief. I thought of Mayhew, I could still picture everything about him with complete clarity. I was hardly overcome by grief. Memories of John, his unpleasant attitude, his rudeness, his shorty shorts, the stooped way he ran with his shoulders hunched up. I can remember thinking the wrinkly skin on his upper arms could do with a bloody good iron. And now, bastard or not, he was gone.

'Well,' Jess said, judiciously, 'there'll be a long list of suspects.'

# Chapter Two

Jess had left; Slattery had told her he wanted to interview me alone and we sat opposite each other in the silent restaurant.

'So what happened?' I asked. I wondered if it was an argument that had got out of hand, John was a pugnacious kind of guy. Maybe he had confronted a fly-tipper, in which case he would have died a hero's death, in my eyes at least.

'How did…' I didn't like to say how did he die. That sounded morbid. I didn't have to, Slattery guessed my question correctly.

'He was shot with a crossbow bolt,' he said, 'at point-blank range by the looks of things.' He shook his head wonderingly. 'I mean, now I've seen everything. Not what I expected when I was called in. You don't happen to know if he had any current enemies, do you, Charlie? You were in the same running group as him. Did you notice anything amiss, or did he happen to mention anything?'

'I'm sorry,' I replied, shaking my head. 'Nothing in particular springs to mind. Look, this has been a bit of a shock. Give me some time and I'll see if I can remember anything he said or anything else that might be of relevance.'

Slattery looked deep into my eyes, I think more because he liked the look of them than to see if I was lying. 'I'd be grateful,' he said, then he finished his coffee and stood up. 'Thanks for the coffee, I'll keep you in the loop. It kind of centres my thoughts talking to you Charlie.'

As I let him out I said, 'I'll keep my ears open.'

'Thank you.'

I watched him walk away down the common heading for the wood and the crime scene. I shook my head and thought about how I had met John and where I should begin. I knew a lot more about him than I'd let on to Slattery, and not just him.

John had been involved with highly suspect people. One of them I knew was a potential killer. But now was not the time to tell Slattery that.

Begin at the beginning I suppose. On an April morning, three weeks previously.

My knowledge of John Mayhew was bookended by rhubarb. I had met him thanks to the maître d' at the Michelin-starred place in the village, just round the corner from where I lived and worked in my restaurant. It had been the second week in April and with eerie synchronicity it had also been a Wednesday and I had also been prepping rhubarb in the kitchen.

I chopped the stalks into two cm sections and weighed what I had, about a kilo. I put them in a pan with 200 grams of sugar, five to one is the ratio I like to use. I went to the cupboard where I keep the herbs and spices. I was going to add a few star anise for a hint of background flavour, 100 ml of water and then on the stove.

I stared into the cupboard; it was far from bare but it didn't have what I wanted. 'Shit.' I was annoyed. I organise my things in alphabetical order, the shelf I was looking at had a gap in between Smoked Paprika and Sumac. No Star Anise. I asked Murdo if he'd seen it. Shake of the head.

'What's it for anyway?' Murdo asked, pointing at the pan. 'That rhubarb compote?'

'It'll go with the panna cotta,' I enthused. 'They'll look great standing in the middle of the rhubarb. They'll be all white and wobbly and they'll be surrounded by the pink of the compote, sprig of green mint on top for garnish, fantastic.'

'Sounds good.'

'It will be.' And to make matters even better, it was local, seasonal, organic produce fresh from my friend Esther's vegetable garden. It ticked all the boxes. Well, it would, if only I had the star anise. I didn't want to drive to the shops, an hour out of my busy day. Then an idea came to me.

'Hold the fort, Murdo, I'm going to go and borrow some off Strickland.'

'Give him my regards.'

Upstairs, I pulled off my chef's jacket, dragged a T-shirt over my head and left my restaurant, the Old Forge Café, and lightly jogged over the common to the other restaurant in the village, the imposing King's Head, once a large country pub, now home to the Michelin-starred Graeme Strickland, the Napoleon of haute cuisine, as I liked to think of him. Mainly because he was short and a megalo-maniac rather than Corsican or fond of tricorne hats.

I knocked on the front door and was let in by the maître d', Tristan Smith.

'Charlie!' He looked delighted to see me. Tristan was a posh kid. Not outrageously so, just well-spoken and assured, good-looking in a public school kind of way, semi-glossy. He also had the floppy hair and the chinos and brogues to match. I thought of him as a kid, but he was about thirty and had done stints at a couple of Gordon Ramsay places. He was dark-haired, slightly taller than medium height, with a neat, dark beard and was generically handsome. He looked like a man in one of the catalogues that I get sent periodically for up-market outdoorsy leisurewear, normally accompanied by a leggy, slender wife with perfect teeth as they look delightedly in unison at some view or other. Tris was also very good at his job – you would have to be if Strickland employed you.

I'd eaten there a while ago. Strickland had owed me an apology and said it with food rather than flowers, which was a nice gesture. It was then I'd seen Tris in action, directing the service of the food and wine like a conductor of a small orchestra, not missing a beat and treading that fine line that lay between professional politeness and obse-quiousness. He obviously had a way with the female clientele in particular, and I noticed that he had clearly memorised biographical details, asking after their children, jobs, husband, dogs, holiday with polished ease. I was impressed. He made people feel welcome but not in a fawning, unctuous kind of way.

'What brings you over here, Charlie?' he asked with an engaging grin. I explained and he said immediately, 'I'll go in the kitchen and get you some. It's a bit of a madhouse in there today.'

He went away and left me alone in the dining room where I floated in a kind of sea of envy. Michelin stars are awarded not just for the food. Consistency, flair, the chef's personality and the overall dining experience go into the mix. Strickland did not go in for minimalism. The King's Head was classic. The furniture was flawless, the tablecloths heavy, ironed linen, the walls, some exposed brick and beam, others a kind of light creamy-grey alabaster effect. There was an eye-catching floral display on a table by the door, geometric in its execution. I contrasted it unfavourably with my shabby old tables and chairs, relics of the previous owner. I must do something, I thought to myself. Not for the first time.

Tris returned with ten pieces of star anise wrapped up in clingfilm. I could smell the heavy aromatic odour through the plastic. As he handed them to me, he said, casually, 'You run, don't you Charlie?'

'Er, yes.' It was true, I ran a few kilometres six days a week.

'Me too.' He hesitated. 'Look, I'm starting a little local running group that will meet on Sunday mornings. It's just for fun really. Your wine supplier Cassandra is coming, so you'll know someone already. Are you interested?'

'How far do you run?' I asked. I had no wish to sign up to serious, agonising distances. He frowned, thinking. 'Between five and ten k, certainly no more than that, usually nearer the five mark.'

13

I thought for a moment. I was certainly interested. I'm good at being self-motivated, but it's easier if there's a group of you. You stretch yourself more. I was conscious of the fact that I tended to do the same routes and the same times again and again. And it would be good for me to meet some other people for a change. I was in a rut, both in running terms and socially.

'Yes,' I nodded, 'I am.'

'Good. We meet on the common on Sunday at eight.' He gave me a high wattage, professional smile. 'See you then.'

# Chapter Three

That Sunday morning was cool and grey, an unwelcome return to more usual British weather. We met up at 8 o'clock, as instructed by Tris, by the bench on the village green. Looking around me was like looking at an image from a picture-postcard book of a traditional English village: the green fringed by houses, and of course my café/restaurant; the play area halfway down the common next to the boundary hedge; the huge blue sky arcing overhead and views across the fields and woods to the neighbouring village, Frampton End. Trees and hedges marked the demarcation line to the adjacent meadow where horses were kept. Above us a couple of red kites with their distinctive V-shaped tails soared high on the thermals. At the bottom of the common, like a convention of undertakers, rooks and crows wandered around solemnly hunting for food.

There were six of us in the running group: myself; a guy called Matt who worked in IT; John, an elderly man in his late sixties; my wine supplier, Cassandra; a woman called Suzi; and Tris.

Tris introduced me to my fellow runners. 'Cassandra you know.'

'Hi Cass.'

'Hi Charlie.' She smiled her rather charming, slightly toothy grin. I had known Cassandra for over a year now. She was an independent wine supplier specialising in the unusual, more off-beat varieties from a varied group of countries. Since she'd taken over my wine list, sales had improved dramatically, as had customer satisfaction. I'm clueless when it comes to the stuff. I'm good with food, crap at wine. I can tell you the quality points of meat, fish and veg, I can sniff a ripe and ready to eat cantaloupe melon at 20 paces, but wine is a closed book to me. The only red I can recognise is the stuff served by the local pub, the Three Bells, because it's so disgusting. Luckily, Cass knew her stuff. She was tall and slim, in her mid to late thirties, with long dark hair and large soulful eyes. Andrea, my Italian boyfriend, who likes art and knows a thing or two about it, said she looks like a pre-Raphaelite heroine. I hadn't got a clue what he was talking about, so he brought up an image on his phone of women painted by some guy called Burne-Jones. Porcelain skin, long dark hair, soulful expressions. Yep, she did look like a Burne-Jones kind of girl. 'A tragic heroine in the making,' Andrea had called her.

Cassandra, or Cass as I usually called her, had a long jaw and a wide mouth; when she laughed (she didn't behave like a tragic heroine, no matter how much she might have looked like one) she showed a lot of very white teeth. She wasn't conventionally good-looking but she was very attractive. She was Strickland's ex as well, which was interesting. I didn't know the whys and wherefores (I had heard it said he had dumped her) but I can imagine finding life as Strickland's girlfriend practically impossible. She was a real find as a wine supplier. Pre-Cassandra, my wine list was utterly un-inspired, chosen by me on price and whether or not I thought the bottle looked nice. Now it was something to be proud of. Another interesting thing about her was that she was a wine dealer who didn't drink. I never asked her about it, it was none of my business. When I was a kid I knew a boy who was training to be a butcher and he was vegetarian. It takes all sorts.

'And this is Suzi... Charlie.'

'Hi.' Suzi was about thirty, Tristan's age group. Everyone was, except me – mid-forties – and the old guy who was standing to one side watching on blearily with folded arms and sour disapproval. Suzi didn't have a runner's build the way Cass and the men did. She was sturdy, with a notice-ably large chest. Good, I thought, that'll slow you down. I knew that I wasn't going to shine in this group but I didn't want to be trailing along, way in the distance. She also had, like just about everyone these days – I was unusual in this respect being ink-free – a tattoo. It was a colourful hummingbird at the base of her neck. It was very pretty. Quite unusual, I thought.

'This is Matt...' Tris made an introductory gesture with his open hand. A tight smile from Matt, another thirty-something. He was tall and slender but muscular. I'd had a boyfriend once, very briefly, who had done calisthenics and I recognised the build, very strong but without the hypertrophy that say, a weightlifter or bodybuilder has. Matt was intimidating. He had a shaven head, not because he was going bald, you could see the dark stubble on top, but presumably because he liked it that way. He had slightly protuberant grey eyes and a reserved, quiet air. Despite this, or maybe because of it, he looked rather frightening, almost psychotic. But to be honest, what really stuck out were his shoes. Not literally, he didn't have freakish feet, but he was wearing those shoes that have toes, like a glove has fingers. They were lime-green, Day-Glo; it looked like he had frog's feet.

'And, last but not least, John.'

This was the old guy. He wasn't wearing hi-tech weird shoes, but he was wearing very short shorts, the kind that were popular in the 1970s. I guessed that he was probably a former club runner who had competed at some high level. He looked the kind, there was a certain rock-hard arrogance lurking under that ageing bodywork.

'Hello John,' I said with a warm smile, a smile that was not reciprocated. If anything the expression in his eyes was one of dislike. Sod you too, I thought.

'Okay, guys,' said Tristan with a warm, encompassing grin, 'warm-up time.'

He led us in about five minutes of stretching exercises, lunges (boy do I hate lunges). I took a surreptitious glance at my fellows. Suzi was struggling like me, Matt kind of sprang from right knee bent, left on the ground to left knee bent, right on the ground, as if his legs were springs. His facial expression was one of calm concentration. It was a calisthenics move, very tough to do. I huffed and puffed.

Hip rotations, heel to butt, well, no problems there, ditto arm rotations. Tris had good biceps, Matt's were like anatomical drawings. I knew that they were called biceps because they're really two muscles, not one as you might think. You could actually see that in Matt's arms, the divide was visible, he had so little body fat.

I carried on with my warm-up, quad stretches and ankle flexion. Tris certainly knew his stuff. After about five minutes more, we finished. 'Okay, guys,' Tris said, 'we'll be doing just a seven k today, a loop round Frampton End,' this was the neighbouring village whose church spire you could see in the distance, 'not fast, this is a slow run. Any questions? No? Off we go then.'

Just a seven k, I thought, mentally groaning. A couple of kilometres more than I usually ran these days. Well, I told myself, this was the point wasn't it Charlie, you wanted to stretch yourself, you only have yourself to blame. We set off running down the common and then over the main road at the bottom, passing a lay-by that now contained a stained double mattress and some tipped black bin bags disclosing their contents of splintered wood and ripped up wallpaper. I wondered, as I always did, what kind of arsehole deliberately desecrates the beauty of the countryside like this for the sake of saving a few quid down at the dump. The problem was getting worse and worse, not simply with the fly-tippers (who at least had some kind of rationale behind their actions) but also the litter that pock-marked the sides of the road. Fast food packaging and cans tossed out of car windows. It enraged me, like gobbing in the face of Mother Nature.

I tried to forget this depressing reality as we turned up a footpath into a field. Our legs pounded along at a rate that was fast for me. We ran through Potter's Wood, which lay between the two villages. The green leaves above our heads were a gentle, glowing sylvan cover over the track we were running along. It felt like being underwater somehow. As I ran, I reflected on the adjective Tris had used to describe the run. 'Slow' is a relative term. It may have been slow for the others, to me it felt anything but. To say it felt like a sprint, well, that would be an exaggeration but it was uncomfortably swift. Still, as I told myself, that's what I was here for, to push myself, not to just plod along securely within my comfort zone.

I glanced at my fellow runners. Tris was leading but would turn around and shout encouragement to the two slowest, me and Suzi. John, the old guy, seemed perfectly happy, his hairless, skinny old legs effortlessly covering the ground, and Matt was, of course, running like a well-oiled machine, his expression a perfectly blank mask. Cassandra at first had seemed well within her comfort zone. Tall and leggy, she looked to have the perfect build, but as we approached the 25-minute mark she was starting to fade and fell in beside me and Suzi.

She grinned her toothy grin at me. 'I'm not feeling it today, Charlie.'

'Me neither,' panted Suzi.

A significant gap was widening between us and the three men. Tris noticed it and must have said something because their pace dropped and he ran back to us.

'There's only a couple of k left,' he said, joining us, 'you can do it... just think of yourself as a car and drop down a gear... you can run a bit slower, it's still running, we're not trying to make the team.' Obediently we slowed even more. There were some further encouraging slogans from Tris – 'the only run you regret is the one you didn't do' – that kind of thing.

'That's it...' Tris said, enthusiastically. Tris was certainly growing on me, none of the PE teacher about him. He must have been studying a manual of coaching psychology. It sounded very professional. We ran along a bit. Suzi's breathing grew noticeably more laboured, unhappiness etched on her face.

'There's only one k left,' he said, glancing at his watch, then looked at Cassandra and me. 'You two can run off now, I'll help Suzi over the line.'

'You. Go. On.' Suzi gasped, pain written over her pretty features.

'Okay,' Cassandra said, 'see you back on the bench, Tris.'

We both accelerated away from the two of them as they settled down to a walk. Now we were alone, Cass turned the conversation to business and she told me about some incredible value South African wines that she had access to. They were a Cabernet Sauvignon and a Chenin Blanc that, because of the low value of the rand, were a really good buy.

'I'll bring them round when I call in at your place next time,' she said. 'Tris said he'd be interested too.'

I looked at her in surprise. 'I didn't know that you were supplying the King's Head? I thought Strickland used someone else.'

'Graeme uses a variety of suppliers. He likes to play them off against each other.'

I thought that was why she had avoided his restaurant, because of her hurt feelings. Maybe she was over that now, it must have been three or four years since they had split up. Almost certainly with his characteristic ruthlessness.

She may have guessed what I was thinking because she sighed and said, 'We've obviously got a history, but I decided to let bygones be bygones. Anyway, I need the business. Tris is obviously more interested in the higher end of the market than you are, but he does like to keep a few cheaper wines for those who've decided they're already spending enough as it is.'

'Obviously,' I said, without rancour. Strickland's clientele could afford three or four hundred pound bottles of wine, mine certainly couldn't.

'Great, bring some round, I'm in.' I had faith in her.

'Okay.' She nodded. 'I'll see you in the week; I'll let you know when later today.'

So we finished our run and I walked the short distance back to the Old Forge Café, my restaurant and home. I made myself an espresso from the machine in the dining room, and was sipping it when there was a sharp knock on the restaurant door. I was surprised, my staff would go round the back, it was too early for customers. I walked over, unlocked it and opened it.

There was a man I didn't know on the threshold. He had shoulder-length silver hair, a casual blue suit and an open-necked white shirt with no tie. He was stocky with a bull-neck. Short, but he had an air of almost aggressive self-assurance which counter-balanced it. My first impression was one of immediate dislike.

'Are you Charlie Hunter?' he asked.

'Yes, but we're closed,' I said, firmly. I was suddenly very aware of the fact that I was dressed in sweaty running clothes. Not a great look for a restaurateur.

'I know' – his voice was sharp and to the point – 'I'm not here as a customer.'

That threw me slightly. 'Well what do you want then?' I asked with a touch of asperity in my voice.

'Your help,' he said simply.

There was something in the way he spoke those two words that made me know he wasn't talking about food.

'You'd better come in,' I said.

We went inside and I indicated a chair. 'Please…' He sat down heavily. I sat down opposite him and evaluated him. He was wearing expensive-looking ox-blood colour leather loafers with his suit. He had a bit of a gut on him which strained his shirt, not a good look. His face looked like one of the less crazy Roman emperors; he had the nose as well as the attitude. Imperious. Arrogance and latent aggression hung around him in a cloud as thick as his aftershave. If he had been there as a customer I would have put him down as the type likely to make a complaint, just for the hell of it.

'So,' I said, 'how can I help you?'

'My name's David Summers.'

He had quite a coarse voice, London or thereabouts, none of the well-educated smoothness of Tris Smith. A working-man made good, I thought to myself. He was obviously making his own evaluation of me as he looked me up and down. I was conscious of the dark ring of sweat around the neck of my running top and under my arms. My hair was stuck to my scalp. I felt I looked a totally unprofessional mess.

'And you are Charlie Hunter?' Obviously making sure that this sweaty woman was indeed the boss.

'I am indeed.' I wondered where this was going.

'You were recommended to me by Edward Hamilton.' He looked at me questioningly as if a mistake might have been made somewhere along the line.

'I'm…' I said. Who? I tried hard to think of an Edward Hamilton but came up with nothing. David Summers noted my confusion.

'The lawyer,' he explained testily, in a tone that said, 'Sharpen up!'

'Oh, yes…' I remembered now. He had been Lance Thurston's lawyer, a slightly intimidating man. I'd rather liked him. Lance was a well-known podcaster who lived locally. I had done some work for him about a year ago, both a catering event, his birthday, and a personal matter; I had helped to get him off a murder charge.

'Would you like to tell me what this is about?' I asked, intrigued. Was I going to be hired for catering or to clear someone's name?

I could hear movement now in the kitchen followed by music drifting through the door as Murdo started work prepping for Sunday lunch. I say, drifting, it was more of a thunderous racket. I recognised the gentle strains of 'Life Sentence' by Malevolence, one of Murdo's latest enthusiasms. David Summers frowned. Perhaps he wasn't a fan of metalcore. Maybe he would have preferred some Tool instead. I had become an unwilling follower of metal.

'It's about my daughter,' he said.

'What's the matter with your daughter?'

'Right now, nothing.' He rested his hands on the table, the fingers bent over, the knuckles shining through the skin. 'Nothing at all.' He took a deep breath. 'But I am very much afraid that her fiancé is going to kill her.'

My eyebrows arched, my eyes widened. That was unexpected.

'What?' I said, startled by what I had just heard. Especially the 'going to'. Like it was a scheduled event.

Summers explained. 'My daughter, Lizzie, is engaged to be married. I did some digging about her fiancé, I had my suspicions about him, and I think he plans to murder her.'

I frowned. This sounded terrible, but what did he expect me to do about it? I didn't know his daughter and I didn't know the man she was going to marry. I don't know what David Summers was thinking, but I wanted no part of this.

'Look,' I took a deep breath as I backed away from the situation, 'this sounds an awful situation for you and your daughter, but I'm not sure how I can help.'

He considered what I had just said and then, with the air of a man laying down a winning hand in poker, said, 'This fiancé,' a pause, a heartbeat, 'he's a friend of yours.'

I stared at him, confused, disbelieving. 'What! Are you serious?'

He nodded. 'Absolutely.'

'Who?' I asked. Various images of people I was close to flashed through my mind. My boyfriend, Andrea. DI

Slattery, the policeman who lived across the common from me. My godfather, Cliff Yeats. The man sitting in front of me smiled bitterly and put me out of my misery.

'Tristan Smith.'

# Chapter Four

I opened my eyes wide in what I felt was almost a panto-mime of surprise.

'Tris! Are you sure?' It seemed highly unlikely to say the least. Of all the people that I knew, this floppy haired former public-school boy seemed the unlikeliest candidate to be a killer.

Summers nodded. 'Quite sure.' He pointed a commanding finger at my coffee machine behind the bar. He had the air of a man used to being obeyed.

'I'll have an Americano and I'll tell you all about it.'

I obligingly made him his coffee and an espresso for myself, the smell of the coffee drifting through the restaur-ant. The slightly chintzy decor and early morning sun made it an incongruous place for these revelations.

'So, please go on,' I said as I put the cups down on the table in front of us and took my seat opposite him.

And he did. It concerned Elizabeth Summers, his daughter. 'Lizzie' as she was known, was now coming up to her birthday. 'It's on the first of July; she'll be twenty-four.'

'What's she like?' I asked. He seemed puzzled by the question, threw out some generalities about his daughter, few of them flattering. Maybe he was one of these judgemental parents, but a kind of hostile judge. I gathered that she was not what you would call intellectual.

'What does she do?'

'She works at Stanley Wood eco-centre,' he said. I nodded. I knew where it was, it was just off one of the neighbouring main roads; I had seen the sign for it probably hundreds of times. It lay at the bottom of a turning but it was a dead-end road that just led to the eco-centre.

'What do they do there?' I had always been curious.

'They do stuff with schoolkids.' He shrugged. 'It's an educational place. They take them on trail-walks, put up nest boxes, visit schools, that kind of thing. It's all very commendable.'

He didn't look like he was particularly happy about it. He'd managed to make the word 'commendable' sound like it was a bad thing. I was beginning to have my initial feeling that I didn't like him justified. He was not overflowing with the milk of human kindness.

'What do you do, David, may I ask?' Something exploitative, I thought to myself.

'Property,' he said. 'I make a lot of money.' Ha! I thought, I knew it. He pursed his lips. 'That is what attracted Smith to Lizzie.'

Silence. I was tempted to ask, the property or the money? Just to annoy him, but I didn't.

I finished my coffee. 'Go on,' I prompted.

'Look, there are some things that you need to know

about Lizzie.' He straightened up in his chair and shook his head for emphasis, then he pushed his fingers through his leonine locks. I was beginning to think he was a bit over-proud of his hair. Men are often self-impressed with weird things, like guys in bro T-shirts flexing their biceps to try and impress women. Summers' barnet certainly didn't impress me, my hair's great.

Not content with the hair action, he pushed the sleeves of his jacket up so I could admire what I assumed was a very expensive wristwatch with several dials. I'm not keen on men with showy watches, I think it's compensatory. I wondered what the different dials signified.

'It pains me to say it, but she is not the brightest,' he confided. 'I had her tested. I thought maybe she was autistic or something, but no.' I got the impression he would have liked her to be on the spectrum; she had disappointed him again. She didn't have a rare condition, she just wasn't very clever. I was beginning to feel a bit sorry for Lizzie. He continued. 'She is though, extremely caring.' He repeated the word for emphasis. 'Caring, gentle and always trying to help.'

'Hence the eco-centre,' I said.

'Exactly.' He pulled a face. 'Glis glis, hedgehogs...'

Last year he had taken her to a leading London restaurant for lunch on her birthday, and there she first laid eyes on Tristan Smith.

'She started eating there regularly.' He sighed. How could she afford it on her eco salary, I wondered. He noticed my interrogative glance. 'She gets a good allowance. I later learned she was going back just to look at him. Eventually he noticed her...'

29

They started dating and they had been engaged now for about six months. The expression on Summers' face made it clear what he thought of that.

'They moved out here when he got the King's Head job. I will freely admit he's a persuasive little bastard. I think it suited him too because it got her away from her friends' group; she doesn't really know anyone out here apart from work colleagues. She's isolated.'

'And you think that Tris wants to kill her? Why?'

'He is after money, Charlie,' he said. 'I'm a wealthy man.'

'How do you know it is for your money?'

He gave a somewhat cold smile. 'I'm a realistic man,' he said, 'I'll be frank.'

I knew he would be. He was the kind of man who would say that, usually with great relish I guessed.

'Look, Charlie, when I was younger – I won't lie.' He sighed. 'Lizzie was a grave disappointment to me. I wanted a trophy daughter and I didn't get one.' Poor you, I thought, how dare she. How dare she not be stunningly attractive and bright. 'But I'm nearly seventy, I've got a heart problem,' he waved a hand, 'stents… diabetes, I've had prostate cancer, I'm running out of road. Lizzie is all I have. When I go I can't look after her. I can't protect her. This needs sorting out now.'

'Okay…' I said in an unconvinced kind of way.

'Before it's too late.'

'I see.'

He carried on. 'He's very good-looking and my daughter isn't.' Summers said tetchily. I frowned. Surely there was more to a relationship than this. He continued the ruthless demolition of his daughter's looks by seasoning it with a sprinkling of self-awareness. 'She inherited my looks, not her mother's and she's going to inherit my money. That's the problem.'

'Is that a problem though?' I tried to put across my point. 'Surely, attraction doesn't depend purely on looks. And why shouldn't money be as valid a reason to find someone as attractive as, say, personality? Both rely on a certain amount of luck, don't they?' I warmed to my theme. 'You can be born pretty or rich or with drive or brains, it's down to chance. You play the hand that life has dealt you.'

He nodded. 'There's a certain amount of truth to that,' he admitted. 'Ordinarily, maybe I'd have gritted my teeth and let things be. I could have accepted that, that he was interested in her money.' He sighed again. 'And if he was a good enough husband, gave her a couple of kids and a happy home life, well, I would have thought, okay I'll pay for that... but for one thing.'

'What one thing is that?'

David Summers settled back in his chair. 'Could I have another coffee?'

'Sure.'

I went round the bar and made him a second Americano then brought it to him and sat down. He sipped it appreciatively and smoothed his hair again. Maybe he thought the coffee would be good for it.

'I can understand what you've been saying,' I said, 'but what makes you think Tris is so mercenary? And even if he is after her money, why do you think he wants to kill her? Maybe he genuinely loves her.'

31

He shook his head. 'Because of this: I found out that five years ago, Smith had married a girl he believed was an heiress. Just like Lizzie.' Then he went quiet. The smell of coffee drifted over the table. From somewhere the other side of the common I heard a lawnmower starting up. He continued. 'Then her father, now his father-in-law, met another woman, much younger, and divorced the wife. The daughter objected, there was a row and he told her he was disinheriting her. So all of a sudden the golden girl he'd married was now without a penny. Cut off.'

'And Tris left her?'

Summers shook his head. 'No, he murdered her.'

# Chapter Five

David Summers left at about 10 o'clock, having added a lot more detail to the Tris Smith allegations. I said I would get back to him that night with my decision as to whether I would help him or not. I didn't really know what to do. It would be a difficult decision to make. On the one hand there was maybe a terrible crime to be prevented (I mentally emphasised the maybe, nothing I had seen or heard during my acquaintance with Tris led to me believe he was violent). I could also earn the extra money that I desperately needed to pay for replacement furniture in the restaurant. This was getting to be a sore point. My last visit to Strickland's place had highlighted just how shabby my tables and chairs were. Before I bought it, the Old Forge had been a failing tea room. I had transformed it food-wise into a good restaurant, but it still looked like a shabby tea room inside and there was only so much you could do with subdued lighting.

So, I had the inclination, did I have the time? Being chef/proprietor of a busy restaurant means a working day that begins at 7 a.m. and finishes at midnight. I had one day a week off and the occasional hour here and there. I was not awash with leisure time and I wasn't sure how I could fit the David Summers investigation into my schedule. Also, I'm not getting any younger, I need time to recharge. I decided to see what my right-hand woman Jess thought I should do.

Another busy lunch, 40 covers between 12 noon and 2 o'clock. We run a special menu on that day – a three, three, three lunch: starters, mains and desserts. Interestingly, the plant-based option, which was an aubergine Wellington, had sold really well, instead of the roast beef. I was beginning to notice a significant rise in my non-meat options, which pleased me because I was putting a lot of effort into vegetarian food. Nice to have it noticed.

We'd cleaned down, Katie, the young blonde waitress had gone home, Murdo was upstairs and I sat in the now deserted restaurant with Jess.

She'd been with me since I took over the place. Pretty, with unruly dark hair and a generous figure, she'd started as my (only) waitress and evolved into my friend, confidante and manageress. She was currently doing a PhD in computers at Warwick Uni. I was uncertain as to what this entailed; to be honest I didn't really know what a PhD was, beyond a vague idea it was one up from a degree and it went on for years. Luckily for me, she could do most of it online from the family home, leaving her time to work for me in the evenings.

We both had a bottle of some Czech pilsner. This was one of Cassandra's clever ideas. She had suggested we stock it. 'This is unusual stuff, Charlie, as well as very nice to drink. Did you know the lager you sell that you seem so proud of is not from Bayern but made under licence in Romford, Essex?'

As always, she was right. We sold a lot of it and it did taste a hell of a lot better than its Essex predecessor.

'How was your run this morning?' Jess asked.

'Oh, it was good...' I launched into a description of where we had been.

'Who are the other runners again? Do I know any of them?'

I ran through their names. I mentioned Matt's distinctive footwear. That triggered a response in Jess.

'Matt,' she said, frowning. 'Is he Matt Spicer, skinny guy? Works in IT?' She looked surprised.

'Maybe.' I scratched my head. 'I only know his first name but he's certainly lean. Do you know him then?'

She nodded. 'If it's him, I do. I've seen him around in those shoes. They are really distinctive, you notice them a mile off. Anyway, about ten years ago my parents hired him to coach me in maths and IT. I didn't really need it, but there you go, parents, eh!'

I smiled tightly. Parents. Always a bit of a sore point. My mum had run off when I was a girl and my dad, who'd brought me up and whom I adored, had died when I was sixteen. I suppose that's why I liked my friend and godfather Cliff Yeats so much, he was a substitute father.

'Parents, eh,' I echoed. 'So what's he like, assuming it's him of course?' He had been kind of intriguing in his buttoned-up way. Which, now I began to think of it, was annoyingly smug somehow.

She frowned thoughtfully. 'He's a bit of a weirdo actually. The kind of guy who makes loners look sociable. At the time I knew him he was doing something in IT for the government.' She tossed her hair back and laughed. 'It was rumoured it was cyber warfare at school, but it was probably some boring old tax thing. There was talk too that he was a secret member of the SAS, which I think is rubbish although he's probably fit enough. He had a passion for exercise.'

'Must be the same guy, my Matt is crazily fit.'

She smiled. 'Well, whether he's a spy or not, he's certainly very good with computers…' She tilted her head. 'Hang on, I'm still friends on Facebook with his wife.'

She hunted through her phone. 'Yeah, here's a picture of them both.'

'That's him.' I looked at the pretty, dark-haired woman with an engaging grin. 'Is she in IT too?'

'God, no,' Jess shook her head, 'she's a schoolteacher. They live up the road in Potter's Hill; she teaches at the local primary school. They've got a couple of kids of their own.'

'I see.' I thought of my fellow runners. We were simply not in Matt's league, nor was he there for socialising, he'd made that pretty clear. 'I wonder what he's doing in the running group?' I mused.

She shrugged. 'I was wondering that, he must be much better than everyone else.'

I laughed. 'Maybe he's besties with Tris.'

'If he was,' Jess snorted, 'I would be amazed.'

'Oh, but the most interesting thing was after the run.'

She looked at me questioningly.

'A guy called David Summers was round this morning, before we opened…' I told her the gist of our conversation. Jess raised a crooked, very dark eyebrow. 'And?'

She stared at me in astonishment as I finished. 'Tris Smith murdered his wife! That's kind of hard to believe, he's a bit of a chinless wonder.'

I nodded. 'Well, that's what Summers told me.'

'When and where did this happen?' Her voice was full of doubt.

'About three years ago, seemingly. Tris and his wife, she was called Cara, were staying up in Argyll in Scotland, some Airbnb place near the Mull of Kintyre. Do you know it?'

She shook her head. I did. I showed her on my phone. 'Look, west of Glasgow, you see that long, thin peninsula which sticks out into the Atlantic.'

'Uh huh.' She nodded.

'That's Kintyre and the Mull is on its southerly tip. Just here.' I pointed at the screen.

'What happened?' Jess asked, raising her eyes to look at me.

I repeated what Summers had told me. 'They had hired a cottage, Airbnb for a couple of weeks. The night she died they ate in a local pub, the Freemason's Arms. Witnesses, including the waiting staff, testified that she had got quite drunk. They went home. According to Tris they had a nightcap, he went to bed. She carried on drinking.'

'Did she have a problem with alcohol?'

'Tris claimed she had an alcohol problem,' I said. 'He said he woke up in the morning and she wasn't in bed with him. He raised the alarm and her body was found later at the base of a nearby cliff.'

'What did the inquest say?'

'It was decided that her death was accidental,' I said. 'David Summers thinks Tris pushed her off. The incident, accident or murder, happened in the summer. You can imagine it, "Let's go for a romantic stroll and look at the ocean". It's light late in the evenings in that part of the world. It would have been lovely, then BANG, a shove in the back and you'd be falling down onto the rocks.'

Jess shivered. 'That sounds a horrible way to go.'

'Well, Summers is worried that history is going to repeat itself.'

Jess looked sceptical. 'Well, why doesn't he tell her, and by extension Tris, he's leaving his money to charity. Then he will either dump her – if he is after her money – and if not, Tris won't have any motive to harm her.'

I sighed. 'That's what I said, but when she's twenty-four, which she will be in July, she inherits a lot that's been held in trust. Summers can't stop it.'

She pulled a face. 'Oh, but... yeah, but, Tris Smith!' Her tone was incredulous. 'I mean look at him, he seems so...' she hunted for a word.

'Wussy?' I suggested.

'Yeah, I can't see it myself, him killing someone.'

'Perhaps he didn't,' I said. 'Mr Summers seems a bit of an arsehole quite frankly, it could just be wishful thinking on his part.'

'Well, exactly.' Jess rubbed the tip of her nose thoughtfully. 'And the inquest found it to be accidental after all.'

MURDER AND THE MAÎTRE D'

'I agree.' I sighed. 'Shall I just say no then?'

'Whoa.' Jess held up a hand. 'Did he say how much he'd pay you?'

I nodded. 'Five hundred a week guaranteed for two months, and a five thousand pounds bonus if I can find enough evidence against him to stop Lizzie marrying him.'

'So you could earn almost ten grand from this.' Jess looked at me, then around the restaurant. 'Furniture money... money you don't have.'

'I know.' I hesitated. 'But it seems unethical somehow.'

'It is not unethical,' Jess protested. 'Does he want you to investigate this? Yes or no?'

'Er, yes. He said Edward Hamilton, Lance's lawyer – do you remember him? – was very impressed with me and seemingly, according to Summers, he's a hard man to impress.'

'Well, there you are then.' Jess was exasperated now. 'You discovered the person who committed the crime that his client was accused of. You got Lance off. Now you can do the same for Summers. If you find Tris is innocent, you lose his bonus but make a few thousand. If you find he's guilty and you stop the wedding, you gain big time. Money, and you will have prevented a crime.' She picked up my phone and slid it across the table to me.

'Call him now.'

So I did. 'David, Charlie here. Okay, I'll do it... Thank you... When can we meet up to discuss things... you're away till when? Okay see you then. Bye, have a good trip.'

I looked at Jess. 'Done. He's away on business for a while, but when he's back, we'll sit down and formulate a plan.'

'Good,' she said, with evident satisfaction. 'The die is cast.'

# Chapter Six

On the Tuesday as I finished my run with a sprint, powering up the slight gradient to the top of the common around which the village was built, I saw a figure I knew well sitting on a bench near the communal notice board. The same bench that the running club had met at on Sunday. I slowed as I approached her.

'Good morning, Charlie,' Anna Bruce said. Panting with exertion I sat down next to her.

'Hi, Anna. Nice to see you.' It was true, I was pleased to see her, I liked her a lot. She had become a valued part of my world. She was a professional psychic for want of a better term, catering mainly to the corporate world. I could never have imagined that businessmen would consult people like her; didn't they have economists for that sort of thing? But the Earl of the village (and my friend Bryony's boyfriend) who was some kind of fund manager, (whatever that may be), told me that Anna with her tarot cards and I Ching coins was as accurate, if not more, than market analysts at spotting trends.

I was wearing shorts and a sweat-stained top, Anna,

perfectly made-up, in white jeans that matched her short hair, and an expensive-looking floral print top. She looked immaculate as always. Tranquil, in command and masterful. I was slightly in awe of her.

'How are you?'

'I'm good.' I felt slightly worried. I normally saw Anna at times of crisis, either in my own life or others. She was like the breeze that portended the hurricane, the rumble before the avalanche.

'You've got a client, I take it,' she looked at me questioningly, 'in a non-catering capacity.'

'That's correct,' I said, thinking of David Summers. Damn, she was good. How could she know this? I didn't really believe in the supernatural, but I made an exception where she was concerned.

Anna sighed. 'I won't explain how I know,' a minatory note crept into her voice, 'but I am here to warn you. There's a woman in danger, Charlie.' She smiled humourlessly. 'Not you for a change, but it's definitely a woman, a young woman.'

'I know who you mean.' It was obviously Lizzie. I was suddenly very glad that I had accepted David Summers' job offer. A silence fell between the two of us.

If you had taken a photo then and there, it would have looked idyllic. The chocolate-boxy village, the two women, one, older than the other, obviously giving sage advice. Some kids in uniform waiting at the crossroads behind us for a school bus, two or three dog-walkers in the distance, crows, jackdaws and rooks pecking away peaceably in the grass away from what few people there were around, the well-kept hedgerows. You wouldn't have known we were discussing a potential murder.

Anna carried on. 'These things don't always happen, they can be prevented. Sometimes I see potentialities rather than certainties, nothing in this life is set in stone.' She smiled again, this time with genuine warmth. 'The future is kind of hard to see.'

David Summers and Lizzie were obviously in the forefront of my mind as I asked what had she seen. The answer was not reassuring.

'I saw blood and death, a great deal of blood. It covered her. So, whatever you are doing, I hope it succeeds in preventing the situation.'

She stood up and smiled. 'On that cheery note I shall leave you. But if you've been having any kind of doubts, then don't. Unfortunately I can't put a timeframe on it, it could even refer back to the past as well as the future, I don't know, but you are connected, that much I do know.'

I got up too. 'Well, thanks for the warning, Anna.'

'That's okay, I just wish I could be more specific.' She pulled an apologetic face. 'Take care.'

She touched her fingers to her lips and blew me a kiss. I watched her walk over to where her car, a Mercedes sports, was parked and she drove off.

I took a deep breath and walked back to the restaurant. As Jess had said the other day, the die was cast.

Sunday came round again with frightening speed. Once again I found myself by the bench, on the green with the other runners. The major difference being that this time I felt myself watched by the spirit of Anna, and of course, I was in my new role, working for David Summers. I found myself, as I always did, relishing the role as an investigator. I love uncovering secrets.

That's not necessarily a praiseworthy thing. One of my besetting character flaws is curiosity. Like Pandora, I would have opened the box. Like Bluebeard's wife, I would have walked through the door into the forbidden chamber. And, like umpteen gormless but cute young women in horror films, I would have gone down to explore the strange noises in the cellar in the creepy house in the woods, or thought it a good idea to have a peek in the grimoire bound in human skin and barbed wire, clearly labelled 'The Book of the Damned'.

It was very much a repeat performance of the last run except this time I was looking at Tris with fresh eyes. He was certainly in excellent physical shape. His body was lithe and lightly muscled, it was a runner's build. And as he ran you had the unmistakable feeling that there was a lot of power under the hood. This time last week I would have looked upon this as a favourable asset that he had, not that I was remotely attracted to him, but now I viewed this as a danger. How easy would he be to fend off, should the need arise, I wondered. Quite difficult to do, especially if you're drunk by a cliff edge. I think it was then that the desire to see the place where Tris's wife had died, began. Just with this seed of curiosity.

We chatted briefly, about business and his boss (and my friend) Graeme Strickland, about how demanding he was. 'True,' I said. I liked Strickland, and his cooking ability was tremendous; he was ten times the chef I was. And of course he had charisma. Personally I felt privileged that he enjoyed my company and respected me. Loyally I remarked, 'But he is very hands on...'

'I'll say,' Tris said, feelingly, 'last week we had two chefs off and he worked six eighteen hour days, he slept on the floor in his office in a sleeping bag.'

'Well, yeah, there you are then.' But he likes that, I thought to myself. And he is driven like crazy, an obsessive. He thinks Destiny wants him to have three stars and he's only got the one.

Tris laughed. 'Yeah, that's true...' Then he changed the tone of the conversation; his voice grew serious. 'Funny how he used to go out with Cass.'

She was running ahead of us, her dark hair tied back, bounced as she ran. She had marvellous legs. Mine aren't bad, hers were exceptional.

'Not really,' I said, offhandedly, 'Cass has got class.' That was true and Strickland recognised class when he saw it.

'True again,' he said. He looked back, I did too. Suzi was struggling again. She appeared to be in considerable pain. 'I'll drop back and give her some encouragement if that's okay with you,' he said. 'I think she needs it.'

'Sure.'

Cass was now ahead, talking to Matt, and after a while I found myself running with John, the old guy.

'Nice to see you again,' I said, brightly and untruthfully. John didn't reply. He gave me a rheumy look of withering contempt. I found that I was really beginning to dislike John.

'This is a come-down,' he grumbled. He had a deep, gruff voice, educated. 'I nearly made the Olympic Team for Montreal back in seventy-six, now look at me. Running with you lot.' He glared at me as if missing the team had been somehow my fault, even though I hadn't been born. When he scowled at me I noticed he had to wrinkle his eyes painfully to see me, I suspected his vision was not exactly eagle-eyed.

I was fed up with his grumpy old man schtick, his rudeness. 'Oh come on, John, lighten up, you're running with three beautiful young women,' I said.

He glared at me. 'You're no spring chicken, don't fool yourself.' Sod you Methuselah, I thought, you horrible old bastard. He increased his pace and left me behind. I was quite happy with that, I certainly didn't want to run next to him anymore. Miserable senile git. I wondered why Tris had invited him along, which he must have done. Not for the bants as they say.

Well, I shall bloody well find out, I thought to myself.

Later, after the run was over, I invited Tris back to my place for a coffee. As well as clearing up the mystery of John, I wanted to see what Tris was like at close quarters. Being disliked by David Summers was not necessarily such a bad thing. Maybe Tris was no murderer, for all I knew it could be Summers himself and the victim not Lizzie at all.

We sat in my restaurant and he sipped delicately at a cappuccino while I had my customary espresso. I noticed while I was making the coffee and small talk, Tris was looking around very carefully like a professional evaluator. Maybe he was comparing his current surroundings with the King's Head, which would be like comparing my old Volvo estate with Strickland's Maserati. I asked him what the story was with John.

'It's true, he nearly did make the UK Olympic team,' he confirmed. 'He was a really good athlete, but he lost out to Brendan Foster and a guy called Ian Stewart. He is still really bitter about it.'

'Well,' I said, 'he seems bitter about a lot of things. Why on earth did you invite him along?'

'A couple of reasons I guess. I felt a bit sorry for him. He ran a little investment company, he lives in Frampton End. He did a lot with crypto, not Bitcoin, some of the other ones that went bust. He lost a lot of money… so all he's got is running really. The other reason is, he is really remarkably knowledgeable about the sport and I've got a ten k coming up that I want to do well in and I really value his advice.'

'Oh.' Well, that was that explained then.

'So if you could bear with him.' Tris gave me a charming smile, one that he had practised probably thousands of times in hotel dining rooms. 'I'd appreciate it.'

'Sure, I'm okay with it.' It was water off a duck's back. 'I've had to take a lot worse in my time.'

He finished his coffee and looked around the restaurant. 'It's nice in here, Charlie,' he said appreciatively, 'I'll have to bring Lizzie over for dinner.'

'Is she your girlfriend?' I said innocently. I was taking no chances, I didn't want him to know that I was aware of his life, just in case.

'Fiancée.' He gave me a grin, boyish this time instead of

charming. I was getting tired of Tris's smiles, it was like he had a drawer full of them and he would pull the most suitable one out when he needed it. 'She's a great girl.'

He stood up and stretched. 'Well, thanks for the coffee and the chat, maybe we can do this again next week.'

'I don't see why not,' I said and let him out.

I watched him jog away athletically from my premises. I was none the wiser about him. So I did not know where I stood on the Tris Smith question. He was beginning to coalesce now in my mind as a personality. But I found him essentially insincere and unconvincing, as if he were playing a part but for no discernible reason.

After Sunday service and the clean down, I went over to my friend Esther's. The panna cottas had gone down extremely well and I needed some more rhubarb. She let me into her large house and ushered me into her living room.

I sat down on the sofa. Esther gasped a little as she lowered herself onto a chair. She needed the arms of the chair to get up, if she'd sat on the sofa I think she would have been trapped there, floundering like a starfish when it was time to rise. If I had to define Esther in a word, that word would certainly not be lightweight. She was a large woman in her sixties, given to wearing voluminous, colourful, kaftan style dresses to hide her bulk. But she was as sweet-natured as she was overweight, and bright too, as a framed degree portrait from her college in Oxford showed. It was a much slimmer Esther in the frame although the future could be glimpsed in the noticeable chubbiness beneath the gown and mortarboard.

'What you need is a nice cup of tea,' Esther said judiciously, 'and some biscuits.'

She disappeared into the kitchen and I sat in the living room and looked at the military prints on the wall, not Esther's taste but those of her husband, Roy, an ex-soldier. She returned, pushing the tea things and a large plate of biscuits on a hostess trolley. If I asked any of the kids who worked for me what a hostess trolley was, I doubted they would know what I was on about. I marvelled at it, its floral design and shiny tubular frame. It was like a relic from another age. She handed me tea, offered me a digestive biscuit which I declined. She ate a couple with relish then said, 'You haven't forgotten that ages ago you agreed to do the food for us for Litha?'

Litha was the pagan name for the summer solstice. Esther was head of the local Wiccans and they were having a big celebration. The solstice was for me, just another day, this year it happened to be on June 20th. It was a Thursday, which could have been better. It was always a busy night at the restaurant and I'd have to get some cover in. But for Esther and her fellow pagans, it wasn't just another day, it was the day of the celebration of summer. The highlight of the year, like Christmas or Easter for Christians.

'I haven't forgotten,' I said. I was doing the catering and it was a big job, 120-plus people. For me it was the chance not only to make extra money, it was a showcase for my talents. I do catering for parties and events and a lot of the women (they were mainly women) in the Wicca community were quite well-heeled.

'Oh, before I get some more rhubarb for you, do you

want to see the diadem that I get to wear at the ceremony?' Esther asked, coyly. She so obviously wanted me to say yes, so, 'Go on then,' I said.

She disappeared and returned with the diadem, prosaically contained in a hat box. 'It's in here,' Esther confided. She looked around suspiciously, as if thieves might be lurking and then opened the box, brightly coloured wooden bangles clacking on her beefy forearms.

She took the diadem wrapped in tissue paper out of the box and she peeled the paper back reverentially.

'Here we are,' she said, holding it up for my inspection.

The headpiece was a bit like a very elaborate wedding tiara, several filigreed layers of silver set with pearls and precious stones. The jewels sparkled and flashed in the sunlight from the windows. It was very beautiful.

'Wow,' I said, impressed. 'Are those real?'

'Real enough,' she confirmed. 'They're mainly semi-precious stones of course, but the pearls are real. It's over a century old.' She sat back in her chair and continued. 'The founder of our order, Agnes Fernshaw, she was initiated by Gerald Gardner himself!' I wondered who he might be, obviously someone famous in Wiccan circles. 'She was wealthy and had a couple of expensive pearl necklaces which she had reset, together with the other stones to create the diadem.'

'So it's purely symbolic?'

She frowned. 'No, not entirely. Agnes would have conducted a ritual, maybe with Gardner himself, to imbue it with power, and as it has been worn countless times during important ceremonies, so its power will have grown.'

She must have seen the scepticism in my face. 'So yes, it is symbolic, like King Charles's royal crown and sceptre are, but for us it's more than that. We believe it has real power.'

She put it back in its box. 'I'll be crowned with it at the festival, to symbolise the Great Mother.' She smiled. 'It's a huge privilege and an honour to know that I am entrusted with the leadership of so many practitioners.' She closed the lid firmly, then turned to me, picked up an old-fashioned print diary and leafed through it.

'Will you be able to make May the thirteenth at ten for a meeting, an inter-coven meeting, to finalise the food?'

'Sure, what day is that?' I asked.

'A Monday.'

'Definitely.' Mondays were my day off, the restaurant was closed.

'That's settled then.' She smiled. 'So, what have you been up to Charlie? Roy was walking the dogs and told me he'd seen you with a bunch of other runners.'

I told her about the running group, but not about the business with Summers and Tris. I wondered if she knew John Mayhew at all, she was younger than he was but not by that much.

'John Mayhew!' she said with a mixture of alarm, dislike and surprise. 'Miserable old so and so?'

That was an accurate description. 'Yeah.'

'I'm surprised he dared to return here.' Her cheeks had turned red, this happened on those rare occasions when she was angry. 'He's been living in Spain.'

'Yes, I gather he's a businessman.'

'Pah!' Esther expressed her contempt for that idea. 'No dear, John Mayhew is not a retired businessman. He's a convicted fraudster, and a lot of people round here hate his guts.'

# Chapter Seven

A week passed in a blur of cooking and prepping for cooking. Murdo had a couple of days off during the week, so although I was twice as busy I was able to escape the barrage of death metal in the kitchen and listen to more pleasant music. Beech Tree FM appeared to be embracing a more contemporary vibe. I listened to a lot of Charli XCX and Chappell Roan. To my ears a vast improvement on Blood Incantation, which seemed to have been on constantly. The frequent startlingly (to my ears) raunchy references by the women singers to the opposite sex made me pine for Andrea. So I called him on the Thursday night. I knew he was in London for a few days on business, staying in the flat he had there in Clerkenwell. I was hoping he might be able to come down and see me, or I could go up to London on the Sunday night. Like Chappell Roan I was Hot to Go.

'Charlie, hi…' He sounded unusually guarded, which was unlike him.

'Hi, look, I'm going to be free Sunday night, any chance that you might be able to join me?'

There was a pause, then, 'I'm not sure, Charlie, I've got a lot of paperwork to wade through.'

I frowned, this was not how I had envisaged the conversation going. I could feel my excitement ebbing away. I was now no longer Hot to Go, more tepid.

'Can't it wait? We haven't seen each other for ages,' I said plaintively. Silence. 'Hello, are you still there?'

'Yes, I'm still here…' he said.

'I thought it might be nice… just you and me. We could go walking on Monday, the countryside's looking lovely.' A certain amount of desperation there.

He sighed. 'Charlie, I'm very busy right now, these are very serious people I'm dealing with and it's a delicate negotiation, lots of details, lots of lawyers. Look, I'll call you some time next week, okay?'

'Okay,' I said, unhappily, 'ciao.'

'Ciao.'

He ended the call. Well, that was slightly unexpected in an unwelcome kind of way. Andrea could usually fit me in around his schedule. These days he tended to work on short-term advisory contracts for banks and investment companies and that meant he could more or less always find a couple of days off here and there. He also sounded uncharacteristically snappy, he was one of the most laid-back people that I knew.

Oh well, I thought, there's nothing I can do about it. He can join me if he gets the chance, he knows where I am.

The run on Sunday went spectacularly well for me. Buoyed by my irritation at my boyfriend – I'd offered myself on a plate and he'd turned it down, how annoying was that – I felt weirdly energised, channelling my frustrations into a lung-bursting, leg-aching effort. I moved up the pack ahead of my fellow women and Tris. He had spent very little time with the other two men, which was unlike him. I guessed he wanted to bathe in the admiration of Cass and Suzi.

I locked myself in just behind John, whose thin, hairless old man's legs were tirelessly carrying him along just behind Matt. Occasionally he screwed his head round over his shoulder to glare at me, like an angry tortoise. Esther had been vague on the details of his alleged fraud. 'I don't really understand these things dear, but you only have to look at him to see he's a wrong 'un, and now he thinks the danger is over he's got the gall to come back here again. He doesn't give a damn for anyone, the man's a monster, he's got no conscience…' Sod you, you vile baby-boomer con man I thought, I'll show you! As we neared the finish line, the bench on the common, I increased my speed and sprinted past John to come second. I looked at my watch, a personal best for me. Suck on that Andrea, I thought jubilantly, even though he was not remotely interested in my running, and pointlessly, like he would ever know or care. John, however, glared at me in hatred, bested by a woman. I smiled sweetly, at the horrible, scrawny old person. My cup runneth over.

The following day, a Monday so the restaurant was closed, I got back from the cash and carry I use sometimes about lunchtime. I parked my car in my space round the back of my restaurant. I was still mulling over my personal best from the day before. My legs still ached. That made me think of John Mayhew whom I had beaten. I still recalled the fury on his face as I'd passed him. What a nasty man he was. And it wasn't just his personality. As revealed by Esther, that air of contempt that he had for me was not personal, it encompassed all the human race, we were shills for whatever snake oil he had been peddling. What had got into Tris that he should invite him to join the runners? Maybe Tris was planning on conning us out of some money and had turned to an old master for tips. No, that thought was unworthy. I did think it very likely that John Mayhew had persuaded Tris that he was simply a local businessman with an unfortunate past, and I'm sure he wasn't lying if he had told Tris he didn't have many friends. Then I wondered... I managed to stop myself speculating about John. It wasn't healthy.

I tried to think of something else. Ruminating took years off your life, I had heard someone say this and it had the ring of truth. I sat in the old Volvo for a moment and looked at the Old Forge Café as if I were approaching it for the first time. To appreciate what I had as a kind of mindfulness exercise.

What I saw was a pleasant old-fashioned building, white-washed walls with a slightly crooked tiled roof and sticking out from that, the tell-tale sign of any restaurant, the kind of big industrial chimney like a ship's funnel that is the outlet for the extractor fans in the kitchen. Outside the front door, flanking the entrance were two large terracotta pots that contained bulbs that earlier in the year were blooming with crocus, narcissi and snowdrops but right now were blazing with scarlet geraniums. In the car park

I had a small three-sided gazebo with some chairs and tables for the smokers among my customers. That too had planters and tubs with summer bedding plants. We were in Britain after all and it's important for us to wring every drop of pleasure from the summer which, let's face it, often disappoints.

I walked up to the front door and checked the menu in its glass box. The set menu, the à la carte and the lunch menu with traditional sandwiches (but done well and on good quality bread for a change), quiche – much maligned, unfairly in my view, I love a quiche. There was the occasional exotic item to make you think, oh, I'd like to try that, and a few clever cheffy touches so that you could tell that I'd been around and knew what I was doing.

It looked like it was a handsome, classic creation that had plenty of power under the bonnet and more than a hint of confident competence. Like its owner, I thought, complacently. I thought of Andrea. I had a classy boyfriend: wealthy and good-looking. Go me!

I unlocked the door and walked in. All was quiet. Murdo would be visiting Lucy, his girlfriend who was head chef at St Anselm's, one of the colleges in Oxford. I sat in a chair, looking at the decor, savouring the peace.

The restaurant could hold about 30 people. I looked at the rather crappy furniture I had inherited (I'd done the best I could with quality tablecloths) and I reminded myself that I was investigating Tris Smith on behalf of David Summers to pay for some new stuff. Motivation is half the battle.

# Chapter Eight

I sat down in the restaurant with David Summers at 9.30 the day after. He was wearing a jacket and tie with a pair of cream linen trousers. The effect on him with his bull-neck, stocky physique and flowing hair was to make him look like a retired former villain now living the good life. We agreed terms and conditions then I got down to practicalities.

'David, I need to get to know Lizzie better and Tris too...'

'That's a good idea. How are you going to do that?'

'Can your daughter cook?'

'No.' He looked at me in a puzzled way. 'She's terrible. Why?'

That's a relief, I thought. But even if the answer had been yes, she's superb, it wouldn't have mattered. I'm a professional and any good amateur would be keen to learn how we do it as much as what we do.

'When's her birthday?'

'July, July 1 to be precise,' he looked confused by the question. 'Why, what does this have to do with anything?'

'Well, tell her that you've bought her five cookery lessons from me as an early birthday present,' I suggested. 'That way I'll be alone with her in her house and she'll open up about things.'

'Charlie, that sounds like an excellent plan.' He nodded happily in approval.

Good, I thought. 'When does she work? It's part-time, isn't it?'

'Yeah, that's right.'

I nodded to myself. Part-time was fine, she'd be able to fit me in. 'Fine,' I said. 'If she agrees, we can do one a week over the next five weeks. That way I can find out a lot more about Tristan from her as well as from other sources. Does that sound reasonable?'

'Totally.'

'Good. Well, that's sorted, hopefully. Now, here is where things could get problematic. I want to go up to Scotland to see if I can find out a bit more about Tris's wife's death.'

'Why?' He frowned.

I explained that it might reveal things which could be used to discredit Tris in Lizzie's eyes. The truth of the matter was that for some reason I had a burning desire to know more about the fate of the deceased Mrs Smith. I felt it might confirm one way or another whether Tris really was a killer or if it was just David Summers' skewed perception. This caused grumbling which I had been prepared for. I was content to do it just for expenses. Eventually he agreed.

'I remember when he told me about her dying...' he said.

'He brought it up!' I was surprised.

60

'Yeah, he was trying to make me believe how precious Lizzie was to him after all the tragedy he'd had in his life with women. Apparently, his mother died when he was a kid, then there was this guff about his dead wife. That didn't fool me for one moment!'

I nodded. Summers was reliving the conversation, he was incandescent with rage. 'And then there was all this psychological bullshit that he'd learned at uni...'

'Which uni?' I asked.

Summers shrugged. 'Some poncey college at Oxford. I never went to university.'

I wondered if he was going to say 'I was brought up in the School of Hard Knocks.' I was a bit disappointed when he didn't.

'Lizzie, of course, is awestruck by his so-called genius. He's always telling her how clever he is and quoting someone called Deleuze. Who the fuck is he when he's at home?' he demanded, angrily.

'I have literally no idea,' I said. 'Anyway, cooking lessons.' I tried to nudge him back to the main purpose of the visit.

'Okay, then, I'll be in touch after I've spoken to Lizzie.' He stood up. 'Edward was right about you. I'm glad you've said yes. For the first time in ages I've felt I've done something positive.'

I watched him go and went to join Murdo in the kitchen. I opened the door and a deafening wave of sound washed over me. I looked at Murdo, busy cooking off veg.

'Are ye in the mood fir some classic Opeth, Chef?' he shouted above the din.

I sighed; it was going to be a long shift. While Murdo

and I were prepping for lunch, I asked casually, 'Oh, Murdo, are you going to be calling Lucy?'

'Yeah, why?'

'Could you ask her if she knows anyone in the Psychology department there?' David Summers' anti education rant had given me an idea.

'Sure, will do.'

Time to go hunting myself, this time in the thickets of Tris Smith's youth. See if I could find anything to use against him. I had done the obvious, gone through his Facebook and Instagram posts but they all appeared to be squeaky clean. Tris was clearly too bright to put compromising stuff out there, but when he was younger he might have created a few skeletons in the closet that I could use against him. Or so I hoped.

An hour or so later Murdo's phone rang. 'Yeah, hi babes… sure… here she is.'

He handed me the phone. 'Lucy.'

I looked up from where I had been probing the beef joints, 50 degrees, that would do. The warmth of the kitchen would heat them up by a few degrees making them a rich pink when I sliced them. I took the phone from him.

'Hi, Lucy…'

The gravelly tones of Murdo's girlfriend drifted out of the speaker.

'Hello, Charlie… Murdo said did I know anyone from the Psychology dept. Yeah I do, a bloke called Vernon Taylor. He's some sort of behavioural psychologist I think.'

'How come you know him, Lucy?' I was curious. 'Is he part of the staff?'

The college kitchens cooked not only food for the students and faculty, kind of canteen style, but they also did fine dining for the college dinners where guests from other colleges, visiting academics and anyone who looked like they might be persuaded to give the college some money were entertained. The menus were discussed with the Bursar and in Lucy's case the Master, because he liked her. So Lucy knew quite a few departmental heads as well as the obvious bigwigs like the aforementioned Master of the College and the Bursar.

'Nah, he done a bit of research on me and my brigade. Hooked me up to a little machine that measured electrical impulses on my skin to see how stressed I was getting… he told me the results – my stress was really low,' she laughed heartily, 'but my brigade's was really high… I said that's because they was a load of useless wankers, particularly the men, so no wonder they were stressed. I says to him, look Doc, you want me to move that dial, you just lock me in a room with Jason Momoa, it'll be off the fucking scale, let me tell you… the things I'd like to do to Aquaman!' She gave a filthy laugh.

'What did he say?'

'That his budget didn't extend to flying Hollywood A-listers in, but if ever their paths crossed, he'd be sure to let him know,' she said proudly. 'His words exactly. I live in hope. Meanwhile Murdo will have to do.'

'I see. How long's he been at the uni?' I was so hoping his path would have intersected with Tris Smith.

'Ages… fifteen years or so.'

I felt suddenly optimistic. Quite a few students every

year would do Psychology, maybe 100 or so I guessed, but there was a chance he might have come across Tris. It was worth a shot. I would be very interested to know what he would have made of him if they had met.

'Do you ever see him or speak to him?'

'No.'

I felt immediately disappointed, but then she said, 'He gave me his number though, said he was always free if I wanted to speak to him, said I was a "unique individual". Do you want me to call him for you?'

'Yes please. Tell him it's in connection with someone called Tristan Smith.'

'Sure, will do. Oh, remind Murdo that I'm officially a "unique individual", as well as the hottest thing ever in chef's whites…'

'I surely will, Lucy. Thanks very much.'

'See ya Charlie.'

She ended the call. I handed the phone back to Murdo. 'Thanks. Oh, and Lucy said that I was to remind you that she was a "unique individual".'

'Aye well, that's certainly indisputable.' He grinned. 'What's all this about Tris Smith then?'

'To be honest, Murdo,' I said thoughtfully, 'I'm not really sure.'

# Chapter Nine

And so, on the Wednesday afternoon, I found out from Slattery that John Mayhew had been murdered. May Day was of course, traditionally a day of celebration and renewal, like the old-fashioned maypole, but it's gone out of fashion. That the traditional beginning of summer should have been marked by a death, no matter how deserving the recipient, seemed to me an ill omen. At work of course, my staff speculated wildly during the evening shift.

I also had a message from Tris on a group chat that he had set up, cancelling Sunday's run for the next fortnight, resuming on the nineteenth. So we could mourn Mayhew. Well, I for one wouldn't be doing much grieving.

I was hoping to learn more from Slattery and sure enough he turned up at my place at 11 o'clock that night. 'I heard John Mayhew was involved in some kind of investment scandal.' I told him about the conversation with Tris Smith, and Esther's description of him as a fraudster.

Slattery nodded and confirmed it. 'That's very true. It was a few years ago now and, yes, quite a few people round here did lose money. His car got keyed a few times, people blanked him in public and he moved away, Spain I heard. He had property out there. He kept his house in the village though, just shuttered it up. Then about four months ago he came back. I guess he felt it had all blown over. And to a certain extent it had. People had died, moved away. Newcomers had moved in. It's not the same community that it was.'

'So you don't think it was someone local who shot him?' I said. 'One of his victims?'

Slattery shook his head. 'I have absolutely no idea at this stage of the investigation. It seems unlikely. Why leave it all this time to exact revenge? He was around for a while after the fraud went to trial, nobody did anything then. No, this looks more professional, in my opinion.' He shrugged. 'We'll see, my money is on his business associates.'

The next day I had a text from David Summers to tell me that Lizzie was delighted by the idea of cookery lessons. Even better, he had forwarded the money for them to my account. Could I possibly go round the following Tuesday afternoon, to her house, and he added an address in the village up the road. Fine, I messaged back, I'll be there.

But it wasn't just Lizzie that was on my mind, or Tris for that matter. Earlier I had gone for an easy run at about half seven in the morning. By easy, I mean the kind of pace where you could still chat to someone without effort. I was slow and relaxed as I ran along. It was still cool and quiet in the narrow lanes with their high hawthorn hedges reducing the sky to a narrow azure strip. A couple of red kites wheeled effortlessly high overhead, silhouetted against the blue above. As I jogged through the wood on the other side of Frampton End, I saw a jay fly across my path, its pinks and blues clashing with the light green tones of the beech leaves above. Then, in perfect counterpoint to the beauty of nature, in a lay-by I passed shortly after, some arsehole had dumped three black bin bags, their torn plastic sides disgorging bathroom waste, towel rails, broken bath panels and bags that had contained grouting and such. I felt quiet rage surge up inside me against these soulless eco-vandals. As I had thought before, on more than one occasion, it really was a growing problem that the council seemed unwilling or unable to deal with.

When I got back just after 8 o'clock I found Cassandra sitting on one of the beer crates that we use as chairs outside the backdoor of the kitchen; it seemed as if she was staring at the ground in front of her. She looked up as she heard me open the gate. I kind of registered the head movement as I walked in.

'Cass, hi! What on earth are you doing here?' I was surprised but not unduly so. Once or twice she had turned up unexpectedly at my place, full of excitement at a new find that was not going to hang around. 'I can get you twenty-four bottles of this at a fifty per cent discount. I'm not asking you to buy it, I'm ordering you, Charlie, it's a steal!'

From her beaten body language I didn't think it was going to be one of those days. She certainly didn't look full of excitement, that was for sure.

I sat down heavily on the crate opposite and mopped my forehead with the base of my T-shirt. I'd turned my easy run into a speed run halfway round. I absentmindedly sniffed my armpits, not too bad. I glanced across at my companion. That's a bit more than could be said for Cass, she looked like she'd had a really late night. I unlaced my trail shoes.

'I didn't know you were coming today, did I?' I remarked, wiggling my toes in my socks. 'Have I got the day wrong?'

She shook her head. 'No, I remembered I needed to have a word with Murdo. I thought I'd call by as I was in the area.'

'Oh,' I looked at my watch, 'he'll still be asleep at this time.' She was very pale suddenly, well, even paler than she had been. I wondered if she was going to throw up. 'Are you feeling okay?' I was feeling slightly concerned. 'Cass, you look awful, if you don't mind me saying so.'

Her normally glossy dark brown hair was lifeless and limp, there were bags under her eyes, her shirt was crushed and creased, she looked haggard, ten years older than she was. Well, we all have our off days, and whatever was going on, it really was none of my business.

'Bit of a cold,' she said, unconvincingly. Then, 'Don't worry, it's not Covid. I did a test.'

Really? I thought, but I just laughed. 'Thank God for that.' The memory of Covid and lockdown when so many of us in the pub and restaurant business stared ruin in the face was not one I wanted to bring up. The very thought still made me shudder. I unlocked the back door. 'Come on in.'

She followed me up the stairs to my flat above the restaurant and I pointed to the end of the corridor where the lounge was. 'Wait in there,' I said. 'I'll go and get him. If you'll excuse me, I'm going for a shower.'

'Thanks, Charlie.' She smiled gratefully and rather painfully at me. I thought it looked like she had a monumental hangover (maybe she had broken her no drinks rule), but it was not just that. I began to suspect something was evidently troubling her. Well, if she wanted my help all she needed to do was to ask. She knew that.

I banged on Murdo's door, heard a kind of muffled groan from within.

'Cass has come to see you,' I called. 'I'm going for a shower.'

When I came out of my room and went into the living room, Murdo was alone and she was gone. He was wearing one of his band T-shirts; today it was Megadeath twinned with a pair of red boxer shorts. Not a great look. His thin white, freckly arms and legs poked out like twigs.

'What did Cass want?' I asked, towelling my hair dry.

'She's hoping to get an entry into the college wine purchasing,' he said, nonchalantly. 'Lucy knows the bursar really well and I said I'd pass on her details.'

'Oh, I see.' Hangover or no hangover, maybe it was a cold, it was a shrewd move on Cass's part. To get a foot in the door to see the bursar would be very hard without a recommendation.

The rest of the week passed in the usual frenzy of food prep and cooking. Every morning I decided that today would be the day I would try to formulate a plan to investigate Tris further and every day I failed to come up with something. Then finally Tuesday came and I went round to Lizzie's.

# Chapter Ten

'Hi, you must be Charlie!'

Standing framed in the front doorway of the cottage, Lizzie Summers looked a lot like her father. Stocky, plump, quite powerfully built. She had the same thick neck and the same slightly aggressive forward jut to her head. They also shared the same hairdo. Summers was correct in that she was not in the same league in the looks department as her fiancé. Not only looks. Lizzie was carrying quite a lot of surplus weight around. She was wearing black running tights and a large pink hoodie to try and camouflage her body. It was unsuccessful.

'Do come in...'

Home was a small detached cottage in Potter's Hill, a village a couple of miles away from Hampden Green, along a single-track road bordered by high beech and hawthorn hedges. There was a kind of inter-village rivalry between it and the village where I lived. There were some seriously big, expensive houses in Potter's Hill (this certainly wasn't one of them, but even this modest house would have been eye-wateringly pricey to rent) and in my village they accused the Potter's Hill residents of snobbery. I had also heard them blamed for walking their dogs over to Hampden Green and letting them shit everywhere and not clean it up. I don't think there was much truth in that assertion. The two villages disliked each other, but that's the countryside for you, it's not a particularly friendly place and almost certainly never was. Feelings run deep and if you quarrel with someone or they upset you, it's much harder to avoid them than if you were living in a larger community.

I knew most cottages like these had been modernised and heavily converted. Lizzie's place was much more basic. The outside looked lovely. The garden was full of colour from a variety of flowers and shrubs, I had brushed past some lavender heavy with purple spikes covered with industrious, friendly looking bees, and the scent had risen gloriously about me, like being spritzed as you walk through duty-free. Violas with their beautiful heart-shaped flowers, blue and gold, peeked out by some small, feathery ferns. The red-tiled roof was charmingly crooked and mossy, the windows leaded.

I walked in through the open door. 'Lovely house,' I said. 'Is it yours?'

'We rent it,' she explained. She smiled shyly. 'We're engaged.' I thought to myself, this has to be heavily subsidised by her dad. I knew the kind of money Tris would be on, he could afford a one-bedroom flat in Wycombe, the nearest large town. Just about. Nothing like this bijou, if slightly run-down, cottage. 'I don't think we'll buy anything just yet,' she continued. 'We may not even be around here. Tris doesn't really know where he'll be a few years down the line… not that he has any plans to move anytime soon.' Her face softened. 'I think he'd like to go back to London, he's from there you know.'

I looked around the small hallway we were standing in. It was nowhere near as nice as the outside. Staircase in front of me, kitchen at the end, living room to the right. Above would be the bedroom, bathroom and probably a box-room. There was a pile of old junk mail carelessly heaped by the front door. Clothes and some books were on the stairs and a couple of jackets were thrown over the post at the end of the banisters. There was a pervasive smell of damp. She followed my gaze.

'I'm not very house-proud I'm afraid.' She sighed and shook her head, then she smiled, a lovely, gentle smile. 'But Tris doesn't mind.'

I'm sure he doesn't, I thought. However, if your dad is correct, Tris doesn't want to rock the boat yet, not until he's got a ring on your finger, then maybe the tune would change. We'll see what happens, I thought to myself. Pulling away from the realm of speculation, I smiled encouragingly. I was here to give Lizzie cookery lessons.

'Let's look at the kitchen,' I suggested. It would be nice to be on safe ground, at least I knew where I stood and what to do when faced with food and a stove. I would figure out how to get her to open up about Tris as things progressed.

'Sure, it's through here.'

She led me from the small hall with its stained oatmeal carpet and slightly musty smell, into a small galley kitchen. My heart sank. There was very little work surface, what there was, invisible under groceries and other bits of junk obviously separated from the heap by the door. Letters, flyers for pizza delivery, gardening services and official-looking correspondence. The sink was full of unwashed dishes. The problems did not end there. The small four-plate electric stove was dirty and there was a pan where someone had heated up some baked beans and left it on the hob. It was obviously not her housework skills that had attracted Tris. For someone used to 30 years (oh my God! A third of a century, where had my youth gone!) of relatively spotless kitchens, it was a heart-breaking sight. I could have sunk to my knees and wept, except for the fact that the kitchen floor (plastic tiles with a dark swirly pattern to hide the dirt) was sticky underfoot and I didn't fancy getting any closer to it than I had to.

'Will it be okay?' she said anxiously.

Well, it would have to be. 'Look, Elizabeth…' I took a deep breath.

'Lizzie, please,' she corrected me.

'Lizzie, on the days that I come, you'll need to tidy the place up a bit, make sure this space,' I indicated the worktop, 'is free and we'll need the cooker a bit cleaner.'

'I can do that,' she said eagerly, with a kind of puppyish enthusiasm that suddenly reminded me of Francis, my kitchen porter. She gave me that lovely shy smile again. I could see why her dad was so protective of her, so anxious to neutralise what he saw as a threat. Lizzie seemed worryingly innocent.

'That's good then,' I said reassuringly. I had been worried that she might have got a bit defensive about the unhygienic surroundings that she cooked in, but she seemed to accept it with good enough grace. 'Let's go into the lounge and talk about what days will suit you and what you'd like to get out of these lessons.' She looked slightly alarmed. 'Remember,' my voice was soothing, 'they're your lessons and we'll tailor them to your needs and expectations.' That sounded very professional, I thought to myself.

'That sounds wonderful,' she said. 'The lounge is this way.'

The living room at the front of the cottage was a kind of shrine to Tris. I checked out the Tris-obilia. There was a photo on the wall of him in his graduation robes clutching his degree and smiling. Actually, it was more of a self-satisfied smirk than anything else. Tris always did seem very pleased to be Tris. There was a framed award from some sommelier organisation, another from a college in Hotel Studies. There were some cups and trophies, for running, I assumed. There was nothing of Lizzie there at all. I found this rather sad. It was all so one-way. I was staring at a framed photo of Tris in a tracksuit on a podium in second place when Lizzie broke in proudly, 'That was Tris at the British Universities athletics finals, fifteen hundred meters; he represented Oxford.'

'Wow!' I was suitably impressed. 'Was that where he went to uni?' Better to feign ignorance of Tris's background in case she wondered who had told me.

'Yeah, he did Psychology.' She smiled ruefully. 'I never did too well in exams myself.'

'Join the club!' I said cheerily. I'd left school at sixteen and gone to a catering college. I had wanted to be earning

as soon as possible. There were more Tris-related memorabilia prominently displayed in the small room, including
a photo of him with an elderly man.

'Who's he?' I asked.

'Oh that's Tris's dad. He's in a home now, poor guy.
Dementia.' She sighed. 'Very sad when that happens.'

There were no other photos of his family, just the father.

'What about his mum?'

She smiled sadly. 'Tris's mum died when he was quite
young.'

'I'm sorry.'

Lizzie made a kind of helpless gesture. 'Tris's dad never
really got over it, seemingly. Of course, now he doesn't
have any recollection of her at all. Tris visits him as often
as he can, sometimes he stays overnight nearby and sees
him again in the morning. Tris tells me quite often he
doesn't know who he is, but he does what he can.' She
smiled. 'I'm very proud of him. Dementia's a terrible thing.'

I nodded. What could you say? 'Where is he today, by
the way?' I asked.

'He had to go in to work, although the restaurant is
closed in the afternoon,' she said. 'Strickland wanted to go
over some ideas with him, he relies a lot on Tris, you know.
He often has to go in on his days off.'

Strickland relied on no one, least of all the restaurant
manager. And while he had no compunction in working
his staff to the bone, himself included, I had driven past
the restaurant earlier and Strickland's car, a very flashy
Maserati, wasn't there. Wherever he was, Tris was not there.
I wondered where he was.

But I just smiled politely and nodded. 'Yeah, Graeme can be a real bastard sometimes. Anyway, let's talk business now.'

Lizzie and I agreed on the following Thursday then Monday and a Wednesday, four until five. This would give us a finish point in the first week of June. So, that was the timing of the lessons worked out. We also discussed the content of the lessons. I don't normally give cookery lessons but when I do, it tends to be dinner-party themed. Lizzie wasn't interested in those. Most people I have met tend to have an exaggerated opinion of their cookery skills. This was certainly not the case with Lizzie. She had no faith in herself whatsoever. Rather touchingly her dream was 'to make Tris a really nice dinner, not just spag bol or sausages and mash and beans, which is what I can do at the moment. Oh, and I can do fish fingers…'

'Nothing wrong with those three dishes,' I said, encouragingly.

'I know,' she said, wistfully, 'but it would be nice to be able to do something else for a change.'

'Well, I'm sure we can manage that.' Let's be positive, Charlie. She looked so vulnerable, in spite of – maybe because of – her bulky physique that I felt a stab of guilt. The only reason she was getting these lessons was to try and split her up from a man she patently adored. I felt an irresistible urge to do something nice for her.

'Tell you what. Your dad's paying me quite well for these lessons. I'll throw in a freebie. I'll come round on Thursday if you're free and I'll throw in an intro lesson.'

'Oh my God, Charlie.' She was almost in tears. 'That's so kind of you!'

'No, that's okay.'

'Maybe we can work up to something gourmet…'

That might be stretching it a bit I thought. 'Well let's not try and run until we can walk,' I remarked judiciously.

'Duck… like they have in restaurants…' she breathed, misty eyed.

That should be doable, I thought. Duck's fairly straightforward to cook when you know what you're doing.

'Well, we can certainly aim for duck.' My tone was encouraging.

'Really!' She sounded incredulous.

'Absolutely, with an orange sauce, old school.'

She clasped her hands together almost in wonder. 'Thank you so much Charlie.'

I smiled warmly. She might look like her dad, but, unlike him, she was a sweetie. 'My pleasure,' I said.

And there we left it. Lizzie with her dreams of duck to serve Tris. As I drove home I felt happy with the way things had gone today. I had learned a bit more about Tris. He seemed far from the image that Summers had projected of him as a ruthless murderer. So far, I had learned that he was indeed a bright guy, with impeccable qualifications, and a dutiful son. Okay, so he was a bit of an egomaniac, but so what. Maybe that's what he valued in Lizzie, an ardent worshipper, the moon that circled around his sun. And she got to be with someone she patently adored. I was beginning to wonder if Summers was totally wrong about him. Well, if he was, and I found Tris to be blameless, he would just have to suck it up.

# Chapter Eleven

The following day, a Wednesday, was quite busy. It had got off to a fraught start as I was teaching Francis how to make a new salad. I was putting it on as a special for the lunch menu, and if there was any left, it would go on as an evening special. Interesting salads were selling well, not just because of the hot weather but because a lot of my clientele at lunch time were women who tended to be more health conscious than men. So, here I was experimenting with fennel, which was new to Francis, although not to me. I'd normally used it in other restaurants where it tended to be paired with white fish, like seabass, and I think it goes really well with salmon. But today I thought I'd use it in a salad. Francis was finding the new dish, simple as it was, confusing.

'What's that Chef?' He asked, holding a bulb up.

'It's fennel, Francis.'

'It smells of liquorice.' He sniffed it dubiously. 'Can you really eat it in a salad?'

'You certainly can. Now, here's how we cut it.' I halved it and removed the woody stem and then, 'Slice it very finely, julienne style. See… now you do it.'

Francis started cutting it into thick strips. 'No,' I said, 'they're too big. Much finer.'

Clumsily and slowly he copied me. I sighed. It was going to be a long day. Once we had succeeded in julienning the fennel, we added walnuts, radicchio, some rocket, parmesan shavings then a lemon, olive oil and honey dressing.

'Taste it, Francis,' I suggested. Well, more of an order really.

'Do I have to, Chef?' He pulled a face. 'It smells a bit funny.'

'Yes, you do.' I was insistent. 'Remember, we taste everything We're checking the seasoning, the balance of the ingredients. Above all, that we're happy with it. Now… No! We're not savages. Not with your fingers, get a fork.'

'Mmm, it's good.' His broad face under its shock of unruly blonde hair looked almost comically surprised.

'I'm so pleased you like it Francis,' I said, only semi-sarcastically. 'Now, do you think you can remember how to make this? The recipe's there in the file.'

'I can remember.' He sounded confident. I wished I felt the same.

Lunch service went well. The last customers left at 2.15 and we closed and locked the door. I pulled off my jacket and left Francis and Murdo to clean down while I had a Diet Coke with Jess. We'd sold eight of the new salads, which pleased me. Jess took her apron off and pushed her hair back.

'Did you know that Graeme Strickland was in today?' she asked.

'What? As a customer?' I felt a frisson of fear, in case I'd served him something sub-par. 'What did he have?'

'He had the fennel salad,' Jess said with maddening complacency.

'And?' My voice was nervous. Jess was playing with me like a cat with a mouse. She knew how much I valued Strickland's opinions. He was a bloody annoying human being but divinely inspired when it came to cooking. A kind of demi-god of the kitchen.

She relented. 'He said he liked it, that it was well put together, compliments.' She smiled. 'Better now?' she asked with faux-concern. I was.

Then Jess changed the subject. 'There was a thing in the Bucks Free Press online about John Mayhew today. I hadn't realised that he was the guy behind Elektra Investment Management.'

'Who are they?' I had never heard of them.

'They were a crypto investment company and John Mayhew persuaded quite a few people round here to invest. They all lost their money.'

'Did your dad get taken in?' I asked. I knew vaguely that her father worked in finance.

She shook her head. 'Dad said he only invested in ISAs and boring things like that, not Bitcoin or Ethereum. But a lot of people did. I bet he was killed by an angry local.' She nodded as if confirming her own statement. 'That'll be it, I bet you. Someone he swindled. That's why they say he disappeared to Spain, taking the money he'd nicked with him.'

\*

'So do you think he was murdered by an angry local?' It wasn't Jess I was addressing this question to, it was eight hours later and I was talking to DI Slattery who had called in on his way home.

He took a sip of the brandy I had given him. We had been talking about John's death and the investment failure.

'It's possible,' he said, 'but unlikely. I think we discussed this before. That was five years ago now. I know there's that thing about revenge being best served cold,' he pulled a dismissive face, 'but I kind of doubt it. They weren't violent people he defrauded. I don't think any of them have been playing the long game, but I thought about it myself and I actually looked into it. There were some big-time losers, it's true, but most of the local investors lost between one and ten thousand pounds. Is that enough to kill someone over? These people aren't gangsters.'

'Was it a crooked scheme or just bad luck that everything went wrong?' I asked. Tris of course, way back when, had suggested that Mayhew had been the victim, that it had simply been bad luck. I remembered he'd said the company had gone bust and all Mayhew had left was running. No hint of impropriety. I was unclear what had happened.

'It's a good question and one that was asked at the time. One big investor complained to the SFO saying it was a Ponzi scheme.'

'What's that?'

'It's when you use later investors' money to pay back the first investors,' Slattery explained. 'Eventually there is no more money and the whole thing collapses like a pack of cards. Mayhew's defence was that any investment is, by its nature, risky. He also blamed the whole thing on his then business partner, saying he'd been taken in too. That said business partner had minimised the risks. He claimed that he had the proof but it wasn't forthcoming. Anyway, the legal ruling was that it was legit, that the investors knew they were engaging in speculative activity that was high risk. I think it's quite a valid point. If you buy into something as potentially dodgy as crypto, it seems to me you are obviously gambling. Anyway, whatever the rights and wrongs, John Mayhew was cleared.'

'Who was his business partner?'

Slattery made a kind of dismissive noise and waved a hand. 'Oh, some shady property dealer called David Summers.' He paused, stared at me in a concerned way. 'Are you okay, Charlie? You look like you've seen a ghost.'

# Chapter Twelve

David Summers was out of the country until the following week. Not that I wanted to discuss his relationship with John Mayhew, but I felt he was owed a progress report. I was glad he wasn't around, to be honest. I had found out virtually nothing about Tris, nothing that he didn't already know. I hadn't even seen him, running didn't resume until the following week out of respect for the dead fraudster.

After a fairly quiet Thursday lunch, thirty-odd covers, I cleaned the kitchen down, did some yoga, showered, changed and went round to Lizzie's for the first of her cookery lessons. Her freebie.

I parked by the duck pond, just up from the cottage and walked down the side-path to where the kitchen door was rather than use the front door. I tapped on the glass of the window.

'Hi, Lizzie, it's Charlie.' But she wasn't in the house.

'Hang on, just a moment.' Lizzie's voice was coming from the shed that was next to the house. The other side of the path to the backdoor. It looked to be more of a workshop than a typical shed; it was long and narrow. Its door opened and Lizzie appeared, wearing jeans and a T-shirt. A muffin-top of flesh hung over the waistband of her jeans and her arms revealed by her T-shirt were sizeable, as was her chest. She looked faintly flustered as she locked the shed door behind her and put the key under one of several empty terracotta plant containers.

'Best to keep it locked,' she said. 'Tris keeps his wine in there.' She smiled. 'Wasted on me, I don't drink.' She opened the kitchen door and ushered me in.

The kitchen was a vast improvement on the last time I had seen it. She had obviously taken my comments to heart and given it a damn good clean. I was impressed and also a little touched. Her large blue eyes peered at me from under her fringe with happy anticipation.

'What are we going to cook?' she asked. 'Duck?' She sounded hopeful.

I shook my head. 'No, not today.'

'Oh…'

'Don't worry, we'll get round to it. Now, do you know what a Cotoletta Milanese is?' Shake of the head. 'Wiener schnitzel?' Same reaction. I showed her a photo on my phone.

'Oh God, yes,' dawning comprehension now, 'it's delicious.'

'It is indeed.'

'I'm so excited… and look how tidy the kitchen is!'

'I noticed. I'm very pleased.'

'… and Tris bought me a present, he's so thoughtful.' She reached into a drawer and brought out a Sabatier chef's knife, its razor-sharp edge glinting in the light from the kitchen window. It was a very nice knife indeed.

So we got down to business. Together we covered the thin slices of meat (batted out veal) with flour, egg and breadcrumbs (pannéing, as it's called) and shallow-fried one so it was golden brown on each side.

'How do you know if the meat's cooked enough?' she asked.

'It's cut very thin,' I explained, 'so if the outside's cooked, the inside will be as well.'

'Oh, that makes sense.'

I gave her a small dish of pre-cooked new potatoes and green beans that I had brought from my restaurant. 'Put those in the microwave, Lizzie.'

I cut the meat in half for us and divided the vegetables between us then I gave her a lemon wedge.

'It doesn't need a sauce, just drizzle lemon juice on it.'

'And we eat it with new potatoes and beans?' she asked.

'You can eat it with what you like. I just had these handy.'

She nodded. 'I think I'll do the same then.'

We ate the schnitzel, Lizzie demolishing hers with unnerving speed. Then, after she finished, she frowned. 'How do you cook the vegetables so they're like that? Mine are either too hard or mushy.'

'Have you got any? Green beans and spuds that is?'

'Yes.' She rootled around in the crammed fridge and triumphantly produced the beans and then some tired looking potatoes from somewhere in the crowded work-space of her kitchen.

I put them to one side. 'I'll show you in a minute.' I put a pan of water on for the potatoes and one for the beans.

Then I taught her how to make a Victoria sponge. That

took about twenty or so minutes and as we put it in the oven I dropped the potatoes in the boiling water and they cooked as we cleaned down her kitchen. Then I explained how to test them with the point of a sharp knife. 'See how easily it goes in? Now they're cooked, we'll let them cool down and you can eat them later.'

Then I showed her how to cook green beans. 'Now, don't forget to salt the water for the green beans… give them three minutes then taste one… no, that's not cooked is it… it should be slightly firm, but not hard, al dente we call it. A minute more.' We drained the cooked green beans and plunged them into cold water to stop them cooking.

'Now you can have them whenever you want, just use the micro… they'll be good for a couple of days in the fridge.'

The sponge was done. We took it out of the oven to cool.

'Do you know how to make icing?' I asked.

She didn't. I don't think I have taught a more inept person other than Francis. But we got there in the end. She was incredibly happy with what she had accomplished. Then we sandwiched the two halves of the cake together with blackcurrant jam that she had.

'Now you can have that with some whipped cream,' I suggested.

'I can't wait for Sunday evening,' she told me as I packed up to leave. 'Tris isn't working that night and I'll be able to cook this for him. I feel so happy and he'll be so proud of me.'

\*

There was to be no avoiding Tris. On Friday evening, just before service he turned up at my place at 5.45, just before we opened.

Jess came through into the kitchen. 'There's Tris Smith at the front door to see you,' she said. She looked quite angry, as if I'd invited him. Jess had decided on the basis of no evidence other than David Summers' word that Tris was a killer, just waiting to pounce again. She'd told me he had that kind of face, and that 'she could tell these things'.

I wondered what he wanted. 'Tell him I will be right out,' I said. I put down the piping bag that I was holding and looked critically at the cake where I had just written 'Happy Birthday Alicia' in pink icing. I took another, smaller piping bag that I'd fitted with a star nozzle and added several little decorative swirls in blue icing around the edge. It looked really good, though I say it myself. It was Alicia's birthday dinner tonight at my restaurant, a table of twelve on a pre-order. A perfect table to cater for.

I washed my hands and went into the restaurant. Tris Smith was sitting at a table by the door, Jess glowering suspiciously at him from behind the counter. It's unlikely I know, but I could swear that her thick, dark slightly frizzy hair actually rose when she was with someone she disliked or mistrusted, like the hackles of a dog.

He stood up when I came in. I noticed his eyes drop slightly towards my chest as I did so. Evaluating the goods on offer. Well, he'd be disappointed; a chef's jacket and apron leave little to get excited about. It's as discreet an outfit as a nun's habit.

'Hello, Tris, how are you?'

'I'm good, thanks. Lizzie sends her regards. She loved that cookery lesson you gave her; she tells me she's going to surprise me at the weekend. Thank you so much, it means such a lot to see her happy. Obviously, working for Graeme I don't get to spend as much time as I'd like with her, she's such a sweetheart.'

He sounded sincere and I felt another twinge of doubt as to the ethics of what I was doing, pretending to be their friend for purely mercenary reasons.

'What brings you here, Tris?'

'Two things.' He produced his laptop out of a satchel he had slung over his shoulder. It was a very nice satchel, made by Dunhill. Doubtless a present from Lizzie.

'Firstly do you happen to know anyone who could fix this?' he asked.

I frowned. 'Doesn't Matt work in IT? He fixes stuff for you at the King's Head, wouldn't he know?'

'Oh, I don't like to bother him.' He gave me his brilliant smile that made me think, you're lying. I wonder why you're really here.

'What's the matter with it?'

'The USB port at the side isn't working. I tried putting a memory stick in and it couldn't locate it, then I tried an external hard drive to play a film, same thing. I don't know if it's a software or a hardware problem, but I could do with getting it fixed. Oh, and my email and calendar are running slow, that's kind of annoying. If someone emails me it seems to take a while to get through.'

'I do know someone,' I said.

'Is he good?'

'Yes,' I said, 'she is.'

He raised an eyebrow, slightly surprised at the concept that women might be good with computers. Oh, poor old Ada Lovelace, I thought, you lived and died in vain. And without even the brand recognition that her 1970s seventies porn film namesake, Linda, still has.

He handed it over to me and looked deep into my eyes with that fake sincerity which I found so icky. 'Thank you. Let me know what she says, I'd appreciate it sooner rather than later.'

'Will do.' I said. 'What's the second thing?'

He smiled at me winningly and stroked his hair, suddenly looking at me in a hungry, evaluating kind of way that I had never seen before. He rearranged his features to look serious and put a voice on to match. 'You've got the potential to be a good runner, Charlie. I think you have been under-estimating yourself.' I felt myself start to bristle internally. I hate it when people try that approach. I once had a guy come on to me saying, 'You don't realise how beautiful you really are.' Like I was supposed to swoon into his arms with gratitude. Instead I'd told him, 'Yes I do. I'm much too good for you, now fuck off.'

Here was Tris, with what seemed to me to be more or less the same approach. I wondered how it would develop. I raised my eyebrows encouragingly. He carried on. 'But you need some coaching and to be pushed. You need tough love, Charlie to fulfil your potential, which I know you want to do…' I looked at him in wonder, he really was being a prick. He obviously totally misinterpreted my expression. 'If you want, we could go on some runs together, I could give you some pointers.'

I bet that's not all you'd like to give me, Tris, I thought to myself. He smiled confidently.

'That's very kind of you to think of me,' I replied, 'but…' I gestured vaguely at the kitchen door behind which Jess had retreated.

'Seriously though, I think you have the potential to be very good, at a senior level.'

'Thank you,' I said acidly.

He laughed. 'Not that you look it.' His voice changed to a lower pitch, presumably he thought it sounded sexier that way, as he murmured, 'I think you're an extremely attractive woman, Charlie, it would be a pleasure to coach you and to get to know you a bit better.'

I had a horrible thought that this was the genuine Tris talking. 'It's very kind of you, Tris, but I just don't have the time.'

As I let him out, he said, somewhat huskily, 'If you change your mind about us… let me know, I'll be there for you.' That smile again, confident as ever, wildly misplaced this time, and he disappeared off into the warm sunny evening.

I watched him go with a contemptuous frown. This had obviously been a come on, no doubt about it. I marvelled at the way he was going about it, a mixture of flattery and the suggestion that he could, like a knight on a white charger, come and rescue me from my history of disappointing run times. Maybe with another woman it might have worked? What it had done was make me simultaneously cross and queasy. I looked down at the sleek silver laptop and patted it gently. What interesting information do you contain about your owner, I wondered.

Jess reappeared. 'Has he gone?'

'Yeah, he wants you to fix his laptop.' I decided not to tell her about his approaches to me, Jess was hyper-loyal, she would be furious. I didn't want that, I wanted her focused.

'What did you say?' she asked.

'I said, yes, of course.'

She nodded knowingly. 'I take it you want to know what else is on that laptop as well as the problem, whatever it may be.'

'Oh, yes, Jess, that's exactly what I want,' I said slowly and with great relish. 'I want to know all of Tris's dirty little secrets.'

Jess nodded happily. 'I'm your girl.'

'Thank you, Jess, I knew I could rely on you.'

# Chapter Thirteen

I walked round to Esther's on Monday morning after a busy weekend. I was there for the meeting to discuss the food at the forthcoming solstice celebrations. Hampden Green was looking particularly pleasant in the sun. The houses were well-kept, the gardens were well-tended. It was a nice place to live. However, I had been here long enough to realise that dark currents of hatred ran deep in the small village community, perhaps magnified by that very smallness. Like it or not, someone from round here had probably killed John unless it really was one of those mysterious 'business associates'. Living in the countryside can be every bit as nasty as living in London, but without the crowds. As I strolled along, I saw several people I knew and waved at several more as they drove by. It could be any one of them who had fired the crossbow that had killed the miserable old bastard.

I reflected, as I often did as I walked up the long drive to her house, that her residence was not the kind that you associated with witches. I don't mean it wasn't made of gingerbread, nothing fairy-tale like that, just that it was aggressively normal. It was large, conventional, slightly boring. The house, at least the communal parts, was kept in meticulous order by Roy, Esther's ex-Army husband. One notable exception was a small sitting room, which was Esther's personal space. It was absolutely crammed with stuff, heaps of it, teetering, piled on top of each other higgledy-piggledy fashion. Some related to her occult activities, ceremonial garments and equipment, some was just junk she had accumulated. There was also a sewing table (she was a skilled dressmaker) that had a large, high quality machine and bags of fabric, boxes of needles and pins, and other sewing paraphernalia, all in riotous, colourful disorder. I knew it drove Roy crazy, he'd told me so, on numerous occasions. It seemed to me to be a fairly accurate 3D construct of Esther's brain, but I kept silent.

Esther opened the door with a flourish. She looked like a colourful, clothed blancmange.

'Charlie, darling…' She kissed me on both cheeks. Her chins wobbled as she stepped back to look at me properly. There was a lot of Esther. She smelled of face powder and lavender. Today she was wearing an enormous embroidered Scandinavian style dress. Her clothes were always slightly eccentric, but stylish – she always managed to pull it off somehow. I found her majestic, like a galleon in full sail. Her eyes were bright and lively in her expertly made-up face.

'The others are here already.'

'Who?' I asked.

'Just two of them,' she said, 'Chris and Pascale.'

'Chris?' I said suspiciously. 'That Chris?' My eyes narrowed. 'Chris from North Bucks Wiccans?'

'I'm afraid so.' Chris's Wiccans – he was their President –

were an umbrella organisation of various New Age groups from the Milton Keynes end of the county. Esther ran South Bucks Neo Pagans, which was the sister organisation. Both groups met under the one banner to celebrate the major events of the Pagan year. This would be for the Summer Solstice Festival. Not only was I not keen on Chris, a scrawny Goth who fancied me, his wife had tried to kill me about a year ago. It's not the sort of thing you forget in a hurry.

'Chris is fine dear,' Esther said reassuringly. I frowned. It wasn't just the fact that his wife had had a go at me, Chris's ill-disguised feelings towards me kind of turned my stomach. Well, we'll see I thought, pessimistically. We'll see.

In Esther's bright, airy kitchen, I either plated up or cooked off samples of the food that I had suggested for their solstice meet and brought it through into the living room. It was going to be a hot and cold buffet which they would eat after their celebrations were done. It was designed to be foolproof.

So we had a red cabbage salad, tabbouleh, my homemade falafel, vol au vents of varying descriptions (I have a secret fondness for 1970s food), and mini quiches. Hot food was a Moroccan-style vegetable tagine, rice with green lentils (a bit like the Egyptian mujaddara) and a vegetable and lentil curry. For meat eaters we had a chicken casserole. There was plenty of bread from a new bakery in Amersham that I'd taken to using. When I first opened I made my own bread but as I've got busier that's had to be contracted out.

Through the windows at the rear of the lounge, I could

see the enormous lawn. On the night of the party there would be a huge marquee there, a bonfire for the celebration would be built and lit in front of it. If it rained, the side of the marquee could be raised so the assembled witches wouldn't get wet. There would be some portaloos too and a covered walkway so I could run the food out to them before the ceremony got going. Roy had been in logistics in the Army and it showed in his meticulous planning.

The three of them looked at me quizzically as I brought the food in, pushing it in on Esther's hostess trolley (so 1970s again, to go with the quiche)

Chris hadn't changed since I'd last seen him. Well, he was wearing glasses, which he hadn't done previously, otherwise he was just the same. That is not meant in any spirit of praise. He was one of those people who clung desperately to their youth. He still had his Goth jet-black bird's nest hairdo. Today he was wearing a black shirt of some shimmery fabric, a leather waistcoat, black, faux-leather trousers and cowboy boots. The top buttons of the shirt were undone to reveal his scrawny, pale, hairless chest. He still had his ankh on a chain, this had now been joined by a Chinese green jade pendant. For good measure, there was also a large cross round his thin neck. I guess he was hedging his bets spiritually. He had certainly covered several bases here. He had silver bracelets and woven friendship bracelets around his puny wrists. The metal ones jangled when he moved, as he did now, playing with his hair suggestively.

'Hi Chris,' I said brightly, 'nice glasses.'

They weren't of course, they were Bono style, tinted orange with large lenses. I could see he still favoured the odd bit of mascara. I have rarely met such an unattractive man. His clothes, the whole get-up, was frozen in time from say 1980, decades ago. Chris wasn't; he hadn't been cryogenically preserved. He had aged badly.

'Hi, Charlie,' he said, managing to put an unpleasantly salacious accent on the two syllables of my name. He took his glasses off with a theatrical flourish and tossed his head in a kind of devil-may-care kind of way.

It was unfortunate for him that he did so. One of his eyelashes, buckling under the weight of caked-on mascara, must have drooped and penetrated his eye. He swore and rubbed at his face. The three of us stared at him in fascination as he frantically blinked and screwed his face up, trying to dislodge the eyelash, stiffened with the make-up, jabbing into his eye, but making matters worse and smearing the eye make-up both over the lids and below so he now looked less like a Robert Smith clone and more like an Alice Cooper tribute act.

'I brought you all some food to try,' I said, worried that it would all get cold, breaking the spell that Chris's panda-eyed distress had cast over us all.

The other two women bent over the plates I had laid out for them and started sampling the food.

Esther said between mouthfuls, 'Oh, this is Pascale. I don't think I introduced you two, forgive me.' The dark-haired woman perched on the edge of a Chesterfield armchair looked up and smiled at me. She was very attractive, slim, casually and expensively dressed; that dark jumper was cashmere, those high-heeled boots would not have come cheap, neither would the gold necklace.

Talks over the menu dragged on for an hour or so while the three of them quibbled over tiny points of detail and I gritted my teeth and politely nodded agreement. It was their party after all. Everybody seemed compelled to offer their opinion on how the food could be bettered. Eventually we got there, with only minor tweaks to what I had suggested originally. I mentally breathed a big sigh of relief. Cooking the food would be a damn sight easier than getting it approved. That was often the way with parties.

Pascale left, then, as Chris shrugged himself into a black pea jacket he said, 'Sandra said to say hello and you must come over sometime to see us.'

I stared at him in astonishment and disbelief. My memories of her were far from happy. That is a considerable understatement. The recollection of his wife as she strode threateningly towards me, dressed in her oily denims and leather jacket complete with cut-off denim jacket with the colours of her Hells Angel chapter sewn onto it, was not one that was likely to fade in a hurry. She was not high up on my 'people I would like to get back in touch with' list.

'Err…' I wasn't sure what to say. 'Is she still a Hells Angel?' I asked timidly.

She'd been in an all-girl biker gang before, Satan's Sluts, if memory served me right, then had joined a more mainstream local group affiliated to the official Angels. She was proof of the adage, opposites attract. Chris was a sad apology for a man, you certainly wouldn't say that about his wife.

'Oh, no,' Chris said, shaking his head, then he gave me one of his earnest looks. 'She's left all that behind, she's been Born Again.'

'I'm sorry?' Surely he didn't mean that Sandra had gone religious? But he did.

'She's accepted Christ into her heart,' he explained, his eyes boring into mine. I think this look of sincerity was supposed to make me feel hot. I think maybe he had once read an article claiming that women find 'empathetic' men attractive. 'She's been washed in the Blood of the Lamb… as have I, Charlie,' he said, dramatically indicating the cross on his chest., 'How about you?' He suddenly grabbed my wrists and looked deep into my eyes. 'Would you let our Saviour into your heart?'

The look he gave me was not one of deep spirituality. I was wearing a tight top and the Hunter assets were very much on display. I disengaged his hands.

'No thank you, Chris,' I said, primly, 'I'm C of E.'

'But…' he began, looking confused.

'I see the vicar on a regular basis.' That was true, he and his wife often ate at my place. I knew the Rev John fairly well. 'He more than meets my spiritual needs.'

'Well,' he said, huffily, 'you can tell Sandra that when you see her, she's really desperate to see you.'

'I'll check my calendar,' I said, as I pushed him gently outside. I could safely predict it would be full. 'See you around, Chris.'

I shut the door firmly in his face. I turned and leaned against the woodwork staring up at the swirly Artex pattern of the ceiling and I groaned.

Esther appeared, shaking with laughter. 'Drink, Charlie?'

'God yes. Make that a large one.'

Esther poured me a glass of white wine and I relaxed back

on the sofa while she settled her bulk in an armchair opposite. 'Well, thank heavens that's all over.' She exhaled loudly.

'Well, I've known worse.' It was true. Nine times out of ten, presentations for parties go fine, customers are usually happy knowing they are in safe hands, but just occasionally people get ideas that they want turning into food facts – these days more often than not, fuelled by some nonsense they have seen on TikTok. Or things that they want which you just know are going to be horrible. Today the only sticking points had been Pascale's egotism and Chris's low-level perving. Both of which fortunately were fairly far down on my list of aggravating items. 'God, Chris is such an arsehole.'

'Well, you probably won't be seeing much more of him,' Esther said, grimly. 'There are moves afoot to get rid of him.'

'For sleaze?' I asked innocently, 'or crimes against good taste?'

Esther laughed. 'Well, I agree he's guilty on both counts there. No, it's more serious than that. This born-again Christianity thing of Sandra's has alienated a lot of the North Bucks Wiccans. Obviously it's kind of a contradiction in terms. It's a bit unfair on Chris, your partner doesn't have to be of the Old Faith. But, let's face it, Sandra's ruffled feathers and this is just an excuse.'

'Is someone standing against him as the Chair of his local group?' I asked.

'Not yet, but I've heard rumours. Hitherto he's been safe, nobody wanted to challenge him in case it made Sandra cross.'

I nodded. That was understandable. Now Sandra had turned over a new leaf, Chris was a lot more vulnerable than he had been previously.

'Pascale is jockeying for his position,' Esther said, adding judiciously, 'and given that the Wiccans are seventy per cent female, if she challenges him publicly, she'll probably get it.'

'Are there elections?'

Esther shook her head. 'Not for his one. All the Wicca groups, and the Pagans as well, have their own rules. But Chris started that group. That must have been about forty years ago, he's sixty-two now, more or less my age. Back then there weren't so many of us. I think he's President for life, so he should be unassailable, unless a challenger gets hold of the diadem, and that's not going to happen.'

'What, the diadem that you showed me?' I asked, curious now.

Esther nodded. 'There's a story about that.'

'I know, you told me. Agatha Fernshaw.'

She shook her head. 'No, there's more, and it's Agnes, not Agatha. She embellished the story, she said that the goddess had appeared to her in a vision and instructed her as to what the diadem should look like, and that the diadem was to be the symbol of the Head of the Order. The High Priestess or Priest.'

'And what does that mean in practice?'

'It means,' Esther's voice was very serious, 'that it's not just a ceremonial head-dress with some nice-ish jewels. It's numinous, it has soul, it possesses the authority of the goddess.'

'So it's important.'

'Very,' she confirmed. 'Whoever holds the diadem wields the power. That's certainly true for us and probably true for Chris's group. Regardless of the fact that it was made by Agnes from recycled jewellery, she had the gems from her old finery reset, the myth has become very strong. It's why I only wear it at the four important festivals.'

'Well,' I said, looking at the clock on the wall, that was enough time spent on the occult. Who could have imagined that people dedicated to cosmic mysteries would have spent so much time in petty politics. 'I'd better go, I'm watching Francis play cricket later.' Francis, so inept in the kitchen, was grace personified on a sports field. He was a very good cricketer and rugby player and possibly the strongest man I have ever met. That quality had certainly come in handy on more than one occasion. Boy, could he hit a cricket ball. 'At least we got the food sorted out.'

'We did indeed, thank you for that, Charlie,' she said, 'and thank you for putting up with my fellow pagans.'

'A pleasure.'

'I'll go and get your coat,' she said and stood up. I watched her as she disappeared through the doorway to her crowded, chaotic study to retrieve it. I thought some more of Sandra and how I definitely was not going anywhere near her in the near or distant future.

I sat in the lounge idly looking at the military prints that hung on the walls, mainly of World War Two aircraft. I was staring at a British night fighter with a turret spitting tracer fire at a German bomber, the bullet traces crimson and gold against the black velvet of the night sky, when a distraught Esther burst into the lounge.

'It's gone, Charlie!' she wailed.

'What's gone?' I replied, startled.

'The diadem.' Esther looked like Munch's Scream reflected in a fairground distorting mirror. 'The diadem's been stolen.'

# Chapter Fourteen

I got back to my restaurant and heaved a sigh of relief as the kitchen door closed behind me, like an airlock on the bewildering, toxic world outside. Thank God I was home, I thought. Although it was his day off, Murdo was in there, checking on the stock that was simmering on the stove ready for the week ahead. He heard me come in, turned round and gave me a concerned look.

'Are you okay, Chef?'

'I'm fine, Murdo. Thanks for checking on the stock.'

'That's okay.'

'I'll catch you later.' I went upstairs to my bedroom, flopped down on my bed and stared up at the ceiling. I relived the past hour in my memory, hoping for some kind of resolution.

After the bombshell of the discovery of the theft, we had checked every inch of Esther's sitting room, to no avail. Esther had droned on about its history and powers, with me only half listening. I was thinking more about the culprit. The thief was obviously either Chris or Pascale. It couldn't be anyone else. I'd asked her why they could possibly want it.

'I told you just now Pascale is jockeying to take over from Chris. If she has the diadem, that will give her the leverage she needs. Chris will be out.'

Esther found an emergency packet of jelly babies down the side of her chair and popped a handful into her mouth while she recapitulated the local Wiccan politics so I would understand the gravity of the situation.

'North Bucks Wiccans was his baby, Charlie, but now the baby's grown up.' Esther's voice was sharp. Not only had she been robbed, she had been betrayed. She carried on resentfully. 'Pascale is young, pretty, popular and don't forget, the majority of the Wiccans are women. She'll produce the diadem and say the goddess has chosen her. Chris will be toast.'

'I see.'

'Likewise, if Chris produced it, Pascale wouldn't dare move against him. He'd use the same argument that she would. It's a very powerful symbol indeed.'

'But surely you'll tell everyone she stole it?' I protested. What good could it possibly do? The Wiccans were not credulous peasants from the Middle Ages, they were doctors, lawyers, housewives, account managers.

Esther frowned. 'Weren't you listening earlier? One of its priestesses, Rebecca Anson, told everyone the goddess gave it to her in a wood! We believe in the supernatural Charlie, we're pagans! And if we don't, well, people will think finders keepers.'

'Losers weepers,' I tactlessly added.

'Exactly.' Esther's eyes filled with tears. Confirming the truth of the saying.

'Don't worry,' I said, adding rashly, 'I'll get it back for you.'

So now I found myself committed to investigating Tris Smith for David Summers, and the diadem theft for Esther. And I had the business to run.

'You,' I told myself, 'are a glutton for punishment.'

I continued to lie on my bed, and within a minute or so I was fast asleep.

When I awoke there was a message on my phone from Jess to meet her at the Three Bells at 6. I looked at the time, it was 5 o'clock. I blearily got up and showered then walked the short distance over to the pub.

I arrived before she did and sat in a corner with a Pils wondering what this was about. It was unusual for us to meet here, we saw enough of each other at the Old Forge Café. I hoped nothing was wrong.

At about 6.05 she arrived, looking fresh in a summery dress and Converse sneakers. She got a Coke and came over to my table, she looked totally serene. Thank God, I thought, not bad news.

She sat down opposite me.

'So Jess, what gives?'

She flashed a beaming smile at me showing her pearl-white perfect teeth, testimony to expensive teenage dental care.

'I've been reading Tris's correspondence, it's very interesting.'

Now she had my attention. 'Interesting in what way? Not sleazy?' I was thinking of his approach to me the week before.

She leaned forward, her voice low. 'No. If there is, that's

all in a folder in images that's security protected that I haven't managed to open yet. No, this was in his inbox. Tris has plans to open a restaurant of his own and guess who the backer was going to be?'

'I have no idea.'

'John Mayhew.'

'Seriously?' My eyes widened. 'Was there any falling out between the two of them?'

'Yeah.' She sipped some Coke. I heard the clack of pool balls from the table in the bar where some kids were playing. 'Tris had advanced John ten k seemingly.'

'But I thought if John was a backer then he was supposed to be providing the money, not vice versa?'

'So did Tris. John had asked him to send the money because his accounts were predominantly in Spain where he had been living and there was a delay caused by Spanish banking regulations and "his people" as he put it, wanted the ten k as a gesture of goodwill. This would, in turn, unlock a million or so.'

'And it didn't, I take it?' I sat there marvelling at this. It looked like John Mayhew was back to his old games of defrauding people. Tris with his high opinion of himself, would, I suspected, have made a tragically easy mark.

'No. Then there was an angry exchange of emails. Tris asked for the money back and John refused, saying he was keeping it as he had invested a great deal of time and money schmoozing the "backers" and he felt he could no longer trust Tris.'

'Wow.' I was incredulous. 'So he took Tris for ten thousand! When did this happen?'

'It's all fairly recent, probably it started a few weeks before Tris put the running group together and continuing up until Mayhew's death.'

'Wow, he royally shafted Tris. I wonder why Tris invited him to join his running group?'

Jess shrugged, 'Maybe he was planning revenge, you know the saying about keeping your enemies close to you…'

'I hadn't thought of that,' I remarked.

'That's what it looks like to me. So, if you're looking for a motive for John Mayhew's murder, there you go.'

I digested this as I walked home half an hour later. How that must have hurt, not just financially but it would have wounded Tris's ego hugely. He was a man who obviously thought a lot of himself, and judging by his attitude, very much liked to be in control of things. And here he was, humiliated, deceived and ripped off by some horrible old baby-boomer. Was that enough of a reason for Tris to kill him? Well, it wasn't my call, but I would certainly pass this on to Slattery when I next saw him.

# Chapter Fifteen

My request via Lucy for a meeting with the Oxford University psychology lecturer who had overlapped with Tris had borne fruit with amazing speed. It was almost as if he had been waiting for my call. After I got back home from my drink with Jess, I had an email giving times when Dr Taylor was free for face-to-face meetings in person or electronically. I voted for in person, and I was given the time of Friday morning at 9 o'clock.

On Tuesday morning I was doing a speed run before work. It was a good day for outdoor exercise. The good weather we had been having meant that the paths, which could be horribly muddy in the rain when you slipped and slid and invited sprained ankles at every step, had completely dried out and were firm underfoot. The idea of a speed run is to incorporate a series of short fast runs at an eight out of ten effort, in my case for a minute, then drop back to your usual pace. I was aiming to do eight of these with a minute's slow pace in between each burst.

While I was finding it difficult to imagine Tris Smith as a killer, despite what Jess had said, I found it surprisingly easy, however, to picture David Summers as one. Mayhew had been obviously up to his old tricks and I knew that he had had links in the past to Summers and that they had probably fallen out. Was Mayhew threatening Summers with his return? Lizzie's dad was a much more formidable figure than Lizzie's fiancé. I also, I have to admit, felt uneasy about doing work for a man with a 'shady' reputation. Although it was true Summers had paid me some money, I was still concerned about being ripped off in the end. I had been stiffed quite a few times over the years by clients and it was a horrible feeling. I simply did not trust David Summers.

I was wondering whether or not I should just call the whole thing off. I didn't think that Tris was going to kill Lizzie. Yes, I completely bought into him marrying her for her money but if we were to talk violent crime then I was suspecting David Summers of killing John Mayhew. Maybe the missing evidence alluded to by Slattery had turned up at last and Mayhew was pressuring Summers. It was an interesting scenario. But, I thought, that was Slattery's problem, not mine. My problem was whether or not I wanted to carry on working for a man I didn't like and certainly didn't trust.

I was going nowhere mentally with this rumination, so I concentrated my mind on enjoying the run.

That wasn't too hard to do. It was fun. The path I was running along was a narrow footpath lined with cow parsley. The colours of the Chilterns were fantastic at this time of year, very delicate pale greens, and when you ran under the beech trees, the tender young leaves diffused the sunlight through their light-green foliage. It felt like being underwater.

I pounded along the hard trail, inhaling the elusive, gentle fragrance of the lacy cow parsley flowers and, less happily, more and more conscious of my bursting bladder. As well as two double espressos I had drunk a mug of tea. When I'd put my running shoes on earlier, I had thought to myself, I kind of need the loo. No. By the time that thought had arisen I was outside, I'd double-laced my shoes, set my Strava on my phone to log my run. I didn't want to take my shoes off and go back inside then put them on again. It'll be fine. I'll be back before I know it, I thought.

Well, that certainly wasn't the case now. I really did need to go. It was 7.45 now, there was no one about. I slowed to an uncomfortable, pelvic-floor tightening walk. Things had reached the point of urgency. I looked around. I was now on a path that ran through some woodland near the Earl's property. The surroundings were beech and rhododendron. Some of the latter were all sinuous trunks and branches, smooth and curved, useless to hide behind, all their foliage was above head height. But there were some kinds of bushy specimens of the rhododendron family and there were a couple growing close to the path. Perfect. Behind one of those I would be invisible. I left the path, disappearing behind them and squatted, concealed but somewhat ill at ease. To be discovered would have been highly embarrassing.

After what felt like an eternity, I finished, rearranged my clothing and had just put my hand on a branch to move back towards the path when I heard voices. Shit! Although I was perfectly decent, emerging from a bush was really… well, people would guess. I crouched again, waiting for them to pass.

It was a man and a woman, and then I recognised the man's voice, low-pitched, confident, public-school. I could hear their feet now on the path; then, through the leaves I saw Tris hand-in-hand with my wine buyer.

My eyes widened. Tris was seeing Cass!

They appeared to be arguing and they came to a stop just the other side of the rhododendron. I hardly dared to breathe but I needn't have worried about them noticing me, they were intent on one another. I saw Tris slide his left hand up Cassandra's arm and he tried to touch her breast with his right. She pushed it away.

'No, Tris.' Her voice was soothing rather than outraged. Damn, I thought. She seems kind of on-board with this. I don't know why I expected her to be shocked, I suppose because I was. What are you doing with this creep, Cass? was my thought. And I had projected my feelings onto her. Then I heard her say, 'I want you, but I can't…'

'Why not, Cass,' Tris urged. 'I'm crazy about you… you're all I think about.'

'It's like I told you on Saturday… I can't, I won't do it with a man who's with another woman, it's not right.' Through the leaves, I saw her shake her head firmly. 'You're engaged.'

'Cassie, I love you,' he said, urgently, entreatingly, 'and I want you so much and I know that you feel the same way about me. I do love Lizzie, but in a different way, and when the time is right, we'll go our separate ways. But I don't want to hurt her.'

You mean you don't want to lose sight of the Summers money and be kicked out of your chocolate-box cottage, I thought. He continued. 'I don't want to jeopardise our chances, we've got something special and you know that…'

She shook her beautiful head. 'I love you too Tris but it wouldn't be right. I hear what you say about Lizzie…'

He shook his head impatiently. 'That doesn't matter, her and me. It's you and me that's important. I'll tell her in good time, I don't want to upset her. I've told you how close to the edge she is.' That startled me; was that true? Lizzie hadn't seemed highly strung when I had met her. 'I don't want her to do anything rash, I want to separate in gentle stages.'

'I'm sorry.' Her voice was firm. 'It matters to me, Tris… if you tell me it's over between you and her, then yes. I want to be with you, but I don't want to be skulking around in woods or round at your place keeping an ear open in case I hear her key in the lock.'

'You've got a flat,' he protested.

Another head shake. 'I don't believe in lies, Tris. I'm in a twelve-step programme, we have a strict policy of honesty.'

I remembered then that's why she didn't drink. She'd told me she was getting a little too fond of the wine she was selling and had stopped before it became a problem.

'Okay, okay,' he held his hands up in an attitude of surrender. 'I'll see what I can do.'

She leaned forward and kissed him and his face was obscured by her long, dark hair. It was a long kiss. This time she let his hands roam free. Then she pulled away from him. 'You do that.' She took a step back from him and folded her arms. 'It'll be sad for Lizzie, but anything is better than living a lie. Lies can kill.'

'I know, I love you Cass.'

They kissed again, passionately and moved off.

Oh my God, I thought. I had never suspected this. It's a horrible feeling when someone you like and admire starts going out with someone you feel is totally unworthy of them. It's surprisingly common. Okay, it was hardly Beauty and the Beast, but still. Whether or not Tris was a murderer, he certainly was not a man to be trusted. Certainly not a man I liked. I suddenly felt a bit more kindly disposed to Summers' dim view of Tris. Overall, however, I felt despondent. Cass was a friend of mine and I could not condone her behaviour. I could also see how Tris was trying to guilt-trip her into sex and paint himself as a man concerned by the mental health of his partner to explain why he was being so devious.

I gave them five minutes so I wouldn't be seen by them and then emerged from my rhododendrons. I walked for a little bit and then broke into a slow jog. They must be free of the wood by now, I thought. Then ahead of me I saw a blur of movement. Not them again! But no, it wasn't. This was someone in a green T-shirt. I followed at a distance. I had no wish to encounter anyone. Soon the wood would end and we would be on the edge of a large field. I could lurk by the edge until they were out of sight and then carry on my way.

The trees ended and I could see the green T-shirted figure striding along the path about 50 metres ahead of me. I recognised who it was. Matt Spicer, his shaved head glinting in the sun.

# Chapter Sixteen

'So, what are we going to cook today, Charlie?' Lizzie asked on Thursday afternoon when I arrived at the cottage with a bag for life full of assorted food. It was difficult to act normally, now that I knew Tris was trying to sleep with my friend, co-runner and wine merchant. Not to mention me!

'I thought we'd make two different pasta dishes,' I said. It's cooking, Charlie, I told myself sternly, the show must go on.

'Oh good, that sounds great. Tris loves Italian food,' she exclaimed. That's not all he loves, I thought, gloomily. 'What are we going to make?'

'Okay, can you make Spaghetti Bolognaise?'

'Oh yes.'

'And how do you make it?'

She told me. A tin of mince from the supermarket, a tin of tomatoes and lots of Worcester sauce. And a stock cube. That was crucial seemingly. 'I learned that from the advert that chef did on TV, it makes all the difference,' she said proudly.

I nodded. 'I'm sure it does, Lizzie, but I think we can maybe improve slightly on that.'

I took out an onion, celery, a couple of carrots, a couple of cloves of garlic and some good quality beef mince. I showed her how to chop the vegetables finely. 'This is called a soffritto Lizzie, it's from the Italian verb "soffriggere" to fry. It's the Holy Trinity for a lot of Italian dishes.' We went on from there, making a stock with a cube, adding the tomato puree and tomatoes. While the sauce was reducing Lizzie asked, 'How long do I cook it for?'

'Ages,' I said. 'Just keep stirring it so it doesn't catch and burn on the bottom of the pan.'

Then I showed her how to make a vanilla panna cotta.

'What's this?' she asked, pointing at a small blue packet.

'It's leaf gelatine. Four leaves sets just under six hundred ml, give or take. We'll be using about five hundred ml of liquid, a mixture of cream and milk, so we'll use three. We want it kind of wibbly wobbly, and we'll make a compote with those frozen fruits of the forest berries.'

I smiled as we made the panna cotta, remembering the first time I had let Francis loose on it. I had shown him carefully exactly what I wanted doing, checking every step of the way. When I looked at the dessert section in the walk-in fridge later I was pleased to see a dozen panna cottas on the shelf. I took one of them and shook it gently. No movement at all. I then got a teaspoon and tapped it, it was like tapping a tennis ball, no give whatsoever. You could have prised them out of the dariole moulds and flung them against the wall, they would have bounced. I dug the spoon in, I had to exert a lot of effort. They were the consistency of jelly when it's in its cube state just out of the packet, before you've added water, not after, which is what you want. You could chew your way through Francis's.

'Francis,' I called him over as I came out of the fridge, 'how much gelatine did you use for these?'

'Fifteen sheets, Chef,' he said, with a hint of pride, 'just like you told me.'

'No, Francis' – my tone was surprisingly gentle – 'I said five.'

'Oh…' he looked faintly surprised, 'does it matter?'

Counting to ten and breathing deeply. 'Yes, Francis, yes it does. Now, throw these away and we'll make them again properly.'

We had no such drama today. Then finally I showed her how to make spaghetti con aglio e olio, spaghetti with oil and garlic, a quick dish with parsley, chilli and oil that is my go-to when I'm hungry but can't be bothered to cook. This was the dish that the two of us ate together after we'd finished.

'That was so nice, Charlie… thank you.'

'That's okay. How's Tris?'

She smiled lovingly. 'He's fine, bless him, he works so hard. Strickland is such a hard taskmaster, and then he's often out on these long training runs, or away down the gym.' I nodded. 'Well, that's catering for you, Lizzie.'

Too busy trying it on with Cassandra and God knows who else, I guess it ate into his leisure time. I looked at her trusting, innocent face. Maybe it was just better to say nothing, ignorance is bliss. I thought of Sandra and her new-found passion for the Bible. I remembered the woman accused of adultery and Christ saying to the assembled crowd, 'Let he who is innocent cast the first stone.' I had a history myself that was far from blameless. I know for sure I'd been the other woman on at least one occasion.

But I was being paid to investigate Tris, not to judge him.

It was time to go and I stood up. 'I'll see you next week then, Monday, four o'clock.'

The following day I had my meeting with the lecturer at Tris's former university. I had been looking forward to this very much. In my line of work, cooking, it's unusual to come across university graduates, not unless their lives have taken either a tragic, professional disgrace, or totally unexpected turn. But from what I've gathered, as a student you're obviously young and still developing as a person. I had seen the grown-up version of Tris, I was excited to learn what the embryonic Tris had been like. So now I was sitting with Dr Taylor, Lucy's psychologist admirer.

'So, tell me again why you're so interested in Tris Smith?' he asked me, politely.

'Was he one of your students by any chance?' I asked, hopefully.

He nodded and smiled sourly. 'Oh, yes… yes he was.'

Dr Vernon Taylor sipped his tea, Lapsang Souchong. I recognised the weird smell that reminds me of hot water bottles for some reason. He studied me over his desk and I blew gently on my tea, Earl Grey, to cool it, and in turn studied him. He was tall and slim, verging on gaunt. He was a good-looking man, in shape, with silvery hair and

120

very piercing blue eyes. His office was small and overlooked the Woodstock Road. He was obviously a neat man, his desk was bare except for a screen and his laptop. There was some abstract art on the walls and a large green spiky pot plant in a corner. The atmosphere was very Zen. I liked it.

I decided to be completely frank. Dr Taylor's gaze was steady and slightly un-nerving. I felt that if I started lying to him or spinning the truth he would see through me. I guess his job was studying the human psyche after all.

'I'm a chef by profession,' I said, 'like Lucy, which is how I know her. But for various reasons, I have been hired by a man called David Summers whose daughter is engaged to Tris Smith. He told me that Tris's wife had died in mysterious circumstances. He suspects foul play.' Now I had Dr Taylor's full attention. 'He wants to end the engagement because he's worried his daughter will be next. How true the murder accusation is, I really don't know, but I'm doing some work on that. In the meantime I would really value your opinion on Tris.'

'So, he's expecting you to dig the dirt on Tris Smith.' He frowned. 'But even if you succeed, I can't imagine it necessarily affecting his fiancée. She would just dismiss it out of hand.'

That was more or less my opinion, but I would still do the job I had been paid to. Even if it was fruitless. Mines not to reason why. I did need new furniture.

'I'm sure you're right,' I agreed, thinking of Lizzie and the collection of Tris artefacts. She'd invested a lot in him emotionally, she wasn't going to give up without a fight.

But we weren't here to second-guess what Lizzie might or might not do.

'So, Dr Taylor, what was he like as a student?' Probably wonderful, I thought. Tris seemed to be one of those people who sail through life. But Dr Taylor shook his head and sighed.

'To be honest, Charlie, I've been expecting to have this conversation for a while now.' I leaned forward in my chair, he certainly had my attention now. 'That's why I answered your call so promptly.' This was not going to be the start of a rave review for Tris Smith. He then qualified what he was about to say. 'Character psychology is not my field, let me make this clear at the outset. My speciality is stress and how it affects the body and mind. That was, of course, how I met your friend Lucy. But…' Here we go, I thought. I took a deep breath to focus.

Dr Taylor looked at me keenly and said, 'Tris Smith is the most narcissistic human being whom I have ever had the misfortune to meet. When you align this with what I suspect is an abnormally high sex drive, bad things happen.'

Don't hold back, Doctor, I thought. I knew, or suspected, Tris had a thing for the ladies but not that it was out of hand.

'Did any bad things happen here?' I asked.

'Yes.' He nodded. 'I have no proof, but two students dropped out of my course because of him. One left university, rumour had it that he had assaulted her. Whatever occurred, it was enough to give her some form of breakdown. The other switched courses and managed to get a restraining order put on him that he was not to go within a hundred metre's distance of her college.'

'And he wasn't sent down?' I was amazed.

The academic shook his head. 'No, there was no real proof. And, I suspect HR squashed it because they feared institutional damage to the department. Easier to hush the victim up rather than go for the perpetrator. Anyway, be that as it may... As far as I understood it, he incapacitated both women with drink or drugs. That part was consensual, he hadn't spiked their drinks. However, the sex wasn't. They were in no way capable of giving informed consent.'

'And he got away with it then.'

'Oh yes, and I gather he seemed to expect to get away with it. There did not appear to be any doubt in his mind that he would. But essentially it boils down to whom do you believe. Anyway, no legal action was taken against him and the university more or less hoped that the issue would resolve itself. But I think now he felt he could really get away with stuff. His invincibility was confirmed.'

'I see.' Was I surprised to learn this? Probably not was the answer.

Dr Taylor continued. 'Then he switched his seduction methods. I had stopped teaching him by then, much to my relief. A couple of girls in my tutorials had asked if they could switch because of him. Anyway, fortunately for me, he switched to Behavioural Psychology. I knew one of his tutors; she came to see me with an essay that he had written called "Gamification and Seduction, from Casanova to Simenon".'

I had heard of the first one, I'd seen David Tennant doing him for about quarter of an hour on some show or other. I rarely watch TV. 'Who's the Simenon guy?' I asked. I'd never heard of him, some actor?

Apparently not. 'He wrote the Maigret books,' explained Taylor. 'He claimed to have slept with over ten thousand women.' I wondered what the Maigret books were. I'd heard of Magret de Canard, it's a very expensive kind of French duck. Maigret was probably something different altogether.

'My God!' 10,000 women. He was obviously Tris's hero. 'And he wrote an essay on this!' I marvelled. What is the world coming to!

'Oh yes.' Dr Taylor nodded. 'His tutor showed it to me. It was practically a blueprint on how to get women into bed by exploiting their weaknesses. He even had an acronym for getting someone into bed, it went, "IEA". It stood for "Identify. Exploit. Achieve."' He sighed sadly. 'I strongly suspect this was his big thing, zeroing in on areas that he felt the target of his seduction was weak in.' He shook his head in bafflement. 'You know, Charlie, sometimes I think the majority of my students have no idea why they are studying Psychology other than it sounds fun. But Tris Smith knew why he was here, he wanted to give himself an edge in using women, for sex mainly, but also I suspect for massaging his self-esteem and, I gather this fiancée has money, for profit.'

'I see,' I said, thoughtfully. Still processing this. I had lifted the rock, I should have been prepared for what had crawled out.

'So am I right about the fiancée?' he asked. 'Is she rich?'

'She is,' I confirmed, 'and also not the sharpest pencil in the box.'

He nodded. 'And maybe not the most attractive?'

'Probably not,' I admitted.

'It's a terrible combination and I think her father is quite right to be alarmed.' He smiled sadly. 'She sounds like Tris's dream woman. Like many narcissists he'll be deeply insecure, and with this poor girl he'll be able to use her money, bask in her admiration for his physical attractiveness and, best of all, assert his intellectual superiority. Does that sound right?'

I thought of the framed photos of the running team and him in a mortarboard and gown, holding his degree. 'Bang on.'

'Bet he doesn't tell her he left without a degree,' remarked Dr Taylor, casually.

My eyes widened. 'What! You're kidding me!'

He looked surprised. 'Has he been claiming he has one? Presumably for professional advancement then?'

'Yeah,' I spluttered. 'He's even got a framed photo of himself all dressed up in robes, holding his degree.'

'Well, you can hire those no questions asked, roll up any old sheet of paper and put a ribbon around it. No, he got kicked out in his second year, repeatedly failing exams. Now that is something the university will do something about, thank God. He was essentially lazy and not too bright, despite his assertions to the contrary.'

Wow! I thought, that was going to come in useful as a weapon to use against him. If I felt mean and whistle-blew, Strickland would sack him for misrepresenting his qualifications.

'What does he do for a living?' Dr Taylor asked.

'He works in catering.'

'Not as a chef, surely! That sounds like too much hard work for Tris Smith.'

'No, front of house.'

'Somewhere upmarket, I dare say.'

'Yes, it's Michelin starred.'

'The ideal environment for him to prosper.' He leaned back in his chair. 'It showcases his charm and his good looks. He's no idiot despite failing his exams, and he's got a pool of waitresses to hit on as well as possibly wealthy women who doubtless form part of the clientele.' He steepled his fingers. 'You should try and ask how he appears to his work-mates. I suspect he won't be able to stop boasting about his conquests; young males would be a particularly appreciative audience.'

'I'll definitely do that,' I said, 'and I think you're exactly right about his job.' I added, 'It definitely gives him power over people. There's a two-month waiting list at the King's Head; he'll be able to select the tables, good, bad and indifferent, the regulars will be sucking up to him; yes, you're right, ideal.'

'Good. Well, now you know everything I know about Tris Smith.' His eyes flickered towards the clock on the wall. I sensed my time was up. He added, 'He's a deeply flawed human being, that's for sure.'

'Well, thank you, Dr Taylor, you've been incredibly helpful.'

He smiled with genuine warmth. On impulse I fished out one of my business cards from my handbag and gave it to him. 'If you're in the area, or if you need a caterer...'

He took it and put it carefully in his wallet. 'Now, is there anything else about him that I can help you with?'

'Just one thing...' I hesitated. 'Do you think he would be capable of murder?'

'You mean do I think it likely he murdered his wife?' He thought for a moment. 'How did she die?'

'She fell to her death off a cliff while drunk. So I've heard.'

He rubbed his chin. 'I don't think he would have the courage to go ahead and murder someone in cold blood, but, if, for example, they were walking together and she stumbled, I could easily imagine him giving a little shove. He'd tell himself that it was probably what she wanted, she was a tormented soul and now she was at peace. Or even kid himself, tell himself that she slipped and he tried to help but inadvertently dislodged a rock or something. People like Tris often lie to themselves and come to believe their version of the truth. Even though they know deep down it's totally fictitious.'

So, that was a yes to the possibility of him killing his wife. I threw out more or less at random the idea he might have killed John Mayhew since we were on the subject of murder. 'What about shooting someone?'

'Shooting someone?' He looked surprised at that.

'One of his running club members was shot with a crossbow. Do you think...'

'Charlie,' he said reprovingly, 'I think you're letting your imagination run away with you. He is a nasty piece of work, in my opinion, but a crossbow killing? That sounds like hit-man stuff. I suppose he could kill someone like that,' he emphasised the 'could', 'he could do it from a distance and not have to see the bloody consequences. I don't think he'd ever get his hands dirty. But it doesn't sound like him to me.'

His eyes drifted upwards towards the clock on the wall for a second time. I got the hint and stood up.

'Thank you so much, Dr Taylor, for all your help…'

'That's okay, I'm rather glad to be of assistance.' He stood up and we shook hands. He came round the desk to let me out of his office. 'I think that Tris Smith is a highly dangerous young man, and, I for one, would be very concerned for anyone unfortunate enough to become involved with him,' he paused, 'particularly his fiancée.'

Driving back home down the motorway towards High Wycombe, I thought of what I had learned from my visit to Oxford. Dr Taylor had thought that Tris could be a potential killer, and I was slightly concerned for Lizzie. Not hugely. I thought of his modus operandi, IEA. Tris had Identified the Golden Goose, that is Lizzie. Exploit. Well, he was certainly busy doing that, living well off her money, basking in her worship, casually cheating on her, but he hadn't finally got to the Achieve. He hadn't got hold of her money yet, or the money she would inherit when her father died, so murder would make no sense. But despite what Dr Taylor had said, he did have beef with John. Could I imagine him hiding in a bush and firing a crossbow at someone? Well, let's just say the jury was still out on that one.

However, I did now know with certainty that Tris was an unscrupulous womaniser, maybe sex addict would be a better term, although I kind of felt that sounded like what he was doing was uncontrollable. I doubted that. From the word go he had devoted himself to the pursuit of women, finding any psychological chink in their armour that he could exploit to his own advantage, to gain leverage. With Lizzie, it would be her lack of self-esteem. And, I supposed, she was used to pleasing men; her dad and now Tris.

At least now I had something solid to give to David Summers. I decided to go up to Scotland the following week. I hoped to learn something about Tris's wife's death that had perhaps been missed during the initial investigation.

I'd already had the green light for funding from David Summers, now I would see if Strickland would lend me Patrick who'd worked for me before to cover in my absence. I could also do what Dr Taylor had suggested and see what people at work made of him. Seeing Dr Taylor had energised me. I could feel the excitement that I got when I felt I was on the trail of some breakthrough.

One thing was for sure. Tris was far more dangerous than I could possibly have imagined.

# Chapter Seventeen

On Sunday morning, as I joined the Hampden Green Runners at 8 o'clock, it was with a sinking heart. Tris was there with Cassandra. I studied him with great attention in which was now mingled suspicion and dislike. I was coming round to the David Summers view of things. I was baffled too as to what all these women seemed to find so attractive about him. And Cass wasn't stupid, either. That was the scary thing.

I tried looking at him as if I had never seen him before, maybe that would help give me a handle on things. I had always been aware that Tris was handsome, with his neatly trimmed dark beard and regular features, but now it occurred to me that it was the kind of face that was almost instantly forgettable. If he was a food item he'd have been something like a piece of poached salmon with a cucumber coulis. Nice enough, but essentially rather bland. Then I recalled that particular dish was a long-standing part of my own menu, and it sold very well. Particularly to women customers. Perhaps people liked bland. The coulis had red chillies in it, little scarlet flecks of them: it was deceptive, it seemed cool and almost creamy, and then BAM, you got a punch of chilli. Maybe he was like that, some hidden depth to him that could catch your attention, despite yourself.

Or maybe the blandness made it easy to project whatever characteristics you found attractive in a man onto him. Like a blank canvas or screen. I still couldn't imagine him as a killer. He wasn't nice, but that did not make him a murderer.

Matt was the next to arrive. Ferociously lean with those long, defined muscles. he looked much more like my idea of a killer. It was as if he were made of wire and moulded plastic. He also had the kind of expressionless face that assassins have in Hollywood films. Easy to imagine Matt's finger curled around a trigger. The two men started talking about marathons. I heard bits of their conversation.

'So you're sub four hours, then Tris?' I heard Matt enquire.

'Yeah, but I'm not doing one this year, I've just got too much on my plate.'

Yeah, I thought, and too much going on with trying to get Cass into bed as well. I thought of Lizzie, so pathetically keen to cook him a nice meal And tonight was the night. I wondered if she'd make him the schnitzel. I hoped she wouldn't cock it up if she did. I suddenly thought, I'm surprised he isn't trying it on with Suzi as well.

As if on cue, I saw Suzi park her car by the side of the common and come running over. 'Hi, everyone,' she said breathlessly.

Tris gave her a welcoming smile – a complicit smile, I thought, which she returned.

'Okay, people,' Tris said, 'seven k today. We're going to run in a loop to Frampton End, then down to the main road, along it for half a mile, then up the hill to Elmer's Pond, then back in a loop via the footpath near the Earl's house, everyone okay with that?'

'Sounds good to me,' Cassandra said.

'It's a good hill that, up to Elmer's Pond,' Matt said matter-of-factly.

'Oh God, is it steep?' asked a worried Suzi.

'Yes,' Matt answered coldly. He had a strangely wooden face, it was not built to show animation, let alone warmth. I remembered what Jess had said about her schoolfriends joking he was a spy. He wouldn't make a good spy, I thought, he looked too abnormal, spies were supposed to blend in, weren't they? I recalled my earlier musings. He could have been a killer employed by the CIA or someone. Do MI6 or whatever they're called employ assassins? Probably not. Matt would never be cast as James Bond anyway, he lacked charisma and he was still wearing the running shoes with individual toes.

'Okay, let's go,' Tris said, enthusiastically. 'We'll do a warm-up pace for ten minutes and then pick it up. If it gets too much for you, Suzi, I'll wait for you at the bottom of the hill, the others can just run past and we'll all meet up back here. Sound good?'

'Sure does.' Suzi flashed him an apologetic grin. Was it my imagination or did I notice Cass intercept this and frown. We set off in single file with Tris leading, across the fields to Frampton End. It was a cold, chilly, blustery morning, most unlike the recent weather we had been having. It certainly didn't feel like May, and there were very few people around. The run to the neighbouring village was uneventful. We went along the main road and then turned into the path that led along a valley with the large houses of Elmer's Pond visible at the top of the escarpment. From where I was running I could see the well-known populist podcaster Lance Thurston's house, or more specifically, the beech trees at the bottom of his garden. I felt a glow of achievement, I'd been part of the campaign to stop him chopping them down for, of all stupid reasons, the purpose of building a helipad.

I was in the rear, the group was no longer in single file. Matt and Cassandra up front. Just ahead of me were the other two. I could see Tris's face, animated as he ran beside Suzi as they chatted to each other. I thought back to Lizzie's shrine to him that was the living room and I remembered his photo in his graduation robes. He did have some balls really, passing himself off as a graduate.

As soon as I got home I called David Summers.

'David, Charlie. I need to go up to Scotland to check on the death of Tris's wife. Can you send me some money?'

I could easily afford it myself, but I was far from certain Summers would honour our verbal agreements. I was worried about being screwed over. Needlessly, it seemed.

'Sure, send me your bank details. Would a grand cover it?'

'Yeah, more than cover it.' I was pleasantly surprised. 'I only plan to be away for three nights then I'll meet you at the end of the week and let you know what else I have found out.'

He seized on that remark like a terrier. 'So you've found out something about him already?'

'Oh yeah. You'll be pleased with what I've discovered, but I'm not going to let you know until I get back from Scotland.'

'But I might not be around! I'm a busy man!' Summers protested. 'Couldn't you just...' he pleaded.

'No, David.' I said firmly. 'Now I've got to go, I open in a couple of hours.'

While Murdo cooked the roast beef off, made gravy and Francis did the Yorkshire puddings, I made the vegetarian starter, an Italian dish called Melanzane della Nonna, Grandmother's Aubergines. Andrea, my Italian boyfriend, had given me the recipe, it was his grandmother's, so I could cheerfully put it on my menu. I'd done an online search for this dish, there seemed to be umpteen variants. They all contained more or less the same ingredients: capers, olives, aubergine, tomatoes and garlic. I'd cut the aubergine into slices, put them in a colander and was salting them. I put the colander in the sink as it would get damp.

'Why are you doing that?' Murdo asked, he'd been watching me with curiosity.

'It draws out the moisture so the aubergine doesn't drink up the oil when you fry it.'

'Oh...'

I paused with my knife in hand. 'I've heard you can microwave it before cooking,' I mused, 'it has the same effect seemingly. Maybe I'll give that a try.'

Murdo fiddled with his phone and doom-laden heavy

metal thundered from the speaker in the kitchen. He had other things on his mind besides aubergines. As did I, such as boyfriends who didn't seem to appreciate me stuck in a kitchen while they criss-crossed Italy looking after the finances of the super-rich.

'It's Rotting Christ's new album,' he said enthusiastically, 'it's called Pro Xristou... they're a wee bit auld, but they still rock!'

Lucky old me getting to hear the latest Rotting Christ. Whatever Andrea was up to, he wouldn't be doing that! So we carried on with the MEP list to the barrage of sound as selected by my sous chef. During a lull in between tracks I said, 'Murdo, are you still friends with Patrick?'

Patrick was a chef with Strickland at the King's Head, a very good Chef de Partie who had once covered for me in my absence. Strickland would, I was sure, lend him to me again to cover for me for the three days I would be away. Patrick would jump at the chance. The King's Head was a Michelin-starred restaurant that demanded perfection. Woe betide you if you cocked up. My place would be like a holiday for Patrick.

I was also curious to see how Tris was viewed at work. Maybe I would learn nothing useful. Maybe it would be pointless, even counterproductive, we all wear a public mask when we're in a professional situation. But catering can be a world of brutal honesty where people don't really care so much about how they are perceived, it's performance that counts and the metric is efficiency and toughness. Can you crank out x number of meals to a specified quality within the allotted timeframe without crumbling. Tris in the predominantly male environment of kitchen banter might reveal hitherto unknown facets of his character.

'Aye, why?' Murdo looked up from stirring a cheese sauce.

'Could you ask him if he'd be free for a drink about nine tonight?' The King's Head was closed Sunday nights. He should be free.

'Aye, fine, why?'

'I want to pick his brains about something.'

'Sure.' He pulled the pan off the heat, took his phone from the shelf and his fingers flew over the screen in that Gen Z way that mine would never do.

'Three Bells?'

'Yeah. Tell him if Strickland won't let him go,' I knew that it was not uncommon for his chefs to work until midnight prepping for the following day, 'that it's Charlie wants to see him.'

He nodded, looking up from his phone and said, 'Oh, he's replying, says sure.'

'Thanks, Murdo,'

''S okay.'

I cut up some onions into fine dice and blanched and skinned a kilo of tomatoes, the big ones that you can get. I could have used tinned, but the flavour you get from fresh is so much better. And the colour, so much pinker.

I thought to myself, well, I'm doing something on the David Summers job. I really ought to do something to reassure Esther as well. I decided that I would text her later to let her know that I would be seeing at least one of the suspects in the near future and that I had not forgotten my promise to her to get her precious diadem back.

'Murdo?'

He gave me a sharp look. I was using that kind of whee-dling tone that people employ when they're about to ask a fairly hefty favour.

'Yes, Chef.'

'I need to go up to Scotland on Tuesday. If I can get cover, would you mind holding the fort for me?'

'No, that'd be fine. Whereabouts in Scotland?'

'Argyll. Do you know it?'

'Aye, I ken it well enough… is that why you want tae talk with Patrick, about cover?'

'Partly,' I said cagily. No need to embroil Murdo in the Tris saga.

Later that afternoon, while I was doing an online search for accommodation for my Argyll trip in my living room, Murdo wandered in. My flat has three bedrooms, one of which I have given to Murdo – I say given, it formed part of his salary – and a pleasant living room overlooking the common.

'Charlie, do you have anywhere to stay in Argyll?' he said.

'No.' I'd just been looking at the internet to see what my options were.

Murdo continued. 'I've been asking around mates of mine in Edinburgh just in case. A chef I used tae work wi' there has bought a hotel down in Campbeltown, you should stay there. He's a nice guy and the food will be good.'

'What's it called?'

'The Davaar View.'

I typed the name into the search bar and we looked at it. It was by the sea, opposite Davaar Island, hence the name. It was small, had a good menu.

'I'm in,' I said.

Murdo fiddled with his phone, put it to his ear. 'Is that you Loyd?... Aye...' His accent thickened noticeably as he spoke to one of his countrymen. 'Ken the woman I work fir? Ay, that's the one... she'll be in Campbeltown Tuesday, have you got a room free... Aye that's grand... Hunter, Charlie Hunter...how many nights?' He looked at me enquiringly.

'Three. Tuesday, Wednesday, Thursday.'

'Did ye hear that? Great... aye, you too, thanks, mate.'

He ended the call and looked at me. 'Sorted.'

'Thank you, Murdo.'

'Glad tae be of help.'

# Chapter Eighteen

Now I had spoken to Murdo and he had said he'd be happy to run the Old Forge Café solo for a few days, Jess had handled the flight bookings for me, and all I needed was to get Patrick's agreement and Strickland's permission, and I was all set to investigate the death of Mrs Smith.

So, later that night I was in the bar of the Three Bells. There were a few people in, mainly youngsters playing pool and a few of the local builders. I went up to the bar.

'Evening, Charlie,' intoned Malcolm the landlord, practically inaudibly, his lined face more or less the same colour as the fire extinguisher that propped open the door to the back of the pub behind him. 'Usual?'

'Please.' I paid for my Pils and waited at the bar until Patrick came in. As one, all heads turned.

He was ridiculously good-looking. It's only when you see someone as handsome as Patrick that you realise how plain everyone else is. There must have been half a dozen local girls in the pub and I swear their mouths dropped open, irises dilated, hands went to hair. Scowls across their faces when he walked up to me. I beamed at the pub, I was the chosen one. Hi girls! I thought, refraining from looking smug.

'Patrick, thanks for coming,' I said as he kissed me on both cheeks. More envious looks. 'What can I get you?'

'Pint of Guinness, Charlie.'

Malcolm poured the drink, I paid, and escorted him over to a table. We sat for a moment chatting inconsequentially as we watched the youngsters gathered around the pool table. Young people liked the place for the pool, the lock-ins and Malcolm's ID policy, which was you didn't need any.

'So, what did you want to talk to me about?' Patrick asked.

'Two things really.'

'Okay, what are they?'

'Tris Smith,' I said.

He looked surprised. 'What about him?'

'What's he like?'

Patrick frowned as he considered the question. He was Murdo's age but a lot more mature. His boyfriend was ten years older than he was and he took Patrick to things like exhibitions and classy restaurants, encouraged him to read improving books and other cultural niceties. Not unlike me and Andrea, although he'd given up on the books. They're not my cup of tea.

'Professionally he's good,' he said. 'He really knows his stuff when it comes to wine, and suggesting what goes with what. And he's very knowledgeable about the food. He does his homework so he can advise the customers on what dishes they might want to eat, he knows what's in all the sauces, he never needs to say, "I'll go and ask the kitchen."'

He nodded. 'So I would certainly rate him professionally. Ten out of ten.'

He took a mouthful of Guinness and pulled a face. 'Unlike this, this is a bit rank.'

'It's the Three Bells,' I said gesturing helplessly.

'Of course, I'd forgotten.' He laughed. 'It's been a while since I've been here.' Patrick's boyfriend, a London interior designer specialising in restaurants – it was how they'd met – earned a high salary, and Patrick, on his days off, frequented classier places than the Three Bells, although to be honest, just about anywhere was classier than the Three Bells.

'So, Tris is fine professionally. How about on a personal level?'

'Mmm' – Patrick frowned – 'not so great. He's one of those men who boasts about how many women he's slept with, like he keeps a tally... I mean... really! Sometimes he boasts about it to me, why would I even care? It would be hard to find someone less interested.'

I frowned. So he was sleeping with a lot of women then it seemed. His thing with Cass was not sounding like a one-off. Or maybe he was all talk and no action. I've met plenty of men like that.

'Does he hit on the waitresses?' I asked.

Patrick shook his head. 'No, he's got more sense. He's certainly not stupid. Strickland would fire him if he did. No, he's too smart for that. But just to give you some idea of what he's like: I was working with this kid the other day, it was end of shift and we'd all had a couple of drinks. Tris can't handle booze, he's pissed after two glasses of wine.

Anyway, my mate was showing me a picture of his girlfriend, just her face, and Tris comes over, and he's like, "What are you looking at?" And my mate's like, "I'm showing Pat my bird", and he's like, "Let's see". Then he goes, "Not got any hotter pix?" So my mate was like, "What?", and Tris gets his phone out, and he shows us this picture of this girl, stark naked on a bed. "That's who I'm banging," he said.' Patrick shook his head. 'Classy guy...'

Oh God, I thought, I hope it's not Cass, being trotted out like a trophy whore. 'What did she look like?'

Patrick thought. 'Dark hair, brown skin, maybe Asian or Middle Eastern, big boobs, tattoo of a hummingbird here.' Patrick touched the base of his neck. Oh, God, it's Suzi. How could I have been so blind as not to have seen this?

'So, Charlie, I wouldn't give him a job if I were you.'

No, I thought, I certainly wouldn't. The more I got to know about Tris, the less I liked him.

'So,' Patrick said, 'that's the first thing. What was the other thing you wanted to ask me about?'

'Would you mind covering for me for two or three days this week: Tuesday Wednesday and Thursday. I have to go up to Scotland unexpectedly.'

He scratched his head. 'I'd be okay with that, I enjoyed it last time, me and Murdo running the place, but you'll have to ask Napoleon.' I was interested to note that it wasn't just me who had noted the resemblance from the Ridley Scott movie.

I looked at my watch, it was half nine. 'Is he still at work?'

'He was when I left twenty minutes ago. We're prepping

the desserts for the beginning of the week. There's still a way to go.'

I stood up. 'I'll run over and see him now, get him to let you go for a couple of days next week. Thanks, Patrick.'

'Good luck.'

I walked round the corner of the common to the King's Head. The lights were off in the restaurant and I went round the back via the car park to the kitchen. I noticed that Strickland's Maserati was still there. I let myself in through the back gate, walked past the bins and rapped on the glass door of the kitchen.

A harried-looking junior chef who looked about twelve let me in. He seemed to know who I was. I stepped over the threshold and removed my boots at the door and in my socks walked into the kitchen, which was about three times the size of mine.

Strickland in his chef's whites was bending over a table. He looked up at me.

'Charlie, there's a punnet of chestnut mushrooms over there, chop them up for me, duxelles style,' he barked.

'Yes, Chef,' I replied, only semi-sarcastically. I washed my hands and the kid silently handed me a chef's knife.

'All of them?'

'All of them.'

I set to work. For a minute or so there was silence apart from the rat-a-tat of my knife on the chopping board.

'You can go now, Alfie,' Strickland commanded.

'Thank you, Chef.' The boy looked close to tears as he left the kitchen.

'That do?' I showed him the mushrooms.

'Good. There's a pan on the stove with some sweated shallot and garlic in, put it on the heat and add them to it.'

I did so and while it cooked down I asked him for the loan of Patrick.

'Why do you want him?' he asked. I could hardly tell him that it was to cover for me while I looked into his maître d' being a wife murderer.

'I have to be away for a few days.'

Strickland was so self-absorbed I didn't think he'd ask why, and so it proved. We blitzed the cooked duxelles in a food processor and then he used a smoke gun to fill the container. The fragrant fumes billowed around inside, drifting lazily over the edges and then he clingfilmed it immediately.

He took a tub out of a fridge, walked over to the stove, put a small pan on and added a couple of spoons from the tub, replaced it.

'Jus,' he grunted. 'There's a tub with fillet steak in the meat fridge over there. Take one out and chargrill it for me.'

'Yes, Chef.' While I did that he took the film off the food processor bowl, blitzed the mushroom mix again, adjusted the seasoning then took a plate out from the cabinet under the pass and added a dollop of the smoked mushroom paté to it.

'Steak's ready,' I said.

'Put it on the plate.'

I did so and he drizzled some jus over and handed me a knife and fork. 'Try it,' he ordered. Wow! The combination of flavours was fabulous.

'That's great, Graeme,' I enthused.

'I know. God, haven't used one of these in years,' he said, indicating the smoke gun. 'Time for it to make a comeback maybe. We'll see.'

I suddenly realised I was starving. I hadn't really eaten properly all day and Strickland's steaks were of exceptional quality. I also realised he hadn't given me an answer about Patrick. 'What about Patrick?'

He looked around the kitchen. There was the mess that had been created during my short time there, then there were other dishes and pans by the stove. Half an hour's worth of washing up.

'Clean down and the answer's yes. I've got some paper-work to catch up on... oh, and do the chargrill and the floors too. Just pull the door to behind you when you go. I'll probably just kip in the office.'

I watched as he stalked out of the kitchen in that quiet, feline way he had of walking. I shook my head and started my menial tasks. At least he'd said yes.

The day after the Suzi bombshell dropped by Patrick, it was time for Lizzie's third lesson. I got there about 4 o'clock. It was on the edge of the village up the road called Potter's Hill. In the late afternoon sun on this spring day, the cottage looked like an illustration from the English Tourist Board website. The small front garden was filled with hollyhocks, lupins, early flowering dog-roses and other brightly coloured plants that I couldn't identify. I guessed the rent would be astronomical, David Summers' money at work. IEA, Exploit, Tris's mantra in action. His sinister modus operandi.

147

Lizzie greeted me and led me inside. She was wearing a short-sleeved floral-print dress that unfortunately showed off her beefy arms. I reflected that she might be a match for Sandra Reynolds in an arm-wrestling contest.

'Charlie, what are we doing today?' She seemed very eager; I was rather touched. 'I've cleaned the kitchen like you told me to.'

'Thank you, Lizzie, always work clean, like we say in the industry.'

'I shall remember that,' she said solemnly.

'Good. I thought I'd show you how to make bread, Lizzie, then we can make a minestrone soup and you can give Tris that for a late supper when he gets in from work, together with your homemade bread fresh from the oven.'

Her face lit up at the thought. 'That sounds fantastic Charlie. Will it be sourdough?'

I shook my head. 'No, we can move on to that later. I can give you some of my starter to use, but today we'll just be using easy, dried yeast. It's fast-acting so if we make it now we can let it rise for an hour or so, then knock it back and shape it. That sound okay?'

So we made a simple white loaf and I let her knead it for ten minutes, then while it was proving in the airing cupboard, I showed her how to cut up the vegetables I had brought. 'Small, regular shapes,' I instructed her, 'paysanne, they're called.'

We sweated the veg which she had chopped, added the stock, and while that was cooking we made some lemon and lime posset, one of the quickest desserts I could think of. That took us to the hour mark. I checked on the bread, which was rising nicely. Lizzie marvelled at the sight of it. 'My God, it's got so big!'

'Well, we don't want it to get too big or it will collapse on itself,' I warned. 'Let's go and set the oven and have a cup of tea while it's warming up.'

'Good idea,' she said. She bustled around the kitchen, which did look infinitely better than when I'd first seen it, pleased to be able to do something without me telling her what to do, and we went through into the living room. As I sat down on an old sofa, I looked again at the Tris memorabilia, curated by Lizzie. Tris had that same grin on his face that I had come to know and detest. When I was a kid at school, for English literature we'd looked at a bit of Chaucer and I remembered a line: 'The smylere with the knyf under the cloke'. That described him exactly. If he had shoved his wife off a cliff, I bet he would have had that same self-approving smirk on his face as he did so. Lizzie came in and saw me looking at them.

'Isn't he wonderful,' she said, with a heartfelt smile. 'I'm such a lucky woman.'

You poor thing, I thought, but, as usual, said nothing. I drove home feeling desperate sorrow for her, and, in equal measure, repugnance for Tris.

# Chapter Nineteen

On Tuesday I flew to Scotland. I called Lizzie from Heathrow and cancelled the Wednesday lesson. The flight to Glasgow was uneventful and I hung around the airport for a couple of hours waiting for the next leg of my journey. This was a flight to Campbeltown on a Loganair plane. I don't know what I was expecting, to be honest I hadn't given it any thought whatsoever, but the tiny propeller plane on the runway astonished me. I was expecting something much bigger. I only had a small suitcase as hand luggage so I climbed up the flight of small steps into the cramped space.

You could see the two pilots sitting in front with the complicated-looking control panel on view in between them, at least until one of them reached up and pulled a curtain across, hiding them from sight. The engines roared into action. Through the window I could see the mesmerising sight of the twin blades of the propellers, now only to be guessed at, in a kind of shimmering vortex as they spun round at God knows what speed. We taxied on the runway and then we were off.

I peered out of the small porthole window, ridiculously excited. This was flying as it used to be, low-down and dirty. None of your jet malarkey. I was fortunate: it was a clear day, grey but the cloud cover was above the plane and I could see the ground beneath, the rivers and streams ('burns' I said to myself, that's what they're called up here) that seemed to crawl across the earth below. The ground was a furrowed, crumpled dark green, with grey outcroppings of rock and the mirror-effect of small lakes ('lochs!' I thought, marvelling at my linguistic mastery). This wasn't my first time in Scotland, I'd spent a few weeks there the year before, helping Strickland out. But the west was very different from the east.

I was like a child staring in wonder at the miniature world below. Cars were like dinky toys and, seen from so far above, their movements along roads were cute and purposeful, mesmerising, like watching little ants.

Then the sea, a very deep blue, with Impressionistic streaks of white and tiny boats scattered on it for decorative effect. We flew over a spectacular mountainous island that I later identified as Arran, craggy and majestic, the grey of its rocky shoreline punctuated by yellow beaches. When we touched down at the airport I thought to myself, I have never enjoyed a flight so much in all my life.

Campbeltown Airport came as a bit of a shock. Not so much the fact that it consisted of a large shed, I wasn't expecting Frankfurt International. Nor the fact that it was located in an area of grassland with low hills in the distance, seemingly in the middle of nowhere. It was the fact that Campbeltown, where I was staying, seemed to be about ten miles away according to my phone and with no obvious means of getting there.

My fellow passengers, about a dozen of them, all got into their cars or were met by people and drove off, leaving me standing feeling both stupid and slightly ridiculous, alone in the now empty car park, staring at the grasslands all around and a flock of sheep. A stiff breeze blew in across the moorland and I could smell the sea. I shook my head at my own stupidity. I'd lived too long in cities. Even Hampden Green had a one-an-hour bus service. I'd forgotten that, out in the sticks, the car was king.

An hour or so later and a considerable amount of money lighter, I waved goodbye to my taxi and stood outside the Davaar View Hotel.

I paused for a moment in a light drizzle looking out across the gunmetal-grey waters to the distant shape of what I later learned was indeed Davaar Island, at the entrance to the natural harbour of Campbeltown Loch. So the hotel's name was pretty spot on. The houses were grey stone, matching the loch. Victorian, I guessed. I looked at the surroundings, they weren't picturesque. I saw a park near the hotel and a large, modern grey concrete and glass building that the taxi driver had told me was a swimming pool.

I didn't really know what to make of Campbeltown, it was pretty-ish, but it had an underlying air of melancholy about it, as if it had been forgotten by the rest of the world in general. The fate of so many British seaside towns.

I walked up the broad steps to the hotel and went in.

*

Loyd McFarlane and I were having a drink together as night slowly gathered over the waters of the Kilbrannan Sound and Campbeltown. Murdo had said Loyd was a good chef, and he wasn't wrong. Earlier that evening I had eaten a spectacularly good meal of local scallops with lardons of local bacon and girolles, followed by a venison burger with homemade rowan jelly and fries, then Isle of Mull cheddar and Lanark Blue cheese.

McFarlane ('Please call me Loyd') was probably only a couple of years older than Murdo but unbelievably mature. I felt like I was talking to someone my own age instead of twenty years younger. I think running your own restaurant/ hotel ages you.

'So, what brings you to Campbeltown?' he asked.

'I'm looking into the death of a woman called Cara Smith.' I drank some of the local whisky, a smoky malt from the Springbank distillery. It was delicious. 'She passed away up here about three years ago. She fell off a cliff near the Mull of Kintyre.'

He frowned. 'Why are you doing that? It sounds like a job for a detective. I thought you were a chef?'

'I am.' I gave him a quick resumé of my CV, culminating in my now coming up to four years' ownership of my restaurant. I wanted to establish my professional cooking credentials firmly in the mind of McFarlane. I thought I had a much better chance of getting help from him, not to mention greater attention paid to my food, if he knew that I was a proper chef.

I then gave him a brief rundown of the reason I was here.

'Well,' he said, with a hint of regret, 'personally I can't help you. I was working in Edinburgh at the time and then I did a stint at Gleneagles. But Nicola who works behind the bar might know something. She's local and has been working in bars around here for about twenty-odd years. I'll go and ask her to join us.'

The lady who had served me earlier came and joined us. It was 10 o'clock and there were only a handful of people in the bar. She had a kind face, wore glasses, in her fifties, thin with short, dyed brown hair.

She sat down opposite me while Loyd left us alone and took up her position behind the bar.

'So, what do you want to know?' she asked me. She had a gentle Western Isles cadence to her voice, unlike Loyd and Murdo who were both from Edinburgh and had much stronger accents.

For the second time that evening I explained how I was looking into the death of Cara Smith.

'And you say the Freemason's Arms was where she had her last meal with her husband?' she asked.

'Yes,' I said. 'I'm planning to go along there tomorrow, see if anyone can remember anything, assuming that there's staff there who worked in the place three years ago.'

Nicola shook her head, 'I'm sorry to be the bearer of bad news, Charlie, but the Freemason's Arms has been closed nearly a year now.'

My face fell. I cursed myself for being so stupid. A few minutes on the internet would be all that was needed to have found this out. It looked like my trip up to Scotland was off to a terrible start and could well turn out to be a complete and utter waste of time. This obviously showed in my face, a good job I wasn't a professional poker player.

'Tell you what,' Nicola said, consolingly, 'I'll pick you up tomorrow morning and take you to where it all happened. I remember it fine, particularly as I have an uncle who used to live nearby so I ken the area very well.'

'Thank you so much,' I said, touched by her kindness. At least it would be something.

'It's nae bother.' She smiled. 'To be honest, it'll be quite exciting. Life in Campbeltown can be a wee bit mundane, if you ken what I mean.'

'I can imagine,' I said. Down here, at the end of the Argyll peninsula, you were about a four-hour drive to Glasgow. There was beautiful countryside around you, and the ever-changing panorama of the sea, but I knew that if I lived here, I would start to feel discontented.

I raised this with Loyd when Nicola went back to the bar to call time. What was it like living here all the time?

'I know what you mean, Charlie.' He yawned, he looked exhausted. 'But, to be honest, you know what it's like in the catering trade. I'm too knackered most of the time to notice. I think if you're young, there's obviously a problem living here. There aren't many jobs around, and a definite lack of nightlife and exciting things to do. Social media doesn't help, all those kids posting images of lives that seem unimaginably glam compared to here… But I shoot and I fish and I surf and I like sailing, so I'm kind of made up really.'

He grinned. 'My girlfriend did none of those things. She

had enough and left me...' he looked at me in an encouraging way as if to say, 'How about it?' and I smiled and shook my head. 'I'm spoken for, Loyd.'

It was funny, I didn't mind being propositioned by Loyd; there's often a kind of brutal honesty to be found among chefs. Maybe it's because we don't have time to say things with finesse. Strickland certainly wouldn't bother with romance, he would find it an irritating waste of everyone's time. Probably no wonder Cassandra split up with him. She had told me she was fed up playing second fiddle to food all the time.

So I went up the stairs to bed alone. I left the curtains half open, the sky was not quite dark (it stays light up north much later, something to do with the shape of the earth, or something, Andrea had tried to explain it to me using an orange as the sun and an apple as the earth, a Cox's, maybe there was a grape for the moon. I pretended to grasp what he was on about, but I didn't really understand) and I could smell the sea on the draught coming in where I had left the window ajar. I fell asleep marvelling at the difference between this quiet, seaside town and my own quiet village. I stretched out in bed and realised how happy I was. Then sleep took me.

Seagulls, the noise of engines from fishing boats and daylight woke me up early. After I'd had a spectacularly good breakfast – 'The Full Scottish', the same as a full English but with square sausage which I must say I prefer – Nicola turned up, as promised, behind the wheel of an old, long, battered green Land Rover. I climbed in beside her and we set off down the road, jolting along, through Campbeltown heading south-west towards the Mull.

'So what is the Mull of Kintyre?' I asked her, almost shouting over the roar of the engine and the rattling of the cab.

She looked at me in astonishment at my ignorance. 'It's the tip of the Argyll peninsula, there's a lighthouse down there. Do you know the song by Paul McCartney?'

'No.'

'Oh well, never mind. We drive through a wee village called Southend, imaginative eh? Then along a road to the end. Cara fell to her death from there.'

We drove through the empty, grassy landscape. The sky seemed huge overhead. The fields were criss-crossed with dry-stone walls. There were none of the hedgerows that lined the edges of the fields in Bucks. There was a kind of we're-standing-at-the-edge-of-the-world feeling about this place. What trees there were had grown stunted and mis-shaped from the wind and the salt air. One line of them in particular on the brow of a small hill looked just like musical notes on a page. After a while we passed through Southend and then along the deserted single-track road until eventually we saw the lighthouse.

Nicola stopped the Land Rover and we got out. The powerful breeze buffeted us and I looked out to the blue-grey sea with the occasional streak of silver from the white horses. On the horizon was a faint dark smudge. Nicola pointed at it. 'Rathlin Island, just off the tip of Ireland,' she said.

We walked across the springy turf scattered with rabbit

pellets and the occasional dried sheep dropping, my hair whipped around me by the wind. It was quite exhilarating. I thought, Andrea would like it here. Nothing like this in Italy, well not that I had seen anyway. We could stay at Loyd's hotel for a week. Once everything was over.

There were daisy-like flowers and yellow plants here and there and the occasional gorse bush. We stood at the edge of the cliff and looked down to the rocks below. I shuddered inwardly to think of the terrifying drop and the impact of falling onto them.

'So this is where she fell?' I asked.

'I dinnae ken for sure,' she said doubtfully, 'but if not here then very close by.'

We stood for a while as I stared at the sea and the rocks. I couldn't think of anything sensible to do or say. I guess I had been hoping for some kind of a-ha moment, a blinding revelation, which was not at all forthcoming.

'I think we might as well go back,' I said, eventually.

I had noticed as we had driven through that there was a shop in Southend, a little general store, and I asked Nicola to stop so I could get some tissues. I went inside. There was a slightly fusty, old-fashioned smell. It reminded me of shops of my youth when sometimes Dad would take me to the Essex coast. It sold a variety of disparate things: canned food, shrimping nets on sticks, postcards whose colours bore no relation to the real world, sweets, fizzy drinks that were not the ones you usually saw, for example 'cola' rather than Pepsi or Coke, limeade of a very unrealistic bright green. Kind of inevitably it was run by an old lady.

I bought my tissues.

'Anything else, dear?'

There were assorted bottles of spirits on a shelf behind her. On a whim I asked, 'I don't know if you can help, but I'm looking for information about a lady who died down here...'

'Cara Smith?' she said, much to my surprise.

'Er, yes,' I said startled. 'How did you know?'

'I've been here thirty years, hen. She's the only woman who's died round here in all this time.' She smiled. 'This isnae Glasgow, ken.'

'Of course not,' I said, 'would you mind telling me what you know about her?'

'Not at all. I'm surprised no one has asked before.'

The story she told was slightly odd, which is why she remembered it so very vividly. A young man, very good-looking, she said, well-spoken, polite, English, that she later found out was Tris Smith, had come into the shop and told her that he and his wife were staying at one of the cottages up the road for a fortnight's holiday. He'd bought two bottles of whisky which surprised her. She explained why.

'It's so much more expensive here than in the supermarkets. We only really stock it for people if they've run out and they've got guests.'

Then he had leaned over the counter and confided in her that his wife had a drink problem and he was trying to cut her consumption down. He had asked her not to sell her any booze if she came in. '"What does she look like?" I asked. He told me she was pretty with blonde hair and a Southern English accent.'

160

'Did she come in?' I asked.

'Oh aye, the next day, wanted to buy a bottle of Scotch.' She frowned. 'She wasn't what I was expecting. He was very good-looking and she, well, I don't want to sound disrespectful, but she was a big lass, seriously overweight. I said that we only had the one, but someone had ordered it on the phone. Sorry.'

'What did she say?'

'Here's where it gets interesting. She was fine with that.' She paused and looked at me in an evaluating way. 'Now, young lady…'

'Charlie,' I said.

'I'm Val.' She leaned over the counter, her eyes a bright blue under the white curled hair. 'Now, Charlie, my ex had a drink problem. If you'd told him he couldn't have his Scotch, he'd have gone crazy. At the very least he'd have demanded a substitute, even if it was sherry or Advocaat; he'd've drunk it. But this woman, the "alcoholic", well, she just shrugged. I thought to myself, she's nae got a problem. He's lying.

'Then two days later she comes in again, this time wanting two bottles of vodka, a long story, some Polish friends of her husband, work colleagues, were coming unexpectedly, it was their favourite drink. Well, this time I didnae have to lie, we don't carry vodka. Fine, she says. Then I went away to Inverness for a wedding. When I get back, she's deid.'

'So you don't think she had a drink problem?'

She shook her head. 'Naw, not drink, but food, aye, she was a big lady, no' exactly a wee skelf. She bought three bags of sweeties and two packs of shortbread when she was in. I saw her open the shortbread on the way to the car, shovelling it in her mouth like she hadnae eaten in days. Anyway, later I heard how she'd fallen after she'd taken a drink and the story going round that she had a problem, but I dinnae believe it. I think he made the whole thing up. I think she was set up by him.'

'Did you tell the police?'

Val shook her head. 'No. I was away after the wedding and when I got back, it was all over. I had problems of my own, ken… but every now and again, I'd think about this lassie. I think he told me she had this problem and then kept sending her down to the shop for messages to establish his story, so if someone challenged him he could say, well, look at her behaviour. She wouldn't be around to gainsay him.'

'I see,' I said. It all fitted in so well with what I knew about Tris and with what Dr Taylor had said.

'What's your interest in this?' Val asked. 'Is he planning to marry again?'

'Yes.'

'Well, Charlie, I'd try and stop it if I were you.' She folded her arms. 'I think he's killed one woman, and I bet he'll do it again.'

I thanked her and left the shop.

'You were gone for ages,' Nicola said as I climbed into her Land Rover. 'What were you chatting about?'

'Absent friends,' I said. 'Come on, let's go back to Campbeltown, I'll buy you lunch.'

# Chapter Twenty

I flew into Heathrow on Friday and I was picked up by Jess. She told me that Patrick and Murdo had been 'fantastic, you weren't missed at all'. This was both reassuring and slightly depressing; we all love to consider ourselves indispensable.

Anyway, Patrick left and I took my usual place at the pass and stove. It was as if nothing had ever happened, except now I knew that Tris was a killer, not just a womaniser. I wished that Slattery had grounds for searching Tris and Lizzie's cottage. I was sure he would find a crossbow.

On Saturday night before service I called David Summers. I didn't go into detail about what I'd learned but I described it as 'significant.' He wanted to know more but I told him we'd need to sit down and go over it and I'd get back to him soon to arrange a date to discuss the matter.

'Good,' he grunted. 'I knew I could trust you. I'll get back to you with a time to meet up. I'm very busy right now,'

He wasn't alone. Suddenly I was engulfed in the maelstrom of the Saturday night service and I put it on the backburner. I would also bring it up with Slattery but I knew he'd be sceptical. He had enough on his plate with actual crime without adding potential crimes to it.

I met up with the object of my suspicions on Sunday morning, at the bench on the common at eight in the morning. Tris, Matt, Cassandra, Suzi and me. Tris looked the same as ever, urbane, confident, in command of the situation. I was now firmly convinced that Summers had been right from the very beginning, that Tris had killed his wife, but it was impossible to prove. No new evidence to lead to his prosecution would ever be forthcoming. But had he killed John Mayhew?

'Okay,' Tris said, 'we're doing an eight k road run today. We'll run along to Frampton End, down to Stony Way and along the bottom road to the crossroads, then we'll loop up back towards Hampden Green.'

We all nodded.

'Any questions? No? Okay, but before we start, I would suggest a moment's silence for John. His funeral by the way is next Tuesday at the crematorium, eleven o'clock.'

We stood silently for a minute on the grass while the wind ruffled our hair. Did I detect a smirk on those lips of his? I surreptitiously regarded Cass and Suzi, the other women in Tris's complicated life. They were very different types physically: Cassandra, tall, pale, slim with large, slightly sad eyes; Suzi, shorter, stockier, bustier, with either Middle Eastern or Asian heritage. What was wrong with these attractive women that they wanted to be having a fling with Tris? They didn't lack brains or beauty. I looked at the object of their desire, evaluating him as a lover this time instead of a killer. Tris was fine, Val up in Scotland had described him as very good-looking but I disagreed. He wasn't that good-looking and his body although good, was not that wonderful. His character was obviously deplorable, they both knew he was engaged. It was one of those mysteries, like people believing outlandish conspiracy theories or that the earth is flat. Again, I wondered if I should maybe confront them about it or tell Suzi that her naked body was by now familiar to the kitchen brigade at the King's Head. But I knew that I probably wouldn't. It would only upset her and he would simply deny it. What was she going to do, go round there, pull her top off and shout, 'Do these look familiar?' It was one of those cases where there didn't seem to be any clear-cut obvious thing to do; there was, as they say, no solution, only trade-offs.

The minute was up and we all fell into line, the two men leading, then Tris's lovers, well, one definite and one on his to-do list, and me (also on his to-do list, Hell would freeze over first) bringing up the rear. They chatted away amicably.

I wasn't enjoying my run. I thought to myself as I pounded along, this is definitely the last time I do this. I can't bear to be sharing this close proximity of sexual and moral betrayal, courtesy of all parties concerned, and then have to spend time with Lizzie as if none of this was happening, and I would be seeing her the following day.

Monday came round quicker than I would have thought possible. I spent the morning catching up on paperwork and in the afternoon, I went over to see Lizzie at 4 o'clock as usual. I had to park my car on the road opposite as there was already another car in the space outside her cottage. There was a lay-by there and as I straightened the Volvo I noticed that someone had dumped a brightly coloured zip-up nylon suitcase there. I wondered if the Earl's cameras extended this far and if he had managed to get any of the fly-tippers' vehicle details.

As I walked through the colourful front garden of the cottage, I was racking my brains as to how I could use my knowledge of the probable murder of Tris's wife to good effect. The trouble was, I strongly suspected that Lizzie would either not believe me, or more likely, Tris had himself raised the subject but in a way that would have totally exonerated him. I knocked on the door. She answered, her face swollen with tears. Oh my God, I thought, with a mixture of alarm and hope, she's found out that Tris has been cheating on her.

'Come in, Charlie,' she said. 'I've had a bit of a shock. We'll go in the kitchen.'

I could hear voices from the living room as we walked through the small hall into the kitchen. She closed the door behind her.

'It's Tris,' she sobbed.

Ha! I knew it, I thought. Bastard!

But I didn't. I had completely got the wrong end of the stick. She immediately continued. 'Someone tried to kill him today, at lunchtime!'

'What!' I hadn't bargained on this. 'What happened?'

'He was out on his run, after service, about three o'clock.' Lizzie's eyes welled with tears, she blew her nose loudly.

'It was in between shifts on his split. Someone fired a crossbow bolt at him in the wood. It missed him by a whisker, thank God, and hit a tree just in front of him instead. It's a miracle he wasn't killed!'

First John, now Tris. I was shocked too, but for a different reason. It now rather looked as if he wasn't the killer after all, but that maybe someone had it in for the Hampden Green Runners. It was obviously the same person, the crossbow again.

'I don't know if I could live without Tris,' Lizzie said tearfully, looking up at me from where she was sitting with sad eyes. 'He means absolutely everything to me, he's so kind and attentive and wonderful... I love him so much, Charlie.' She burst into tears again and I put a consoling arm around her.

Oh, God, I thought. This is becoming intolerable. I could easily ignore Tris's affairs if I could keep my distance from him, but I had grown to like Lizzie. Here I was, centre-stage, horribly aware of what was going on. I decided on two things there and then. First, I wouldn't be going to anymore Hampden Green Runners meets. If someone was targeting them, I didn't want to be next on someone else's hit list. Secondly, I would have a word with Cassandra and warn her off Tris. I knew I was risking ending our friend-ship by doing that, people hate being told what they should or shouldn't be doing – particularly when they themselves are doubtless very aware that their actions are morally wrong. She would almost certainly flare up. Well, so be it. If our relationship ended, I could take it. But I could no longer ignore what was going on and be a party to it.

The annoying thing was, I much preferred Cass to Lizzie. I liked Lizzie but I didn't respect her. She was just too much of a doormat. She seemed so utterly dominated by Tris, like she was his handmaiden or something. Just then I heard voices outside the kitchen, there was a knock and the door opened. There stood Slattery and a stern-faced woman with dark hair in a dark blue skirt and jacket who I assumed was one of his colleagues.

He nodded curtly to me then spoke to Lizzie. 'We'll be off now Ms Summers. Thank you for your assistance and we'll leave you be now.'

'Goodbye, Detective Inspector,' Lizzie said, pasting a brave smile on her trembling lips. I felt a stab of irritation. He's not actually dead, I thought, maybe uncharitably. Get over it already. 'And thank you both for all your support. I'll see you out.'

She returned in a short while. 'Charlie, I'm sorry, I don't think that I am up to doing a cookery lesson today, not after what happened.'

That was the last thing on my mind too. I had kind of forgotten about it. 'Don't apologise, Lizzie, I totally understand. I'll be back on Wednesday anyway and we'll reschedule today.'

'Thanks, Charlie.' She threw her arms around me and hugged me. 'You're such a good friend.'

I left the cottage and drove home thoughtfully. I suspected that I would be seeing Slattery soon. When I did I would pass on the information about Lizzie's father and John Mayhew being erstwhile business partners; it could be important. Whoever had killed Mayhew, it certainly wasn't Tris.

That evening I called Andrea. He was in Bologna in a hotel discussing finance for the hotel in Porto Fino.

'What kind of a hotel is it?' I asked.

'Which one?' he asked.

'Both,' I said. I studied his familiar face on my phone screen. He looked tired and stressed, which was unusual for him, normally he treated work with a kind of amused detachment.

He turned the phone away and showed me the room, large and minimalist.

'It's very nice,' I said, wistfully. 'I wish I could be there with you…'

I was expecting the reply 'me too' but he started talking about the other hotel, how exciting it was, Il Maneggio I think it was called, which he told me meant something like 'Stables'. I wasn't remotely interested.

'When am I going to see you again?' I asked, plaintively. 'I miss you!' And I did. Jess's remark about how well the place had functioned without me had got me thinking. A while ago, Andrea had suggested that I find a chef to replace me and I move in with him, working just two or three days a week down in Bucks while I lived in London. At the time I had rejected this out of hand, but now I thought, why not? I'd broach it with Andrea the next time we were together.

'Soon,' he promised, 'very soon, once all this is over.'

I stared at the phone in my hand and sighed. Well, that hadn't gone as I had expected it. 'Once all this is over,' he had said. That reminded me, I had become so occupied with Tris that I'd forgotten about my promise to Esther and the bloody diadem theft.

I poured myself a drink and relaxed on the sofa. My phone buzzed, I had a message. I glanced at it hoping it was from Andrea, but it wasn't. It was from Lizzie. She messaged that Tris wanted to be alone after the near-death experience to 'process it' and she would be going to stay at her dad's near Chichester for a few days. She hoped I would understand. 'Process' my arse, I thought, you just want to be shagging Suzi.

Well, there was nothing I could do about that. I messaged back something soothing. Okay, diadem time. I called Chris, the Goth Wiccan from Milton Keynes. 'Hi, I'm free next week to come over to see Sandra…Wednesday, you say, great, about eleven?… make it twelve and you can be there? Great!' I insincerely gushed. 'See you Wednesday.'

At least someone was pleased to see me, I thought sourly.

# Chapter Twenty-One

On Wednesday, as I drove to Milton Keynes where Chris and his wife, Sandra, lived, I was feeling much less confident than I had pretended a while back. Aside from attempted murder, other incidents included a car-jacking and a fight in the kitchen of the very house I was now headed to. A fight I had won only by shoving a Scotch bonnet chilli in Sandra's eye. It had been a chequered relationship, I reflected to myself as I drove through the pretty backroads north of Thame.

I'd spoken to Sandra as well to confirm on the phone and she'd sounded pleased to see me, but you never really know. Before being born-again, Sandra had been the treasurer of a woman-only Hells Angels gang called Satan's Sluts. To anyone tempted to snigger at the idea of a lady Hells Angel, I can assure them that the reality is every bit as terrifying as their male counterparts. Maybe slightly more so. Sandra, when I saw her last, had weighed in at about 114 kilos, 18 stone in old money. Her arms were big and beefy, she could probably lift me effortlessly above her head. In addition to that she had a kind of feral gleam in her eye of unrestrained violence, which had made me quail with fear.

Sandra was a force to be reckoned with. Samson had slain 10,000 Philistines with the jawbone of an ass, I remembered from Sunday School. She was cut from a similar cloth. It had literally taken a bullet to stop her berserker advance, a bullet not fired by me, I hasten to add. She had survived the shooting, and the subsequent murder charge. I suspected that is what made Sandra sure God was not only looking after her, but had set something special aside in store for her. A mission, a calling.

I wondered how she had changed. Well, miracles do happen they say. And Jesus is nothing if not very much in the miracle business.

I pulled up outside their detached house on an executive-style housing estate. It looked so normal. I couldn't help but wonder what the neighbours made of it all – the former Hells Angel, now the Preacher and her husband, the scrawny Goth Wizard at Number 36. Well, from the outside the house looked much as I remembered it, indistinguishable from all the others. I rang the bell, feeling nervous.

The door opened. A gruff voice said, 'Charlie, how nice to see you again…'

I smiled weakly. 'Hello, Sandra.'

She was wearing a floral top and a mid-length skirt, a pair of flat pumps on her feet and high ankle socks. Her formerly long hair had been cut to her shoulders. It was quite a transformation. The last time I had seen her she had been wearing a cut-off denim jacket over her leather one, greasy jeans, steel-capped biker boots, a black T-shirt and her hair had been a wild, grey-streaked mane. Now she looked, if not genteel, at least refreshingly normal. Well, not all that normal, to be honest. Still sizeable. Like Big Daddy (one of my father's favourite wrestlers) in a wig and a frock.

'Do come in.' She led me through the hall now bedecked with religious imagery, into the lounge.

The weightlifter physique remained, I could see the powerful trap muscles rising from her blouse collar, and those in her bull-neck were like cables. Her large chest was now held in place by what looked to be, via its outline, an industrial-strength bra. That reminded me of something.

I glanced over at the wall that used to have a large black-and-white portrait photo of her from her youth, naked except for an unzipped leather jacket, straddling a Harley. It had certainly been quite something, it had definitely drawn the eye. That had gone.

'Take a seat. I'll go and make some tea.'

She had noticed my glance at the space over the side-board; now there was a luridly painted crucifixion scene, Jesus looking like a faintly zonked hippie, not at all both-ered by the crown of thorns, the lance in his side or the nails through his palms and ankles. She guessed why I was looking.

'It's currently in the bedroom, where it's more appro-priate,' she said, primly. 'I serve the Lord now… Anyway, I'll just go and get that tea.'

The lounge was clean and tidy, there were more religious pictures. I guessed she had gone over to the evangelicals, none of this looked C of E to me. But I had to say, the new Sandra was a vast improvement on the old one. I checked in on my emotions. I was nervous, but I wasn't fearing for my life. She brought in a pot of tea and its usual accompaniments, also a chocolate cake, obviously home-made. It had a 30-degree slant where the top half had risen irregularly in the oven.

'I made this for you.' She took a deep breath then delivered an obviously rehearsed speech. 'I did you a grievous wrong, Charlie Hunter. I know the Lord has forgiven me, but it would heal my heart if you did too.'

I felt quite touched. 'No hard feelings, Sandra,' I said. Which was weirdly true. I'm not one for bearing grudges.

'When I was lying in that hospital,' she said, dreamily, 'hooked up to the morphine pump, I had a vision of the Son of God.' She smiled radiantly. 'He was hovering up in the corner, He was very handsome...' there was a pause and a far-away look while she relived her beatific vision, 'and I told Him that if I survived I would be His bride...' I looked at her. Lucky old Jesus, I thought, with your new Mary Magdalene, 'and I would devote myself to good works.'

Sandra had been shot in the stomach and I'd done my best to staunch the bleeding until the ambulance arrived. Much to my surprise I had succeeded. That had been a highly unpleasant ordeal. Ghastly actually. Blood welling around my wrists while I pushed down on the sodden scarlet rag that had been a wadded T-shirt. Well, obviously it had been worse for her, although she had been unconscious.

'That's very commendable, Sandra,' I said. She poured the tea. 'Black, no sugar for me please.'

She nodded and continued with her narrative. 'And the Lord took pity on me. Not only did He heal me, but He guided the hand of the judge and jury who accepted my not guilty plea and kept me out of prison.'

'That was good of Him,' I said.

'It most certainly was,' she agreed. 'I'm glad we've put that little misunderstanding between you and me behind us. Cake? I made it specially.'

'Yes please...' She cut me a large slice of chocolate sponge. It was overbaked, kind of crusty, and rather dry but I politely said, 'It's lovely.'

She beamed at me. 'It's Chris's favourite. He says I should be on *Bake Off*.'

Does he now? I thought. You wouldn't get a Paul Hollywood handshake for this. I swallowed a chunk of cake and drank some tea, it was making my mouth rather dry. Maybe she'd put too much baking powder in if she'd used plain rather than self-raising flour. I tore my mind away from the topic of baking to harder problems. I wondered how I was going to introduce the topic of whether or not her husband was a thief. I didn't want to upset her.

'What I'm about to tell you is strictly confidential, Sandra.'

She nodded. 'I swear on the Bible that I won't tell anyone...'

I looked suspiciously at her. I guessed that she was no stranger to swearing on bibles usually to say that she was telling the truth, the whole truth and nothing but the truth. She had doubtless been in court more than a few times during her membership of the Hells Angels.

'Okay,' I said, taking a deep breath, 'don't take this the wrong way, please Sandra, but something's been stolen from Esther. It happened while I was there with Chris and Pascale.'

'Chris didn't do it,' she said, both immediately and emphatically.

'I'm sure he didn't, but I need to check, to eliminate him from my enquiries.' The thing about Chris was that he wasn't malevolent in my estimation, but I could certainly see him as impulsive. I had envisioned the possibility of a thoughtless theft, like a magpie stealing gold or a brightly coloured piece of jewellery as they are rumoured to do.

She nodded. 'Check away, but he definitely didn't do it. He can't lie to me, he's never been able to. He blushes when he does, it's always very obvious.'

Momentarily I wondered how she squared this with her conviction he was having all sorts of affairs, but then again the best of us aren't that logical, why should she be? Just then we heard the noise of a car pulling up in the drive and we watched through the lounge window as Chris got out.

'You can ask him yourself,' Sandra said complacently, 'then you can rule him out as the thief.'

It seemed a reasonable suggestion. I heard the key turn in the lock and Chris walked in, wearing a cheap, rather horrible, blue two-piece suit and a tie with Goofy on it. Nothing indicates a lack of a sense of humour more than a comedy-themed tie. He was jewellery free too. No ankhs in the workplace. Not even in the Bucks Council's Leisure department.

He came into the room. 'Charlie, great to see you as always...' I noticed that he didn't try to kiss me on the cheek, which he would have done if we'd been alone. That was a relief. He was very nervous around Sandra when other women were present, understandably so.

'Go on,' Sandra urged, 'ask him...'

'Ask me what?' Chris immediately looked guilty.

'Okay.' I stood up and looked him in the eye. I was taller than him and he quailed slightly as if he expected me to hit him. It was an action that I must confess had crossed my mind on occasions.

'Chris,' I said sternly, 'did you take something the other day at Esther's that didn't belong to you?'

'No,' he said loudly. Sandra and I both looked on in horror and fascination as a tide of red surged up Chris's pallid skin like mercury in a thermometer until he was glowing like a beetroot.

It looked like I had found the diadem thief.

# Chapter Twenty-Two

I drove the thirty-odd miles back from the sterile environment of Milton Keynes to my village in a state of acute bewilderment. When Chris's colour had changed, the human litmus test, white meaning truth, pinky red, a lie, Sandra had initially been enraged. I suppose having claimed that Chris had not been involved and then discovering he had been was all the more upsetting since she'd been convinced of his innocence. She'd jumped to her feet and Chris had looked suitably terrified. I took a step back too, an angry Sandra was a petrifying sight. She might be following in the footsteps of Christ but she certainly wasn't gentle, meek or mild.

'You lied to me!' roared Sandra. 'Falsehood is a sin… Judas!' she hissed.

'I didn't steal it…' Chris stammered.

'What didn't you steal?' Sandra thundered.

Chris looked around him wildly as if searching for either an escape route or an ally, neither of which were forthcoming. I stared back at him, stony-faced. Arms folded.

'Whatever it was you think I stole, I didn't…'

It was like dealing with a child.

'But you did take something that didn't belong to you?' I suggested, in an encouraging tone of voice.

'Yes…' Chris said miserably, looking at the floor. 'Yes I did.'

'What was it?' Sandra demanded.

'I can't tell you,' Chris said, lifting his chin in a kind of attempt at bravery which fooled no one. 'It was for a cere-mony… but if you go in the kitchen, Sandra,' he said in a wheedling tone, 'I'll tell Charlie. She's practically a witch, Esther confides everything to her, but it might go against your faith, darling.'

Sandra frowned as she mulled that over then looked at me. 'Is that okay with you, Charlie?'

'I guess so.' I was interested despite myself to know what Chris was going to confess to stealing. It obviously wasn't the diadem.

'Okay, then,' Sandra said. She looked darkly at Chris and left the room.

'Right,' I said briskly, 'what was it that you took, Chris?' This had better be good, I thought.

He sighed resignedly and pulled something out of his pocket. 'This.'

I took it from his hand and looked at it. It was a woman's silk scarf, small with two stylised, richly caparisoned horses in oranges, yellows and reds. It was beautiful. I looked at the label, Hermès. So, as expensive as it looked. It smelled faintly of perfume.

'Whose is it?' I really didn't need to. It wasn't the kind of thing that Esther would have worn.

'I think it belongs to Pascale.' I saw a faint blush appear, so, a bit of a lie there then. It was fascinating now I knew his secret, it really was like a chemical reagent test.

'You think?' I raised an eyebrow. 'You didn't think, Chris, did you.' I shook my head sorrowfully. 'You knew it was hers.'

'Yes,' he admitted, miserably.

'Why?'

'Okay, I'll tell you.' He looked me in the eye. 'I'm in love with Pascale and she can't stand me, that's why…'

'So you stole her scarf to get even?' I said incredulously.

'No, Charlie,' he shook his head impatiently, 'don't be stupid. I was going to perform a ceremony to summon the powers to grant me their aid in winning her heart.'

I frowned. 'By heart, you mean her body, don't you, Chris?'

'No!' He turned scarlet and plunged on, hoping to leave the reasons behind. 'I needed an article of clothing,' he explained, 'something she would have worn close to her skin. When I went to the bathroom I saw her coat there in Esther's sitting room and I found that in her pocket. I took it.'

'Weren't you worried you would get caught?'

'Fortune favours the brave, Charlie.' Was stealing a scarf brave? Maybe for Chris. 'But she didn't notice. She's loaded, she's a vet, she earns a fortune… she's probably got lots of scarves…' he suddenly looked anxious. 'You're not going to tell her, are you? Or Sandra?'

I glared at him. He really was despicable. However, I didn't want to upset Sandra so I shook my head. 'I won't say anything, but I'm keeping the scarf,' I said firmly. Then a horrible thought crossed my mind. 'You haven't...' I hesitated, searching for a suitable word, le mot juste as Pascale may have said, 'done... anything with it...' I was hesitant, I didn't want to put what I wanted to say into words, 'or on it... have you?'

'No!' No tell-tale blush, thank God for that I thought.

'And you definitely didn't take anything else?'

'No.' No blushing.

'Okay, Chris, you've been honest with me, I'll be honest with you.' I believed completely that he was innocent of the diadem theft. Chris wasn't obsessed with power, just women. 'I'll tell you what's happened. Someone has stolen the diadem from Esther. You were one of the suspects.' I paused, just time for a quick check. 'It definitely wasn't you, was it?'

'No,' he replied firmly. Not even a hint of a blush.

And that was where we left things. So now l had ruled Chris out of the suspect list it was down to Pascale. All I had to do was get her to surrender it, and I suspected that was not going to be easy.

As I drove back to my restaurant I felt quite pleased with the way the morning had gone. I had taken quite a big step forward in getting the diadem back, inasmuch as I knew for sure who had stolen it. Pascale, you thieving bitch, I thought as I parked my car outside the Old Forge Café. Then, how the hell am I going to get it back off her?

I was in time to join Murdo for the tail-end of lunch. I changed and helped him with the last few orders then

I sent him off early and cleaned the kitchen down with Francis who burbled on about how good he had become at the fennel salad. 'You should have seen them, Chef,' he enthused, 'pretty as peacocks...'

At round about 3 o'clock, Cassandra arrived for an appointment to discuss my wine order. She was wearing a two-piece suit, a short dark skirt that showed off her long legs, expensive-looking dark tights and a matching jacket.

'Charlie!' She was delighted to see me. As we talked business and gossiped about people including Graeme Strickland, I realised just how much I liked her. The thought of falling out with her over her choice in men was intolerable.

'So, Charlie, you've been up in Scotland. Was that a break or professional reasons?'

'Oh, a bit of both,' I said, evasively. As I looked at her pale, beautiful face and large, deep eyes, I thought of her name. Cassandra. The original one had been a prophet, way back when, but was cursed so that while her prophecies were always bang on, nobody ever believed them. I thought to myself, I'm in that position with the women in Tris's life. I have learnt that he is almost certainly a killer but they're not going to believe me. If I tell them the truth, all I'll do is alienate them and alert Tris.

So I didn't bring up what I knew about Tris. Any carefully thought out strategies and the conversations I had prepared in my head simply didn't happen. She was looking serenely beautiful with that otherworldly loveliness of hers that was so captivating. I could well understand Tris falling for her, what I couldn't see was how she could fall for him. I bought some wine instead. I don't know if my silence was prudent or simply cowardly.

I think it was the latter.


That evening at 10 o'clock I was having a drink with Cliff, my godfather. I looked at him across the table, twenty-odd stone of muscle and flab, the onyx signet and sovereign rings on his powerful banana-like fingers, the gold tooth, the remaining few strands of reddish brown hair combed across his bald scalp, and I contrasted him with the ethereally lovely Cassandra, Beauty and the Beast. And I loved both of them.

The Three Bells was pretty busy for a Wednesday. There were quite a few young people in, gathered round the pool table. I recognised their faces, if not the names. One I did know, Bryony Mogg, the girlfriend of the Earl of the village was among them, her blonde hair sticking upwards in her cockatoo-like quiff, the tattoos on her body a riot of colour. Her ruby nose stud, a recent addition, glinted in the light from the bar. She saw me, smiled and waved, I saluted her with my glass of lager. I liked Bryony a lot.

I told Cliff about Esther and the theft of the diadem and how I was supposed to help get it back.

'What a load of old cobblers,' Cliff said, dismissing Wicca and a couple of thousand years of women worshipping the goddess in one form or another. Look at the Oracle of Python or the Maenads, Esther would have said. I stayed quiet. No point arguing with Cliff.

'It's good to see you, Cliff.' And it was. He was so reassuring. Mind you, like the vindaloos he so enjoyed, a little

184

of Cliff went a long way. Mrs Cliff found him a bit much at times and periodically booted him out of the Bethnal Green flat and he'd come and sleep in my little box-room for a couple of days.

'So what are you gonna do about Esther's dia whossis?' he asked and sank a half pint of lager without any discernible effort. It just vanished down his gullet seemingly without him swallowing.

'Diadem, Cliff, it's like a tiara.' I shrugged. 'It can only be one of two people. I've seen one of them – Chris – already.'

'What, the geezer that's married to that cross between Hulk Hogan and Catweazle?' He narrowed his eyes. 'She tried to kill you Charlie, twice if my memory serves me, or had that little detail slipped your mind? You went round there? You need your head seeing to.'

'She's been born again, Cliff, she's found Jesus.'

'Oh I see. So that's all right then. It's a well-known fact that religious nutters never hurt a fly.' His words heavy with sarcasm. He shook his head and pushed his glasses back against the bridge of his multiply-broken nose with a pudgy finger on which the sovereign ring glinted. 'Sometimes Charlie I wonder about you... That woman's like an XL Bully, it might let you scratch its head and pet it, but the next minute it's tearing yer throat out.'

'Takes one to know one.'

He laughed at that. 'Touché.' He emptied his pint in one fluid motion, set the glass back on the table and looked at me. 'Now, you can get me another pint, while you're still alive.'

'She's not going to hurt me, Cliff,' I protested.

'Of course not,' he said pityingly. 'Never mind Charlie. Spend your money while you can, you can't take it with you.'

I went up to the bar, I could feel the sticky tackiness of the carpet gently tugging at the soles of my trainers. 'Hello, Charlie…' whispered Malcolm, the landlord, hoarsely across the bar. I had never heard him speak any louder than this, some nights he wouldn't say a word. 'Same again?'

'Please Malcolm.'

He turned away and a voice behind me said hi. It was Bryony who had left her friends at the pool table to join me. She'd obviously come from the gym. She was wearing very white thick-soled trainers and extremely tight beige Lycra cycling shorts. Highly anatomically revealing. Her pink Puffa jacket was slung over her shoulder. She had a matching crop top to the shorts, that emphasised rather than covered her perfect breasts. Despite, or maybe because of, the gym, her blue eyes were kind of unfocussed but as she approached I could smell the faintly compost tang of the weed she'd been smoking.

'Drink, Bryony?'

'Mmm, a half of Guinness please.'

We took our drinks and went and sat down with Cliff. I admired the ink that, courtesy of her scant clothing, were very much on display. The tattoos never failed to fascinate me – maybe because I hadn't got any myself. I particularly loved the one she had on one arm, a serpent and an apple and the biblical phrase concerning Eve and temptation written in Hebrew. It was kind of appropriate inasmuch as

Bryony was a highly tempting young woman and she had seduced a man with a huge amount of money and influence who was her boyfriend. Given the fact he was old enough to be her father, most people used the word sugar-daddy, but who am I to judge? I liked Bryony. She was incredibly sweet-natured, and, despite being perma-stoned and having zero academic qualifications, nobody's fool.

'I'm a rose between two thorns,' Cliff remarked drily. 'I'll leave you two ladies alone and go and have a natter with Malcolm.' I looked at him fondly as he walked towards the bar, the floorboards creaking under his weight.

'Charlie,' Bryony said, 'I bumped into Esther the other day. She looked terrible, like she hadn't been sleeping, and I swear she might have lost some weight, as if she was on a diet. That's not like her at all. I'm a bit worried. Is she okay?'

'Well, Bryony, not really…' So for the second time that evening I related the story of the diadem.

She nodded sympathetically. 'Poor Esther.' She sighed.

'Yeah, poor Esther.' Silence fell.

'So, what else are you up to Charlie?'

'Oh the usual.' I suddenly remembered the fly-tipping that I had seen on my run that morning, a big, multi-stained green double mattress propped against an iron-barred gate to a field had been particularly eye-catching. 'I'm getting so pissed off with people dumping stuff in the lay-bys, the council don't seem to be doing anything about it.'

'James is,' Bryony said proudly. James was Bryony's boyfriend, although the word hardly accurately describes him. In his sixties, he was no boy and the word 'friend' well…

'What is he doing about it?'

'He's got a few of those spy mini cams and he's hiding them in various lay-bys around here, hoping to get the number plates of the vans that are doing it, although I gather you can get fake plates easily enough. He says though you'll probably be able to get the faces of the bastards. Anyway, at least he's trying to do something.'

'Thank God someone is.' I changed the subject to her. 'How about you? I haven't seen you for a while.'

'I've been up in Scotland.'

'Scotland!' I was surprised. Bryony didn't travel much. She disapproved of flying for ecological reasons and so rarely went far.

'Yeah, James took me to go looking for ospreys.' Then she added, maybe she thought I was questioning her eco-credentials, 'We took the train.'

'Ospreys,' I marvelled, some kind of sea eagle I think. 'Whereabouts?'

She frowned, trying to remember, 'I dunno... Somewhere with some kind of bird in the name. Oh yeah. Gleneagles it was called.'

'Gleneagles!' Nothing but the best for the Earl. I felt a touch of envy. Maybe I'd get Andrea to take me, he had the money. After his recent grumpiness on the phone I felt he owed me. I like an expensive hotel.

'Yeah, some hotel or other.' That was Gleneagles put in its place. For me the place was notable for its great head chef, now passed away, Andrew Fairlie. No point in asking Bryony what the food was like. She was nominally vegetarian but would eat fish or meat when she was stoned, which meant she normally ate anything. Then her face lit up. 'We saw a pair… it was like…' she frowned, hunting for an adjective for the osprey experience, but the cupboard was bare. She spread her hands and smiled. 'Intense…' she whispered. She drank some Guinness. 'Like, vibey…'

'Lucky you,' I said, thinking more about the hotel than the birds. I quickly filled her in on what was happening, then, 'Bryony, I am ninety per cent sure that Pascale is the diadem thief.'

'So you really don't think Chris stole it?'

I shook my head and said, 'No, I really don't think so. Aside from passing the blush test,' I explained what that was, 'he and Esther go way back. I think he genuinely quite likes her and, more to the point, I don't think Chris has got the balls for it.'

'How do you mean?' She took a sip of her Guinness.

'Whoever stole it is going to have to stand up in front of everyone and lie outrageously as to how they came by it. Chris wouldn't have the bottle, pure and simple. And I'm not sure Sandra in her current religious phase would have let him get away with it even if he did.'

Bryony laughed. 'I think she might have turned up at our house on Friday.'

'Really?' I was bemused. 'Why?'

'Does she look like an old boxer in a frock, broken nose but with huge boobs, beefy arms, "Born to lose" tat on one forearm and "Iron Horse" on the other, Gothic script above a Triumph Bonneville?'

Typical of the multiply-inked Bryony to focus in on the

artwork on Sandra's arms. I hadn't even noticed, to be frank, I just thought of her as generically scary.

'I think I can say with ninety-nine per cent certainty that that was her. What was she up to?'

'She wanted to know if I had been saved, and if I was interested in meeting the Lord.'

'Blimey.' So she really was spreading the Lord's word as she said she was. I wondered why she was doing it round here and not in Milton Keynes. Maybe she didn't want to embarrass Chris but most likely it was the Lord working in mysterious ways. Bryony continued. 'She went on to say that she was going to be preaching the Word in High Wycombe on Friday at eleven and would I be interested in coming? Also, as the Lady of the Manor, her expression, could I put the word out.' She frowned. 'I'm not quite sure what she was on about... then she said, "No one can say 'Jesus is Lord!' except under the influence of the Holy Spirit," and then she just stood there looking at me.'

I marvelled at this. 'And then what did you do?'

'Well, I didn't know what to say... So I gave her twenty quid and told her to keep up the good work and I'd spread the word.'

'What did she say to that?'

'She said, "We are God's fellow workers and you are God's garden. 1 Corinthians 3." I've been called some things in my time, Charlie, but never, God's garden.'

I considered this. 'It's quite a nice thing to be called, when you think about it.'

'Yes, it is isn't it?' She drank some Guinness. 'I might

get that put on my thigh.' She pointed to the inside top bit, just beneath where the beige Lycra met the skin.

I made up my mind there and then to go and see Sandra preaching. I was curious to see how it would go down. Wycombe High Street did not seem a promising place to spread the Word. I feared she would be sowing her seed on stony ground.

'So it's Pascale then,' Bryony said, reverting to our original topic of conversation.

I thought of the glamourous Pascale, beautiful and with that beguiling French accent. 'Do you know her at all?' I asked.

'Reasonably well,' Bryony said. 'Why?'

'I want to meet her again. I have no idea how it's going to help, but I suppose I want to probe her weaknesses,' I explained. I didn't really know what I meant by that, but I felt I had to do something, the summer solstice was looming.

'Sure, Charlie,' she said with a complicit grin, 'I'd be delighted to assist.'

The following night, Thursday night was a bruising, busy service. I had to frantically make more fishcakes at about 8 o'clock, easy to do during prep time, less simple when you only have quarter of an hour. Ditto a cucumber coulis sauce. About 9.45 we had sent out the last of the main courses and the end was in sight. I went into the bar and brought out a pint of lager for Francis, a white wine for me and a Diet Coke for Murdo.

'Thank you, Chef, my mouth's as dry as Gandhi's flip-flop,' Francis said fervently. He put the glass to his lips and tipped it back. The contents appeared to vanish without him swallowing.

'That's better,' he said, beaming with goodwill at us.

'Thanks, boys,' I said, 'that was awesome…'

My phone vibrated in my breast pocket. I pulled it out and looked at it. It was Cassandra. I frowned. I was shattered and the last thing I wanted to do was have some kind of chat.

'Hi, Cass,' I said. I was surprised to say the least. It's not a good time to call a chef, late on a Thursday night. She should know that, I thought, annoyed. There was a momentary silence then, 'Something terrible has happened, Charlie.'

Her voice had a kind of terrible, brittle calm, like she was holding back hysteria. Oh God, I thought. Lizzie's dead.

'What is it? Are you okay?' Murdo and Francis looked at me in alarm.

'No, it's Tris.'

Tris? What could have happened? I suspected the worst. I felt sick to my core, my heart lurch and then start beating intensely. 'Oh my God, what's he done to you, Cass?'

'Nothing.' Thank Christ, I thought. She carried on. 'He's dead, Charlie…'

'What!' I was incredulous. 'How…'

Her voice was eerily calm. 'Charlie… I think I've killed him.'

# Chapter Twenty-Three

I stared at my phone, disbelievingly. I had absolutely no idea what to say or do so I stood up and paced the small yard behind my kitchen, anything to relieve the pressure I was feeling inside I suppose. Murdo tried to say something and I shushed him frantically with my free arm.

'Are you sure?' A stupid comment I know but I couldn't think of anything else to say.

'He's on the sofa opposite me, Charlie. There's a knife in his chest, his eyes are open, he's not breathing and I'm covered in blood.' She gave a little hysterical laugh. 'I've never been more sure of anything in my life.'

'Oh God, oh God.' I was now walking frantically up and down. 'Where are you?'

'His house.' For one mad moment I thought of driving round there and bringing her back here, fortunately I didn't.

'Go in the kitchen, Cass and call the police,' I ordered. 'I'll arrange a lawyer for you. Don't, for God's sake, say anything until the lawyer gets to the police station.'

'Okay,' she whispered.

'It's very important you don't say anything until the

lawyer arrives okay?' I re-iterated. She was almost certainly in shock, I didn't want her incriminating herself. 'Don't speak without a lawyer present... Do you understand?'

'Yes... I'm in the kitchen now... Okay.'

'Repeat what I just told you.'

She did so. 'I'm so scared, Charlie...'

'Of course you are, Cass... but you'll just have to be strong until the lawyer comes, promise me that. Okay, now I'm going to hang up now. Call the police, then call me.'

'What's going on, Charlie, is she okay?' Murdo looked scared and worried, as did Francis, speechless for once.

'It's Cass, she's in trouble.' My phone buzzed again. 'Right. What happened?' I asked.

'I don't know, Charlie,' there was a pause and she cried, 'I can't remember... I can't remember a thing.'

'Okay, I'm going to hang up, then I'll call you back.'

Murdo and Francis stared questioningly at me, their eyes boring into me as I turned the phone off.

'Someone's killed Tris Smith. I have to go and make a phone call,' then with a calm I did not feel, 'can you two please clean down the kitchen?'

I ran upstairs and found the business card that Edward Hamilton had given me last year when he had been Lance Thurston's lawyer. Andrea laughs at my habit of keeping business cards in an old Tupperware, but I'm so glad I do. Cassandra needed help of a kind that I was not capable of giving, but one thing was blindingly obvious. She would need a lawyer. And a good one at that. Hamilton had struck me as being extremely capable. That's what she needed. The company name was on the card and I called Cass.

'Charlie.' She sounded both relieved and desperate.

'Have you called the police?'

'Yes, they're on their way… what do I do?' she wailed.

'When you're arrested they'll ask if you want legal representation. Say yes, and give this company name and say you want to see Mr Hamilton. Don't, for God's sake, say anything without him, okay. Now repeat what I just told you.'

She did so, then, 'The police are outside. I can see the flashing lights… I'm so frightened, Charlie, I'm so scared.' Her voice was shaking. I felt so sick with worry for her that I thought I was going to throw up.

'That's okay. Mr Hamilton will make everything all right,' I said, fighting back tears and nausea. 'I promise. Now go and let them in and we'll speak soon.'

I ended the call. I then phoned the 24-hour helpline for the law firm and told the nice man at the other end that Hamilton knew me, and that he was to expect the police getting in touch re a Cassandra Jenkins, arrested on suspicion of murder. He was very professional and soothing and I strongly suspected that the bill for the service would be astronomical. I changed out of my sodden, dirty work clothes and went back downstairs where Murdo was finishing mopping the floor.

'Murdo,' I said, 'I've got to go and speak to Strickland, I'll be back about eleven-ish.'

'Okay, Chef…' he paused and looked at me. There was an awkward silence. 'Chef, I need to speak to you about Cass later, it's important.'

I could tell he was being serious. I had never known him speak like that before. 'Wait up for me.'

'I think Jess should be there too,' he said. 'Cass is her friend as well.'

'Okay.' I felt like screaming DON'T TALK TO ME, but I managed not to. 'Sorry I've got to go. Bye.'

I ran across the common to where the King's Head was, just hidden from view around a bend in the road. I looked at my watch, 10.15 Strickland would still be there. His car park was half full and I could see quite a few people still in the restaurant finishing their desserts and coffee and petits fours. His clientele were the rich, the very rich, and normal people who had scrimped and saved for this moment. They were generally in a mood to linger. I went round the back, let myself into the yard behind the kitchen and poked my head through the fly screens. A couple of the younger chefs turned to look at me, one was a new face to me, the other I knew quite well. Billy, the sous was over by the stove.

'Hi Charlie, come in.'

'Hi Stan,' I said to the enormous Polish youngster. His jacket sleeves were cut short, the better to show off his impressive biceps. I turned towards the sous chef.

'Billy… is Strickland around?'

'In his office,' he said.

'Thanks.'

I slipped round the pass and walked down a corridor to Strickland's office and rapped on the door.

'Come in.'

Tonight I thought he was looking more like Napoleon than ever. Not so much facially, but the small build and the megalomaniac self-belief were similar, as was the magnetism that he projected. He shrugged himself inside his clean chef's jacket, gleaming white and beautifully ironed, with his name embroidered on the chest, like the Emperor putting on his greatcoat. I wondered vaguely what Strickland would look like on a horse. Quite ridiculous, I suspected, his short legs would stick out. On a chair by his desk was the jacket he'd been wearing in the kitchen that night, dirty with splashes of food. I identified jus, blood, fruit coulis, oil spatters and fish scales. Strickland liked to make a triumphant circuit of the restaurant at the end of service, graciously accepting the accolades of his fans. He wouldn't want to see them in his dirty work clothes. He looked at me in surprise.

'Charlie! Not a problem I hope?'

'Yes,' I said, closing the door, 'a very big problem.'

I explained what had happened. Strickland looked at me incredulously. 'Let me get this straight,' he said slowly, 'Cassandra Jenkins has killed Tris Smith?' He seemed more annoyed than anything else.

'No, well, I think she was framed, she must have been.'

'But she came to and he was dead and she's covered in his blood? What else can have happened, Charlie?' he said impatiently.

'I don't know, I wasn't there for God's sake,' I said suddenly angry with him. 'Maybe he tried to drug her and she had some sort of weird reaction to whatever it was? Maybe he tried to assault her and she fought back and she's blotted that out of her memory? Maybe it was the fucking mafia or aliens... I don't care. I have no bloody idea,

Graeme, but I do know one thing, there's not a violent bone in that girl's body, and so do you, you went out with her for two years.'

'Three,' he corrected me absentmindedly. Then, fixing me with a gimlet eye, he was nobody's fool, particularly where money was concerned, 'I suppose you want me to pay for some top-notch legal counsel?'

He stared at me in a confrontational way. Strickland was famously aggressive. He'd once thrown the restaurant critic of one of the quality newspapers, some said *The Times*, some the *Telegraph*, out of his restaurant, because, as he'd shouted loudly while escorting him off the premises, 'You don't know your arse from your fucking elbow.'

My heart sank. The last time I had used a lawyer was to buy the Old Forge Café and that had been expensive enough. And that was only conveyancing. If Lance Thurston had used Edward Hamilton he would be very expensive indeed.

'Yes, Graeme,' I said beseechingly, 'that's exactly what I want.'

He lifted his chin in that challenging way he had. Shit, I thought. I braced myself for rejection. Needlessly.

'Well, Charlie, of course she didn't do it.' I gawped at him in surprise, I hadn't expected that. He carried on quietly. 'I put that girl through quite a lot when I was going out with her, I guess this is payback time. Bring it on.'

'You'll pay?' I said, incredulously.

'I'll pay.'

There is a God, I thought. Maybe Sandra's right.

# Chapter Twenty-Four

I walked back across the common in the darkness under the warmth of the dark, velvet sky. There were only two streetlamps in the village, so very little light pollution, and you could see the stars overhead, brilliant in the night sky. I arrived back at my own restaurant feeling hugely relieved. I had been geared up for a huge row with Strickland over this. I had mentally prepared at least three or four powerful arguments for him to pay for Cass's legal aid and then an elaborate series of counter-arguments for when he said no to each of them. And none of this had happened! It was like running with a battering ram at a massive oak door studded with reinforcing nails, like in a castle, only for someone to politely open it.

And it wasn't just the money, I reflected. To have Strickland on your side was a major asset. His enormous self-confidence, his intransigence, not to mention his refusal to ever accept defeat, made him an ideal ally. As I let myself in through my back gate and walked into the now silent and clean kitchen, I wondered, if not Cassandra, who had killed Tris Smith and how.

Someone, meaning it in an unkindly way, had described me once as unstoppable. I had to confess there was a certain amount of truth to the charge. Not only was I like the Terminator, I felt excited at the thrill of the chase and, again, I hate to admit it but it was true, the chance to explore someone else's life, uncover their secrets. I had fallen at first reluctantly into the role of a private investigator. I grumbled about it, but deep down, I really loved it. People lead, or can lead, amazing hidden lives and it was enthralling to uncover them. And when I do get the hint of a scent, I can be like a human bloodhound, unstoppable.

The first flush of excitement was wearing off now, and one part of me wondered if maybe Cassandra had indeed killed Tris. Lizzie was away in Chichester with her dad, and I couldn't imagine Suzi had done this. As I walked up the stairs to my flat I began to feel a growing pessimism and self-doubt.

Murdo and Jess were in my living room, waiting for me.

'What did Strickland say?' Jess asked. I think she had guessed why I had gone over there.

'He said that he'd pay for a good lawyer,' I said, collapsing heavily down onto my old saggy sofa. 'I think she's going to need one.'

'Good for Strickland,' Jess said stoutly. 'She's innocent of course.'

'Is she?' Murdo said, unexpectedly. I stared at him, surprised. I knew he liked her, I would have expected him to be firmly in her corner.

'How do you mean, Murdo?' I asked.

He hesitated. 'Look, you know Cass gave up drinking?'

'Yeah, she told me.' I shrugged. 'Bit of an occupational hazard for someone in the wine trade, I guess.'

'Well.' His voice was quiet, a serious Murdo. I found this quite uncomfortable. It was a side of him I guess I knew must exist but I had never seen. 'She used to talk about it a bit with me, seeing as I'm in NA.'

'What's NA?' asked Jess.

'That's Narcotics Anonymous isn't it?' I said. 'Like AA?'

'Aye,' said Murdo impatiently, 'different substance, same disease.'

'Oh.' That was us put in our place.

'Anyway, earlier this month I was in Wycombe on a night off and I got a call from a mate of mine, Kai, who's the sous at the Burnt Orange, ye ken the fine dining place?'

I knew of it. It was new and did kind of experimental food, molecular gastronomy as it's called, or so I had heard, like a much cheaper version of the Fat Duck. Another major difference is that the Fat Duck is situated in a pretty village on the Thames. Even the most fervent fan of High Wycombe would admit that you couldn't call it attractive. Murdo continued.

'Kai said my wine supplier was passed out at a table, could I get her home somehow. If I didnae, Scott, he's the head chef and owner, would have to call the police to remove her. So I went over there, she was absolutely blootered.' He shook his head sadly. 'Kai helped me get her round the back via the kitchen. She came to but she hadnae any idea where she was. I called a cab, gave him an extra twenty quid as he didnae want her in his car, and we came back here.'

'Why didn't you tell me?' I protested.

'Because she'd have been mortified.' He shook his head, too polite to say Duh! And added, 'Would you want to be seen like that?'

He had a point. No I wouldn't. He carried on. 'I put her in your office and wrote her a note telling her to phone me when she came to. She did, about six in the morning. I came down, told her what had happened, she had nae recollection whatsoever of the night. Then I told her to hide in the dry-store and come out when she heard you go for a run, then wait on the doorstep. Pretend she had just arrived. The rest you know.'

'Oh God, I remember… so that's why she was waiting outside the kitchen door.' What had her excuse been? Something about wanting Murdo to give Lucy a message. It was quite a cunning explanation. I'd fallen for it, hadn't noticed the absence of her vehicle.

'How did she get back to her car?' Jess asked. Practical as ever.

'I'd arranged it with the taxi driver who brought us back. When he dropped us off, he agreed to pick her up from here the following day. Ye ken how difficult it is to get an Uber out here, practically impossible, and she could hardly get the bus. I called him and he picked her up the other side of the common.'

I looked at Murdo with new respect. He'd dealt with a highly charged situation with skill and diplomacy. I would never have credited him with such cunning. Andrea would have said it was Machiavellian, he was some famous Italian guy from back in the day that my boyfriend admired.

'Did she say why she was at the restaurant?' I asked.

Burnt Orange was a curious place to decide to go on a bender, it wasn't like the Three Bells. Now there was a place you could drink yourself senseless without anyone caring, maybe not noticing, and for a fraction of the cost.

'Aye. She said she'd had a row with her boyfriend. He'd taken her there for dinner, he wanted to have sex, but she wouldn't…' Tris, I thought. Followed by, I'm glad he's dead, bastard. 'I told her it was hardly normal behaviour. He wasnae the problem, it was her own heid and that she needed to dump him and get help with her drinking. I said lots of people row, or split up, or get dumped, but they don't get pisht in the very same restaurant afterwards, which was what she'd done.' He sighed. 'I told her she needed to go back to her meetings. I'd looked in her handbag when I got her back, there were two empty half-bottles of vodka in there. My guess is she was topping up in the restaurant when she went to the ladies.'

'And she must have come back to Tris for a repeat performance!' marvelled Jess. She knew all about their relationship, I shared pretty much everything important with her. 'She came to visit him at his home. What the hell was she thinking?'

'Maybe she was going to dump him in person,' I suggested.

'She could have messaged or texted,' Jess objected.

'Well, it doesn't really matter why she was there.' I was getting impatient with this speculation. 'The blame lies with Tris. That bastard had a genius for getting in people's heads,' I said. It fitted perfectly with his IEA ways; Identify – he had identified her drinking to excess as a weakness;

203

Exploit – get her blind drunk and unable to say no or to stop him; Achieve – I knew very well what he wanted to achieve. He was a very dangerous man. I remembered what she had said about not wanting to have sex with him unless he left Lizzie, which he had no intention of doing, not yet anyway. But, whatever had happened earlier that night in that cottage, I had no doubt Cass had gone there of her own accord, he hadn't dragged her kicking and screaming across the threshold.

Murdo had been following our conversation with a look of increasing scepticism.

'So, Murdo,' Jess said, 'what do you think happened?'

'I think he got her pisht, I don't know how. Maybe he spiked a drink with vodka, maybe she thought she could handle it "just this once", who knows. I reckon he thought once she was pisht, which wouldnae take long, he could do what he wanted with her, once she collapsed.' Well, we were both agreed on that then. 'But she didn't collapse. She drank till she went into blackout and didn't know what she was doing. Maybe when he made his move she lashed out with whatever was at hand and then went under again... anything is possible.'

'You think she could have killed him and not even been aware of it!' I said, astonished.

'Aye, that's exactly what I'm saying. I think she killed him in blackout. I hope I'm wrong but...'

I sighed. To kill someone and not even know you had done it. I hadn't thought of that. The way Murdo had described it sounded horribly plausible. 'What a bloody mess,' I said.

Jess came over to me and I stood up and we hugged each other. 'You've done all you can do for tonight,' Jess's voice was soothing. 'You've got her a lawyer. All you can do is wait to see what tomorrow will bring.'

'That's true.' I disengaged from her and stretched unhappily. I suddenly felt absolutely shattered. A wave of exhaustion that I hadn't noticed had enveloped me.

'Well, thank you both for all your help. I'll see you two in the morning.'

# Chapter Twenty-Five

Early on Friday morning I woke up feeling refreshed and energised, then immediately remembered the events of the night before. Cass would be under lock and key in a cell somewhere. Then I had a kind of revelation. My gut instinct when I'd heard the news was that she didn't do it. And now I was certain, despite everything, despite her own self-confessed ignorance as to what had happened, despite Murdo's assertion that she could have killed him and not remembered, I was sure that I was right and that she was innocent. And I would do everything in my power to prove it. That was followed by an unshakeable feeling that I should speak to Anna Bruce. I was beginning to feel like I was in above my head. I messaged her and she replied immediately, telling me she could spare half an hour if I came over between 10 o'clock and 11.

At 9.30 I told Murdo where I was going and drove into Wycombe. I parked my car in the multi-storey by the station. The car park smelled of wee, the parking bays were from an age when I guess cars were smaller so when you were within the lines you had what felt like millimetres to squeeze out of your door, and the lifts never worked. But it was handy for Anna who lived nearby in the town centre in a penthouse on top of a residential block of flats, which offered a 360-degree panoramic view of the unlovely place, or, as the signage as you drove in pointed out, 'The Historic Market Town of High Wycombe'. I guess in the Historic Days, with horses everywhere and a non-existent or rudimentary drain system, the whole of Wycombe had stunk of piss, not just Easton Street car park, so maybe things had improved somewhat.

As I pressed the intercom to be taken up to the penthouse, I reflected being high up, overlooking the town, was a kind of vindication for Anna. She had told me she was from one of the council estates to the west of the town that was a byword locally for being a crappy area. She was now, quite literally, on top of the world, or as top of the world as it gets in the centre of High Wycombe. For some mystifying reason she didn't bill me for her time, maybe because I amused her or because she liked me or because I was maybe tax-deductible as a charity donation. I had no idea, and she never told me. There was something mysterious, Sphinx-like about Anna Bruce, which was obviously no bad thing in a Seer.

A lot had happened since she had warned me way back when, I guess it must have been something like a month and a half ago, and she had foreseen murder and a woman covered in blood. Back then I had assumed this would be Lizzie and not Cass and Tris, but she had been right, just not in the way I had expected.

'Charlie!' She embraced me as I got out of the lift, which opened directly into her hall. It had no button for her floor, you had to be buzzed up by the intercom. It was a luxury lift too and it smelled of Jo Malone scent diffusers, not stale urine, unlike the nearby car park one.

'Anna.' Today she was wearing a dark blue Mao style tunic and trousers. She had a jade necklace and matching bracelets Her short white hair was as crisp as snow, her face not unlined, but her skin was remarkably taut for someone in her mid-sixties. Maybe she was older. Her youthful look was natural. I've met a few people with face lifts and they look decidedly odd. Anna didn't, she looked great. And her presence filled the room.

She led me up a staircase to the top floor of the apartment which had a terrace with bamboo and ferns in planters. She had once explained that she was away too often to make having flowers worthwhile. She could do yoga and Tai Chi on her terrace, there was no one to observe her up here. Only the red kites could see her, wheeling high up in the blue sky, soaring effortlessly on the wind currents.

We sat indoors, the sliding windows open to the view, while a cool breeze ruffled the elegant stalks and narrow leaves of the lime-green bamboo outside.

'Can I get you anything to drink?' Anna asked. 'Tea, coffee, juice?'

I shook my head. 'No, I'm fine. I don't want to take up too much of your time.' I was always aware of how generous Anna was with me, I think an hour with her usually cost about three figures. I got it for free. 'I just wanted your input on what to do about this situation.' I told her about Lizzie, Cassandra and the death of Tris Smith. For good measure I mentioned the diadem.

Anna frowned and a flicker of distaste ran across her face. 'That's terrible,' she said. 'Poor woman, and not to have any memory of what happened.' She hesitated and then asked, 'What makes you so sure that she didn't do it, Charlie?'

'Because I know her really well, and I've also got to know Tris Smith better than most people, certainly better than his fiancée. He's a guy who is mixed up in a lot of murky things.' I gave her a quick rundown of Tris's CV; the history of coercion as far back as student days, the lies about his degree, the murder of his wife, the relish with which he humiliated women by not only bragging about them at work but also by showing his trophy photos, his involvement with dodgy people like Mayhew and lastly, maybe most importantly, the fact that someone had tried to kill him. Obviously he didn't just have an enemy, he had a ruthless one. Anna listened, her face inscrutable, to my exposition.

'Well,' she conceded, 'those are telling points.' She looked at me with her shrewd eyes. 'Anything else?'

'Just my gut feeling that she's innocent,' I confessed.

Anna smiled. 'That's good enough for me, Charlie. You're an intuitive person, you started a successful business on intuition, you've built a good team on it, it works for you. Okay, you can make mistakes, and have done in the past, but I believe in you. You should follow this certainty of yours.'

'Maybe you could hypnotise her?' I said eagerly. 'Then she'd remember.'

Anna smiled pityingly and shook her head. 'Hypnosis is far too unreliable when it comes to memory, Charlie.

Imagined events get conflated with reality, or there are underlying wishes and feelings that take control of the narrative. There's only one way out of this mess, only one way to clear her name. If she didn't do it, someone else did. You're just going to have to find the person responsible.'

'Don't you have any ideas?' My initial feeling of elation at her support had diminished at this. I was feeling very disappointed. I'd wanted her to name the real killer, or give me a massive clue. Then I shook myself mentally and told myself not to be so ridiculous. That was my job, not hers.

'No,' she said decisively, 'apart from the diadem problem.'

Well, that was better than nothing, although Esther's problem, maybe Chris's too, seemed trivial compared to Cassandra's. I looked at her enquiringly.

'You need Bryony's help,' her voice was firm.

'Er, why?' That was certainly unexpected.

'You probably don't realise this Charlie, but Bryony is a very powerful psychic.'

I stared at her in utter disbelief. Bryony was stoned all the time! 'Um, what makes you think that?'

'Well, it's kind of my job, Charlie, it's what I do for a living.' She looked annoyed at my scepticism. She carried on. 'Let me give you an analogy. I take it when you see an untrained youngster working in a commercial kitchen you can probably tell if they're going to be a good cook or not.'

My mind flashed back a few months to a teenager I had met in a hotel kitchen in Edinburgh, an apprentice chef, a girl called Innes.

'Yes, I can certainly spot potential. Definitely.'

She spread her hands out eloquently. 'Well, it's the same

in my field. So can I. I'm good, Charlie, but I make a little go a long way. Bryony on the other hand… when I meet her it's like a furnace roaring behind a metal door. It's awesome… The thing is, she is kind of oblivious to this, but her power is beginning to make itself known.' She smiled. 'Even to her.' She had obviously met her a few times.

'So she's totally unaware of this?'

'Oh yeah.' She nodded. 'I'm not the only one to have noticed. People think the Earl is with her 'cos she's young and hot. Well, there is a certain amount of truth to that, and unfortunately a rich man like the Earl is not short of unscrupulous women throwing themselves at him trying to use sex for access to his money. And he's highly cynical. No, he's with her because he is a powerful man drawn to the power within her. Like recognises like. Maybe he doesn't realise this himself, but it's true. Otherwise Bryony Mogg would have joined that very long list of nubile young women that have trailed behind the Earl in his wake, discarded once he tired of them.'

I digested this for a moment or so, then returned to the problem again. 'So, what does this mean regarding the diadem?'

'If Bryony senses it,' Anna said with finality, 'that's where it will be. You don't need to worry about finding it, she'll do it for you.'

Well, that was hugely encouraging. I felt a palpable sense of relief. It was like a load had been lifted. On that front anyway. Something was better than nothing, even though it did nothing to ease Cassandra's plight.

'I can tell something else is troubling you,' Anna said.

'No,' I was puzzled. 'I think that's everything—'

She held her hand up, silencing me. 'I will tell you things are going to get very challenging for you. Friendships will be strained, maybe severed. Emotional turmoil. Trauma. And maybe some physical danger. You're in for a rough ride, Charlie.'

'Oh…' Shit, I thought. This was not going as I had expected. I was hoping for a Cassandra insight. That hadn't happened, and my own future looked far from rosy. Ignorance is bliss. I was beginning to wish I hadn't come. 'Okay… are you going to tell me any more?'

'No.' She looked at me severely. 'Stop looking so glum, Charlie. If you set up as a private investigator specialising in serious crime then obviously you're putting yourself at risk. It's an occupational hazard, like burns on your arms in a kitchen' – she pointed to a massive red weal on my left arm where I'd caught it on the inside of the oven –'or cuts.' She nodded at my left index finger that was wrapped in blue sticking plaster. 'Now that I've warned you, you will have to keep your wits about you.'

She looked pointedly at the clock on the wall. 'I'm afraid our time is up. I have a client.'

I stood up. 'Thanks for the info about Bryony, and the warning.'

'Just remember, Charlie, things are not always what they seem. I'll see you out.'

Well, that was reassuring, not, I thought as the lift doors opened. I wondered whose friendship I would lose, maybe

Cassandra's, maybe Lizzie's. I hoped it wouldn't be Murdo's. I wasn't worried about Jess. That was rock solid.

I walked down the small hill outside Anna's apartment block to the centre of town. It was market day and there were various stalls filling the High Street. Then I heard a voice I knew well, carrying over the shouts of the vegetable traders and reggae music from the Caribbean food truck.

'… there's a bakery over there, sells very nice bread, but bread goes stale, it has a sell-by date. You all voted recently, but all politics has a sell-by date too.' It was Sandra, standing on a wooden box, haranguing the shoppers. She continued. 'There's a pub over there, it's a shit pub, it sells stale crisps, I know 'cos I used to drink there! But there is one whose bread never goes stale, there's one whose policies are never out of date, there's one whose house is immaculate… that one is Jesus!'

I had forgotten the Lord had told her to preach in Wycombe. She had drawn a small crowd of interested people. She was an arresting sight, her mane of grey-white hair, her beefy, tattooed arms. She seemed perfectly at ease, as if she had been doing this all her life. I stopped to listen. I was entranced. She was a damn sight better than the Archbishop of Canterbury and certainly more eye-catching.

Sandra roared to the small crowd. 'He said "I am the bread of Life. He who comes to Me shall never hunger, and he who believes in Me shall never thirst."'

Ow! I felt a sharp pain in my backside. I wheeled around. There was a man standing behind me, about 40, red-faced, lank dark hair greased back, a faded blueish tattoo covering half his face, wearing jeans and a plaid shirt. He certainly was not suffering from thirst, I could smell the alcohol on his breath. High Wycombe town centre was kind of an oasis for people with drink problems. There were a couple of pubs that opened early (one of them had just been pointed out by Sandra) and there was a hostel just up the road for homeless alcoholics. I glared at my assailant speechless with rage. What do you say to someone who has just pinched you on the bottom? 'Do you mind?' sounded hopelessly supine and old-fashioned. Swearing would have been pointless, my angry silence prolonged itself. Nobody came to my rescue, the nearest people shuffled away. They didn't want to get involved. Where's the Good Samaritan when you need him, I thought.

'Jesus said, "I am the resurrection and the life".' Sandra bent down, picked something up, straightened and waved a large cross in the air.

The man leered at me. 'Show us your tits, darling. Don't get many of those to the kilo.'

I was about to walk away with as much dignity as I could, my cheeks beginning to burn with impotent resentment. He opened his mouth but this time not to speak.

'Aaargh…' and he crashed down on his knees like he'd been Tasered, revealing the man who had been standing behind him. A big guy, heavily built, crimson-faced with anger, his piggy eyes hard behind the thick lenses of his heavy framed glasses.

'Say sorry to the lady, you sexist nut-sack,' growled my godfather, poking the kneeling man with the steel toe of his boot. My assailant was still gasping with pain. Cliff Yeats leaned forward, put his meaty fingers into the guy's hair and hauled him upright with his left hand. I saw the glint of metal as Cliff slipped the knuckle-duster off his right hand into the pocket of his cheap black trousers, held precariously in place by a thick belt under his huge gut.

Cliff shook him roughly by the hair. 'We're waiting.'

'I'm sorry,' sobbed the man.

'You should be more polite to women,' I said, encouragingly.

'I will…'

Cliff let go of him and he hobbled away, one hand rubbing his kidneys. He turned round to look at us, Cliff made a lunge in his direction and the drunk guy turned and fled on stumbling feet.

'Fancy a coffee, Charlie?' he said brightly.

Over a double espresso at Caffè Nero Cliff told me he'd just left one of the pubs singled out by Sandra as 'a shithole' ('she wasn't wrong' was Cliff's opinion). He'd been discussing terms with the management, staff had been threatened by customers, something needed to be done. Cliff would do it, for a hefty price.

'So what brings you to the lovely, historic market town this bright morning?' he asked.

I smiled at the description which I had been thinking about earlier. It was technically true, but anyone expecting to see anything remotely old or pretty would be in for a disappointing time. I told him about Cassandra.

'I dunno how you keep getting mixed up in stuff like this, Charlie…'

'Because she's my friend,' I said, quietly.

'I'm sorry Charlie...' he rubbed his chin, looking crest-fallen. 'I shouldn't have said that.'

'I forgive you, you insensitive fat bastard,' I said, patting his huge hand with the onyx and signet rings.

He smiled. 'You can't call me fat these days, Charlie, it's a hate crime. How's the boyfriend by the way?'

'Andrea's fine, he's in Bologna at the moment. He's had to go to Italy a lot recently, business,' I said vaguely. I wondered if I'd inadvertently offended Andrea somehow. He'd been short with me of late as if he was feeling very stressed. I pushed the thought from my mind. Although he looked classically Italian, his character defied the stereotype. He was unflappable, hard to irritate. I guessed he was in the middle of some deal, he usually was. It was his job after all.

I looked at my watch, it was past 11. 'I'd better get back, Cliff, I left Murdo with all the prep to do.'

I said my goodbyes and walked thoughtfully back to my car. Hopefully the incident with the guy assaulting me was the very thing that Anna Bruce had warned about and the danger was now over. I passed by the place in the market where Sandra had pitched her makeshift pulpit. I felt a glow of warmth towards her. She had been surprisingly eloquent. Any resentment I might have once harboured against her had now totally dissipated, although I still would not want to get on the wrong side of her. She was a violent woman, maybe even scarier than Cliff. And now Jesus himself was in her corner, she would be absolutely unstoppable.

# Chapter Twenty-Six

I got back in time to help Murdo before things got hectic. The work soothed me, I didn't have time to brood over things. This good humour lasted through the next couple of hours. I dealt effortlessly with the mains. Murdo was his usual more than capable self. I was proud of my menu but it didn't stretch Murdo. He had come from a fine dining background, a Michelin-starred restaurant, so working with me was, professionally a bit of a comedown. But he was enjoying himself, he had a stress-free life (highly unusual in this industry) and I paid him well. We were both happy. I so hoped that he wasn't going to be the one I fell out with.

No danger of that with Francis. Francis was perennially good-humoured. At one stage we were ultra-busy, the orders from the restaurant coming thick and fast. I looked over at Francis who was on sandwich duty. It was a hot day and as well as the cooked food we were doing a lot of cold food, particularly salads. We still had the fennel salad, of which he was very proud regarding his mastery; they were indeed 'pretty as peacocks'. He was currently busy assembling a cheese Ploughman's and a Waldorf salad, that's apple, celery, walnuts and mayo.

'Why's it called a Waldorf salad, Chef? He's that old geezer in the Muppets?'

'Um...' I was a bit taken aback by the question. I knew the puppet character he referred to, I could see him instantly in my mind, heckling from the balcony. 'I think it's named after the hotel.'

'He's got a hotel named after him too?' Francis shook his head in wonderment, 'Blimey!'

'Check on! Three steak baguettes.'

'Check on, two Ploughman's, one blue cheese, one cheddar... one Caesar salad.'

'Check on...'

It was remorseless. Francis was getting spanked with the cold food. 'Take over the grill, Murdo, I'm just going to help Francis clear these checks,' I said.

'Are you okay Francis?' I checked, as we worked together, the sweat pouring down our faces. It was about 35 degrees in the kitchen, even with the fans on and the door propped open.

'I'm as happy as Larry, Chef.' He frowned. 'Whoever he may have been.'

'That's great news.'

But no service would be complete without Francis cocking something up. I intercepted a slice of Black Forest Gateau about to go out covered with a fruits of the forest jus that Murdo had made to go with a venison neck starter as a special.

'But it's got fruit in it!' Francis said indignantly.

'Yes Francis.' I wiped the sweat off my face with my apron, 'That is very true, but, and here's the but, it's predominantly heavily reduced game stock and that's not going to go well with cake, is it, now?'

'Sorry Chef.' he said, looking woeful and shaking his head sadly. 'I'm as much use as a pair of tits on a nun!'

'FRANCIS!' That was Jess who had materialised at the other side of the pass.

'It's okay Jess,' Francis beamed at her, 'Father Flanagan said it the other day when I was helping him dead-head those roses behind the church...'

'Well, just don't say that ever again, okay!'

'Okay,' Francis said with resignation as she disappeared back into the restaurant carrying the dessert with its cherry coulis, free of meat juice.

After the lunchtime shift had finished, thank God, that had been hard, the three of us sat in the sun outside. We were talking about holidays. Francis's dream was to go the West Indies and cheer the England cricket team on. I asked Murdo if he was going to take Lucy to Campbeltown to stay at the Davaar Hotel. Murdo laughed at the idea. 'What would Lucy do in Campbeltown, Charlie, other than get eaten by the midges? She likes Tenerife, so do I come to that. I've had enough dreich Scottish weather on my holidays in Scotland tae last me a lifetime, and then some. We had to stay at my auntie's in Ardrossan for half-terms and such, it's on the coast in Ayrshire. They have a saying there, if ye can see Arran it's about to rain and if you cannae see Arran it is raining.' He shuddered. 'I never want to spend another summer in the west coast of Scotland.'

My phone rang and when I looked at the screen it was an unknown number. I took the call anyway, a man's voice. Would I be free this afternoon to meet with Edward Hamilton, Cassandra Jenkins' solicitor.

Yes I would.

Mr Hamilton looked exactly the same as when I had last seen him. In his dark suit, highly polished black brogues and austerely prim features under his bald head, no concessions sartorially to the summer weather, he was the perfect picture of a successful undertaker. The two of us sat in my restaurant with the sun shining through the windows.

'I suppose it must be about a year since I last saw you,' I said.

He shook his head. 'It was last September, I checked.'

'Have you seen Lance at all, since he was cleared?'

He shook his head again. 'And you?'

'Yeah, he's been in the restaurant a couple of times. He was in celebrating his engagement.'

'Who's the lucky woman?'

'It's not a woman. He's marrying Sam Hickocks, the deli owner, the ex-don. Lance's podcast has changed out of all recognition,' I marvelled. He used to be a borderline homophobic, climate-change denier. 'He's embracing all sorts of eco-issues now. Complete 180. Kind of weird.'

'Not really.' Hamilton's tone was that of a man who has seen just about everything, and as a criminal defence specialist he probably had. 'It's called enantiodromia, a complete reversal of a previous stance. Like St Paul who used to persecute Christians, or a couple of prominent right-wing journalists I can think of who used to be members of the hard-left. It's quite common.'

I thought about this some. Maybe Sandra had fallen into that category.

'So how is Cassandra?' I asked.

He looked at me impassively. 'She wanted me to come and visit you to see if you could offer me any assistance.'

'I'll certainly do what I can,' I said. I told him what I had learned about Tris and his history of mental coercion towards women. Including my trip to Scotland and the suspicion of the woman in the shop regarding his wife's death.

'I think it's very likely that if she had married Tris, some "accident" might well have befallen Lizzie,' I said angrily. 'That man was an absolute monster.'

He tutted discouragingly. 'Unfortunately, speculation, no matter how accurate or true, is not going to help Cassandra Jenkins. The fact is, she was covered in his blood, the murder weapon had her prints on it, there was blood under her fingernails and there were no signs of any kind of forced entry to the premises.'

'Had she been drugged?' I asked hopefully.

'No, a tox screen came back negative; however, she did have an extremely high blood alcohol reading. I forget the exact figure but it would have put someone about four times over the drink drive limit.' He sighed. 'Thankfully, she did what you had instructed her to do and didn't consent to an interview and I was able to do everything on a prepared statement, so at least we've avoided any unguarded admissions, cock-ups or incriminating faux-pas of the sort that could come back to haunt us when this comes to trial.'

'What would it take to get her free?'

'A cast-iron admission of guilt from the real killer.' He leaned forward, rested his elbows on the table and fixed me with a hard, penetrating look, doubtless practised umpteen times in various courts and police interview rooms. 'Look, I'll be frank with you Charlie. The case against Cassandra is extremely strong. The main problem is that she has not got any idea herself of what happened.'

I told him about the time I had seen her and Tris together in the woods and what Murdo had said and he made an equivocal gesture with his hands. 'The trouble is, that doesn't help us, does it. If anything, arguably it could make things worse.'

'But he got her drunk to lower her defences,' I protested. 'I think surely if he did that and she killed him as a result of not knowing what she was doing, then it's his own fault? He brought it on himself.' I looked at him hopefully. 'It wasn't murder at all, it was aggravated suicide!' I added wildly.

He smiled thinly. 'It's not a defence I would pin much hope on. You might equally say that she demanded he leave his fiancée, which you admit she had asked him to do, he refused and then in a fit of anger, she stabbed him and then made up the story about not knowing what had happened.'

I nodded glumly. Things were not looking good.

He stood up. 'Well, thank you for the conversation. I'll email you the details of where she is being held and you can make arrangements to visit her.'

I shook his hand and saw him out.

# Chapter Twenty-Seven

Bryony met me at the Three Bells early on Monday evening. We'd said 6 o'clock but she was late and I was having a second bottle of Diet Coke when she arrived. I had been feeling uncharacteristically depressed and thought alcohol would make it worse. I somehow felt, stupidly, that Cassandra's part, whatever it was in Tris's death, was partly my fault. I could have taken her to one side and told her the truth about Tris. I could have told her he probably had murdered his wife, that he was definitely sleeping with Suzi, that he'd made a pass at me, that he was a fantasist (or had a cynical disregard for the truth). I had done none of these things. Maybe they would have had no effect whatsoever, maybe she would have told me to mind my own business, but I would have tried. And I hadn't, out of cowardice basically, in case she stopped being my friend. And now look where we were, Cass was facing 35 years in jail.

I had wanted to talk things over with Andrea. I always valued his opinion, but he was still away in Italy and, rather uncharacteristically, not returning my phone calls. I satisfied myself with leaving him a somewhat sarcastic text message. As soon as I had sent it I regretted it.

There were a few people in the pub at 6.15 when Bryony finally arrived. The tail-end of the builders and tradesmen who knocked off at 4 o'clock and drank there until they went home for dinner round about 6.30. Heads turned as she walked in. She was provocatively dressed as ever, an eye-catching figure. There was a considerable waft of weed around her as we embraced. I wondered if I would see any signs of her psychic abilities.

I asked her what she wanted: a Guinness.

'So, what's all this about Cassandra killing her lover?' she asked me as she sat down beside me holding her half. I told her what had happened, Bryony exclaiming, 'what a bastard' several times as I explained what had led to the fatal, tragic denouement.

'Do you think anything more can be done to help her?' Bryony asked.

I shook my head. 'Seemingly not, short of finding the real killer.'

'So you don't think she did it?'

'No!' I said, rather crossly. I nearly blurted out, can't you tell, what with your psychic powers, but I didn't.

'You know what, I don't think that she did it either.' Bryony's voice was calm and measured. 'And it's quite irritating the way everyone seems to think she's guilty.' I looked at her with grateful surprise – it was as if she had been reading my mind. I was both glad of her moral support and hopeful that her latent powers as revealed by Anna would confirm my faith in Cass's innocence.

Then, before I had any chance to comment, she said, 'Have you made any progress on finding Esther's diadem?'

No I hadn't. With all the excitement and drama involving Tris Smith, I had rather forgotten, well, not exactly forgotten, I'd pushed it to the back of my mind. I suddenly felt maybe here was a chance to do something. Anna Bruce had specifically told me to get her involved, here was the chance.

'No, none whatsoever. I'm kind of stumped as to know what to do,' I said, hoping that Bryony's seemingly latent powers might come in handy, hoping she would have a plan.

'Well, personally,' Bryony said, 'I think it has to be Pascale. You don't think it's Chris. If that is so, it has to be her. In fact, I said I'd go and see her sometime, we could go over there right now, if you like?'

Anything to take my mind off Cassandra. I'd been going over it again and again, pointlessly, in my head. 'Definitely.'

'Okay, finish your Coke and we'll go. You'll have to drive, I've had a drink.'

Not to mention God knows how much marijuana, I thought. 'That's fine by me, Bryony.'

Pascale lived in a town on the outskirts of Wycombe called Prestwood. We drove over there and it was quite a fun journey as we motored along singing to Lana Del Rey, Chappell Roan and Charli XCX. So much cheerier than Murdo's barrage of death metal.

'Why are you going to see her anyway?' I asked.

'I said I'd lend her my copy of *The Book of Shadows*. I'm getting really interested in the Wicca stuff.'

I nodded as if I knew what she was talking about. *The Book of Shadows* almost certainly referred to magic rather than Cliff Richard's old backing band.

We turned off the main road into a cul de sac. Pascale's house was in a small close of executive-style residences of varying sizes. It was not too dissimilar to the kind of executive estate where Chris and Sandra lived. I felt a bit disappointed. Why couldn't they live somewhere more magical? We rang the doorbell. I was kind of hoping for something Gothic as a doorbell chime, but it was disappointingly normal.

Pascale opened the door wearing a T-shirt and shorts. She was wearing nothing underneath her top. I was so glad Chris wasn't here, he would have had a coronary. 'Do come in…' she said.

She led us into the small living room, which was furnished in a kind of boho chic, Indian tapestries and throws on the furniture, folk and tribal art on the walls and incense burning in a holder. There were Mexican Day of the Dead skeletons and skull motif decorations aplenty. This was more like it, I thought. This is more occult. While she and Bryony huddled together on the sofa looking at the book that Bryony had brought, I excused myself and used the loo. That was ultra-normal: walk-in shower, toilet, sink, two laundry baskets, one for coloureds, one for whites. There were some green plants on the bathroom windowsill, it was all very tasteful. I felt a bit disappointed. I had hoped for something to match the downstairs vibe, at least a black bath. I washed my hands and went back into the living room.

She made us some tea, thanked Bryony for the book, then she said to me, 'Is everything in hand for the Ceremony of Litha?'

For a horrible moment I didn't know what she was on about, then I remembered. 'Yeah, it's all in order.'

'Good. We wouldn't want anything going wrong on the most important event of the year.' She gave a smile that I found extremely provocative. There was no way she could have known that I suspected, more than suspected, her of stealing the diadem, but it was infuriating knowing that the absence of what essentially was the crown for this particular group would be humiliating for Esther. And, if she was right, probably mark the end of not only Chris's but maybe Esther's reign too. No prizes for guessing who her successor would be, all hail Queen Pascale. What a bitch you are, I thought.

'No, Pascale,' I agreed, 'we certainly wouldn't want anything to go wrong.' Meanwhile Bryony who had been fiddling with her phone, suddenly stopped as if puzzled and turned her head this way and that like a dog startled by a noise or an unexpected scent.

'Are you okay?' Pascale said. I must say I was concerned too. Bryony suddenly looked far from her normal self. She had gone pale, well, she was pale at the best of times, but she suddenly looked really unwell and I noticed her eyes blink several times. Oh God, I thought, alarmed, it must be some kind of cannabis psychosis. Then she shook her head and breathed deeply.

'I'm okay… Just felt a bit… y'know…' She visibly pulled herself together, breathed deeply several times like someone recovering themselves if they've had a shock, then she asked Pascale, 'Why the book?'

'Oh,' Pascale said, airily, 'Chris is doing a First Degree Initiation on Friday night and I want to make sure of a couple of things. I think he's been doing it wrong...'

'That's a serious accusation,' Bryony said, sternly.

'I know, but I think it's time he stepped down as High Priest. We need some new blood as leadership...' I knew it, I thought, grimly. Esther was right, this is the first of Pascale's power grabs. Now that she's got the diadem she's emboldened. Like some dodgy country getting nuclear weapons.

'Don't let his wife hear you say that,' Bryony said.

'Why?' Pascale said, with a hint of a sneer. 'What's she going to do? Kill me?' Here was a part of the conversation where I felt I had something to offer. I obviously knew nothing about magic, but I did know a great deal about Sandra. 'You wouldn't be the first.'

'What do you mean?' Pascale was confused.

I briefly recounted my history with her when she thought I was having an affair with Chris.

'She came at you with a sword!' She raised a shapely dark eyebrow in surprise. I reflected that Chris was a dirty-minded old pervert but he had a point with fancying Pascale; she was, not to put too fine a point on it, gorgeous. And what a fabulous body!

'She was a Hells Angel at the time,' I explained. I didn't fill her in on the whole story. It was far too complicated. Things had then got ultra-gnarly with another woman who had ended up dead. It hadn't been one of the most pleasant evenings of my life, that was for sure.

'Oh my God!' Pascale said. 'And she didn't go to prison for this?' Her voice was incredulous.

'No,' Bryony said. 'Let's hope no one provokes her.'

Pascale's eyes widened and she shuddered. I could see that she was deeply alarmed by what we had told her. Maybe trying to get rid of Chris now seemed somewhat less of a great idea. I began to suspect that deep down, Pascale might be a bit of a coward.

'So go carefully,' I advised judiciously. Chris was icky but the more I got to know Pascale, the more she rubbed me up the wrong way somehow, so I was finding myself in the unusual position of defending him. I twisted the knife somewhat. 'Don't upset Sandra. She's massively possessive of Chris, thinks all women are out to steal him from her.'

'Chris?' Pascale said, horrified, pulling a face. 'Eeuch!'

That more or less summed up my feelings on the man. Obviously his attempts to seduce her with magic means had been utterly ineffective. 'You may feel that way.' I smiled sweetly. 'She'll never believe you. Just don't do anything to make her jealous.'

Pascale swallowed nervously. 'I'll try not to.' She turned to Bryony. 'Thanks for the book, I'll be in touch.'

She looked at me. 'And thanks for the warning.'

We stood up to leave. 'How's Esther by the way?' she asked.

'She's well,' I said.

'I hope she has everything in place for the midsummer festival?' she asked, innocently.

'Of course she has. She's very much looking forward to it, we both are. And like I told you, as far as the catering is concerned, it's absolutely covered,' I said. 'Not too far away now, is it?'

She shook her head, and kissing us on our cheeks by way of a farewell, said, 'I'll be in touch later tomorrow, Bryony' – she smiled, with no real warmth – 'or should I call you Astarte.'

She showed us to the door and we walked back to Bryony's car and got in.

'Astarte?' I asked.

'It's going to be my Magical name. She's a goddess of love, sex and war,' said Bryony, proudly. 'The first two are definitely me and, as for the third, I'm a fighter for animal rights.'

Well, that was true. She was a tireless eco-campaigner, eco-warrior and vegetarian. I could imagine Bryony as a Priestess, clad in a robe, high as a kite, communing with the goddess. The strange thing about the Wiccans is that they were all perfectly ordinary people, totally sane, yet believing in extraordinary things. But I'd long ago given up trying to fathom what was normal and what wasn't.

She started the car and pulled away from the house. Bryony was quiet for a while and then said, 'There is one thing, Charlie.'

'What's that?'

'The diadem.'

'What about it?'

'I can't really explain it, Charlie,' her expression was thoughtful, her beautiful eyebrows furrowed, 'but I suddenly sensed it. I thought I was going to faint back there, the feeling was so powerful. I know it's there in the house. I could feel it calling to me.'

'Wow,' I said, impressed. I suppose until that moment I hadn't really believed Anna Bruce when she'd credited Bryony with occult powers. 'So it's definitely there then?'

She nodded. 'I'm one hundred per cent certain. Pascale's definitely got it.'

# Chapter Twenty-Eight

Tuesday came and I got back into the swing of things in my restaurant while the problem of Cassandra ticked over at the back of my mind like a stockpot slowly cooking on a back-burner. In between prepping food and cooking during service, when I wasn't thinking of her, I grappled with the problem of how to get the diadem back. In the car driving back from Pascale's I had asked Bryony how she knew. I remembered her words almost exactly, 'I could sense its presence. It's there in the house. I know. I can feel it.' She had turned her face to me and I could see the certainty in it. 'She's one hundred per cent the thief,' she had said with absolute conviction.

The strange thing was, I absolutely believed that she was right. I did have a lingering feeling that maybe Esther could have mislaid it, or some unknown third party might have taken it. Esther had a cleaner for instance, it was not impossible that she had stolen it. Anna Bruce had told me Bryony was psychic and I had so much faith in what Anna said that if she had told me liver and onion casserole (as served for lunch occasionally when I was at school, a dish whose memory still makes me gag in a kind of Proustian way) was nice, I would have unhesitatingly put it on my menu. That's how much I trusted her. If Bryony said she had sensed the diadem was there, the diadem was there. But what could I do? The police would laugh at me. I toyed with the idea of burglary and immediately rejected it. Her house had an alarm for a start, I'd noticed it blinking away below the bedroom window when I'd first visited, and where would I find the diadem if she'd hidden it?

Then on Wednesday I went to see Esther. I told her I still had no hard news about the diadem but I was looking into it. I didn't want to give her any false hopes.

'Oh God, Charlie,' Esther wailed, 'the solstice is almost on us.' She looked at me almost accusingly.

I found that slightly irritating. After all, I hadn't volunteered for this job, nor had I offered any guarantee of success. I held my tongue though, Esther was distraught. The diadem was like a Sword of Damocles hanging over her head. The younger Wiccans probably felt it was time for a change, and if Pascale claimed the throne, so to speak, and possession of the diadem was hers, Esther would probably be toast. Esther was tragically vulnerable. Her whole world, her whole being, lay in the organisation of South Bucks Neo Pagans. She had no children, no real interests outside of Wicca. I felt very sorry for her.

'I know,' I tried to reassure her, 'but there is hope on the horizon. We're not done yet. Chin up!' Maybe I should have said 'chins'. Esther had put on even more weight, perhaps she was comfort-eating. As if to prove my theory she unwrapped a Flake and absentmindedly crammed it in her mouth.

Then she said, swallowing her Flake practically whole, 'Chris, Pascale and Isabella from the accounts committee are coming round on this Monday coming. Would you mind popping over and assuring them that everything is okay with the catering? I want to establish at least a façade of normalcy.'

'Of course I will, Esther, but seriously' – I patted her hand – 'everything is going to be okay. You've only got the diadem to worry about and I'm sure we'll get it back.'

To my horror, I saw a tear roll out of the corner of one of her eyes. 'Esther,' I said firmly, 'I have a plan.' It was a complete lie but it seemed justified to me. 'Stop obsessing about this piece of jewellery. It's not helping. Do something positive, pray to the goddess.'

'Okay, I will. Anyway, I'll be so relieved to have an ally here on Monday. Just run over the details for them, if you don't mind. It's mainly for Isabella, she is an ex company CFO, she has a passion for money and numbers.'

'There's a surprise,' I said. 'Yes of course I'll do that.'

'And there's one more favour. I know it's your day off, you won't want to do this and I know it's a big ask, but Chris tells me Sandra is insistent on coming.' Lucky them, I thought. 'He tells me she thinks he is having an affair with either Pascale or Isabella. She wants to let them see who they would be dealing with if they carry on.' She rolled her eyes. 'I know it's ridiculous but he told me that if he'd said no she would have taken that as proof. You of all people know how possessive she can be.'

'God yeah.' I could almost sympathise with Chris. I wondered how this pathological jealousy worked alongside her new-found love of Jesus, but religion doesn't stop people from righteous slaughter.

'So could you inveigle her away from here, take her to your café for cake or something for half an hour, so we can talk about confidential things... Please!'

'Of course I can.'

There and then I knew how to get the diadem back. It was as if God Himself had struck me with a lightning bolt labelled GENIUS IDEA. I knew then exactly what had to be done.

# Chapter Twenty-Nine

Wednesday evening's service was over, the kitchen had been cleaned down, the mise en place sheets written for the following day, the meat, fish and veg orders done. It was 11 o'clock and I was sitting down in the empty restaurant with Jess, enjoying a glass of Cabernet Sauvignon.

'This is the last bottle of that Washington State Cabernet that Cass supplied.' She took a sip. 'Much as I hate to say it, you're going to have to bite the bullet, Charlie and find another supplier.'

I sighed and swirled around the aromatic red wine around in my glass. 'Yeah,' I said heavily, 'I suppose you are right.' I had been putting off making a decision on finding a replacement for Cassandra, but it had to be done, business was business. I wondered who Malcolm at the Three Bells used, B&Q maybe, paint-stripper was what his wine tasted like. Strickland's other suppliers were too pricey for me. Well, I probably had a couple of weeks before I needed to worry.

'I'll get round to it,' I promised.

'Will you?' Jess was sceptical. 'Some of us do things on

time,' she said, 'even though there's obviously no rush now.' She put a hand in her capacious backpack-style handbag and produced a laptop, which she put on the table. I looked at her questioningly.

'This is Tris's. I fixed the port, it was just a loose connection.' Then she smiled. 'I also found out what the problem with his email was.'

'Well, I don't think you'll ever get paid for it, not now he's dead. I suppose I had better take it back to Lizzie.' I sighed. 'I just wish that Slattery had been more interested in the connection with Tris and John Mayhew, he more or less dismissed it out of hand.'

Jess made a kind of, well, what can you do? gesture then said, 'But I did find some other beefy things on it.'

'Really?' She had my full attention now. 'What kind of things?'

'After I had discovered that deal he had going with Mayhew that fell through, I had a good old nose around on it, while I had it. I wanted to check on what he'd been up to image-wise. He was alive at the time and I was hoping to find illegal porn, something super beefy that would warrant the police so you could tell Lizzie's dad. Have you heard from him by the way?'

I shook my head. 'No, I don't think I am ever going to again. He doesn't need me now Tris has gone, he got what he wanted when he was murdered. He doesn't need any evidence to put in front of Lizzie to put her off marriage, not anymore.'

'So you won't be getting your new furniture then?' She looked sad, as well she might.

'I fear not.' It wasn't a huge blow, but it was annoying. I suppose I should have taken some satisfaction in the fact that I had been proved right over my initial feelings that he wasn't to be trusted. 'Mr Summers will almost certainly be celebrating like crazy, Christmas has come early. He hated Tris, he loves his daughter, and now one has gone and he has got the other back. Couldn't be better really.' I drank another mouthful of the wine. As Cass had promised, it was delicious. 'I kind of knew deep down he'd probably stiff me for payment, I had that vibe when I first met him. It came as no surprise that he was known as a shady businessman. Well, Slattery did warn me.' I drank some more. I never listened, one of my many failings. 'Anyway,' I said, 'Tris's computer…'

'Yeah, I did find some locked files which I accessed.' Jess pulled a face. 'Every time he slept with a woman he made detailed notes, what they did, marks out of ten, how often they did it, where they did it, it was a weird mixture of the disgusting and the bizarre. He also managed to get about half of them to pose naked for him, pictures I guess he would use maybe for blackmail purposes. He was a truly revolting guy.'

I sighed. 'Well, we knew that all along.'

'You were there too,' she said matter-of-factly.

'Where?' I was momentarily confused.

'In his photo gallery.'

PFFFFFFF! I had a mouthful of wine which I kind of spat everywhere in a red vinous spray in shock. 'What!' I shrieked. 'Naked pictures of me? From where?'

Jess laughed, shaking her head. 'No, you were fully clothed. He'd copied them from images of you on the net,

241

from industry dos and things, interviews, articles and that profile in *Restaurant* magazine. They were just his idea of a sort of image board. Or to put him in the mood, I guess.'

I knew the kind of thing she meant. I wasn't famous, not even in catering circles. But I had been around a while and there were plenty of old photos of me if you did a search for my name as Tris had obviously done. At awards dinners (not mine sadly, other restaurants I'd worked in), pictures from way back, pictures from the local papers, that kind of thing. 'Bucks Chamber of Commerce welcomes new restauranteur'. That gives a flavour of my level of fame.

Jess continued. 'He'd listed you under "potential targets".'

'Seriously?' I snorted. I don't know why this should have come as a surprise, I had suspected earlier he was going to make an attempt on my virtue.

'Yeah, he'd made a little plan as to how he was going to go about it.'

Reassured that I wasn't spread-eagled butt naked or the victim of some clandestine sex-tape from a former boyfriend, I was by now totally committed to knowing how Tris's devious, warped mind had worked. 'Tell me more.'

'Okay. There were things like, "win her trust… give her a really pro training schedule, including gym work, move on to massage?", "get her to go swimming, check out her figure in swim suit/bikini, almost certainly v. good".' Well, I thought complacently, nothing wrong with his eyesight. '"Work on Charlie's weaknesses".'

I suddenly thought, this is what would come under the Identify bracket. 'What are my weaknesses according to Tris?' I was intrigued.

She smiled for the first time. 'I knew you would ask that.'

'Go on.'

'Egomaniacal.'

'I am not!' I protested.

'You're the one who wanted to know all about yourself,' she pointed out. 'Seems perfectly accurate to me. Now, what else… "getting old", he had added here, "use that for leverage".'

'Bastard! Well, I'm certainly not as young as I used to be, that's true.'

'"Very self-confident, maybe overly self-confident, could be masking deep insecurities".'

This would come under 'Exploit'. How was he going to exploit my age, tempt me with Werther's Originals? I took a quick glimpse into the dark well of my psyche, nothing in particular peered back. I certainly didn't feel deeply insecure about anything, other than plumbing, electrical know-how or car maintenance, indeed anything about cars. I could live with that.

'You are, and I quote, "obsessively curious, we can use this"…' She frowned. 'I don't get the "we" bit. Must be the Royal We.'

'I am not obsessively curious!' I protested.

'Yes you are Charlie' – she rolled her eyes – 'it's what makes you such a good investigator, you can't help yourself. Duh! And it makes you a really good chef, you're forever wondering, what would happen if we did X. Murdo often remarks on it to me. He says it's one of the reasons he admires your cooking so much, your ability to experiment, as well as make mistakes and then own them.'

'Hmm.' These sounded like rather backhanded compliments to me.

She squinted at the notes she'd taken on her phone. 'That's more or less it... oh, one more thing, "absentee boyfriend – exploit this, suggest he's playing away, maybe say, 'two can play at that game'..."'

Well, I had unshakeable faith in Andrea. He wasn't playing away, I knew that. He wasn't the type. Besides, he had me and my amazing figure. 'Was there anyone or anything else on file?'

'Yes, and this could be very important.'

I stiffened in my seat and she noticed my body language.

'Don't get too excited, Charlie. You know you were wishing there was a credible other suspect for Tris's murder, well, I can give you one.'

'Who is it?'

She looked at me hard-eyed. 'Matt Spicer.'

# Chapter Thirty

Matt Spicer. The name immediately brought forward his image from the back of my mind. Shaven head, intense, super-fit, intimidating. I'd seen him once or twice in the village since we'd stopped running. He'd still been wearing those shoes that look like kind of froggy feet, wet-look plastic or rubber with toes. I think they give you some sort of super-grip on the ground. He looked weird, that was for sure.

'Tell me more,' I said.

'You remember I told you I knew him earlier?' Jess asked.

I nodded. 'Yeah, I remember.' I knew that Jess had history with him. I remembered that she had first met Spicer about a decade earlier, just before her GCSEs. She had shown early promise at maths and IT and her parents had hired him for extra tutoring.

'What was he like back then?' I asked.

'Much the same as he is today. Very quiet and very intimidating. He really knew his stuff though. I got the impression he was not a team worker, that he hated being in the office environment. Don't get me wrong, there are a lot of super-nerdy people in IT, I should know, I work in the field, but he was a really antsy guy. That's why he only does freelance stuff, so he doesn't have to work with anyone. And his wife is very nice.'

'I have never met her,' I said. 'To be honest, I hardly ever spoke to him when we went running, I don't think he likes me very much.'

'Maybe he's just shy, but Abigail, that's his wife, is the opposite, really outgoing. In fact so outgoing that she had an affair with Tris.'

'Oh my God, not another one!' I stared at her in disbelief. 'How did Tris meet her? She's a schoolteacher you said.'

'That was detailed in his notes, he was very thorough. Tris Smith, in his maître d' role, had started doing some promo work for the King's Head, "giving back to the community". He talked Strickland into backing it. There was some sort of restaurant award available and Strickland's a sucker for things like that. He met Abigail as part of a schools initiative. He also knew Matt because he is employed by Strickland to maintain the website and handle the systems they use. And this brings me to the strange thing that I found on his computer.'

'Go on…' What could be stranger than the Abigail revelation?

'I found some spyware that had been installed in Tris's laptop, which would give whoever had put it there full access to his computer files,' Jess said. 'It was niftily hidden. I doubt any normal person would have noticed, but I did.'

'Go you!' I was so full of admiration for her computer skills, a discipline completely alien to me.

'Thank you,' she said with faux-modesty. 'It was why his email wasn't working as fast as it should've been. I was able to find the date that the program was introduced. I bet you any money you like it was the last time Matt was round at the King's Head working for Strickland.'

'When was that?' I asked.

'Over a month ago.'

I did the maths, it was probably round about the time Matt joined Tris's running club. I pondered this. 'Do you think it would have given Matt access to Tris's sex records?'

'I think we can safely assume the answer would be yes.' She frowned. 'And he would have read in horrendous detail all the stuff that Abigail, his wife, had done with Tris. And from what I know about Matt, he probably wouldn't have said anything. He would have dealt with it in the same way he would de-bug a program.'

'How do you mean?'

'Thoroughly, patiently, with attention to detail. Then deleted the bug.'

I could well imagine it. Matt, his face an immobile mask, peering through a bush as he pressed the trigger of the crossbow to kill Tris. It was even possible that he might have killed Mayhew as a diversion so that his revenge attack on Tris would have gone down as another psycho attack on the running group. If he hadn't killed Mayhew, the same logic would apply. He would never be suspected as the killer, it would be blamed on the mysterious Crossbow Killer. Everyone, myself included, had wondered at their relationship but most people would just assume they were friends, work colleagues. I doubt he would have been suspected.

'So you think Matt deleted Tris?'

'Yeah.'

I recalled the time I had seen Matt Spicer just after I had eavesdropped on Tris and Cassandra in the wood. Had he been following Tris, planning where to attack him, where to strike? And was the use of a crossbow not suggestive of an assassin's weapon? Jess had joked about how her schoolfriends had speculated he was a spy and I could remember thinking he looked more like a trained killer. You could buy crossbows without any questions being asked. They were deadly, they were silent, what more could you want?

Jess pursed her lips and then sighed. 'Look, I like Matt, but I like Cassandra more. I wondered at the time why Matt had joined Tris's running group. I think the answer is he was stalking Tris. I think he had read about what Tris had done to Abigail, I'm a hundred per cent sure he had, and I think he was out for revenge.'

'So you definitely think he could have killed him?' I asked. Just to make sure.

'God, yeah, with no compunction. Like swatting a fly.' She took a sip of wine and carried on. 'Matt lives in Potter's Hill, just up the road from Tris. He was aware of all of Tris's movements from his calendar. He'd have known he would be on his own that night. Tris had written in his Outlook calendar that Lizzie was away, staying with her dad. He could well have gone round there, seen what was happening, the unconscious Cass, Tris preoccupied with her helpless body. Tris wouldn't have heard an elephant coming in the room. Not with an unconscious, beautiful woman who had been holding out on him, a totally help-less piece of prey.'

I nodded. I could easily visualise it. Jess was right. And it would be bad enough knowing your wife had slept with another man without reading in excruciating detail about their intimacy. Not to mention the photos. Yes, he would have killed Tris and then cold-bloodedly framed Cass.

Jess continued. 'I've read what Tris had done to Abigail, so would Matt. Oh, yeah,' she said, quietly. 'You've got your suspect now Charlie. Matt Spicer.'

Jess left about 11.15 and at 11.30, just as I was turning the lights out, there was a knock on the door.

I knew who it was immediately. I went to the front door of the restaurant and opened it. 'Come in DI Slattery,' I said.

He sat down without being asked. He looked at me hopefully so I went behind the bar and asked, 'Brandy, Scotch or Armagnac?'

His eyes brightened. 'Armagnac please. I haven't had any of that since the last time I was in France.'

I poured him a hefty measure, brought it over to him and studied him as he swirled the drink around in its glass. He was one of those forceful people who seem larger than life. He was a big guy but the space he seemed to occupy extended far beyond his actual body.

'How are you?' I asked. His name was Michael, but I always thought of him as Slattery.

'Busy.' He drank some Armagnac, then nodded apprecia-tively, swirled it around some more and inhaled deeply. 'This is lovely. Not only have I got the murder of John Mayhew to look into, I'm the SIO on the Tris Smith murder.'

In all the recent excitement I had almost forgotten John Mayhew. He was of course the first of the killings involving the Hampden Green running group. Now, three of them were out of action, two dead and Cassandra in prison.

He hesitated. 'Look, Charlie, I know Cassandra Jenkins is your friend, but really, she is by far the strongest suspect, the only suspect in point of fact as far as I'm concerned. But I would be interested in your take on events on the night in question. You knew them both and you know I value your opinion.'

I poured out everything I knew about Tris, his promiscuity, his manipulative tactics, my guess that he tried to assault Cass when she was unconscious with booze.

He listened carefully as I spoke, then said, 'All this is fascinating, Charlie.' He sighed. 'It doesn't help with the fact that her hands and clothes were covered with his blood and her fingerprints were on the knife.' Which of course was her lawyer's point of view too.

'Have you even considered the possibility that she might be innocent?' I asked. 'Have you tried to find another suspect?'

He nodded. 'Believe me, it's not for the want of looking.'

'Who else have you interviewed?'

'His fiancée obviously. She was staying down near Chichester with her father. The night of the murder, Thursday night, they were at home, both alibiing the other. You know her quite well, do you think she had anything to do with it?'

I shook my head. 'I very much doubt it. She worshipped the ground that he walked upon. I can't see it happening.'

Slattery nodded. 'And did he have any enemies that you knew about, jealous husbands, spurned ex-lovers? That kind of thing? From what you've just told me, it wouldn't be surprising.'

Now was the time to tell him of Jess's discovery. 'What if I were to tell you that I have evidence that someone who lives in the same village as Tris Smith knew that his wife had been having an affair with him, and not only that, had read Tris's detailed notes on what they had been up to?'

Slattery gave me a surprised look. 'Do you mean in full, graphic detail?'

'Yeah.'

'I would be very interested indeed.' Slattery's wife had left him a few years ago for another man. If Slattery had read his rival's account of their love-making in graphic detail, well, I would imagine the consequences would have been dire.

His glass was empty by now. I refilled it and said, 'I'll be back in a minute, just fetching something.'

I went upstairs for Tris's laptop and handed it to Slattery. I explained how I had come to know what was on it and all about Matt and Abigail Spicer.

'Charlie' – he shook his head sadly – 'I'm afraid that as evidence it would almost certainly be inadmissible.'

'But why?' I wailed. 'It's his bloody computer, those are his files!'

'I don't doubt it for one moment.'

'Well, where's the problem?'

'Because Matt Spicer's lawyer would say to us, that's not going in because you can't cross-examine Tris Smith about their veracity. He's dead. These files could have been created by a third party determined to prove Spicer's guilt.'

'So it can't be used?'

'Probably not.' He exhaled heavily. 'Look, I'm not a lawyer. I'll take it on the off-chance but I think the likelihood of it being admissible evidence is practically zero.'

'Do you want me to ask Jess for the passwords or protocols that she used?' I had, of course, no idea of whether that was how she'd got in. He shook his head. 'The lab will deal with it.'

'So a murderer gets to walk free, and an innocent woman gets life,' I said bitterly.

'Charlie.' His voice was gentle. 'You don't know that. The investigation is still ongoing and I will look into this, believe me.'

I let him out and went to bed. In a state of misery, resentment and despair. I had not felt so hopeless in a long while.

# Chapter Thirty-One

Slattery's rejection of the compelling evidence on the laptop was a terrible body blow in my attempts to clear Cass's name. It was beginning to look like a lost cause. But at least I could save Esther. That would be something. So it was the next day after service, I met Bryony in the bar at the Three Bells.

'Thanks for coming, Bryony.'

'Your message was very mysterious.' She raised her beautiful light brown eyebrows. 'I'm intrigued.'

'Bryony, over the weekend, I want you to go round to Pascale's. I don't know how you'll do it or what you'll say, but it's vital.'

She looked at me excitedly. 'Is it to get the diadem back?'

'It is. When you're there, ask to use the loo,' I instructed her. 'In the bathroom there are two laundry baskets. I want you to steal some underwear, a bra or pants, either will do. Hopefully one with a French label. Then get it to me before ten in the morning on Monday.'

Bryony looked at me like I was crazy. 'Let me get this straight, Charlie, you want me to steal Pascale's underwear.'

'Exactly.' I nodded my head.

She pulled a face. 'That's a bit icky.'

'I don't care, Bryony.' I was adamant. 'You are going to have to do it, it's vital. There's only a few days to go to go before the Feast of Litha. Esther needs that diadem or it's going to destroy her. Pascale will have won and Esther will be on her way out.'

'Okay,' she said doubtfully, 'if it helps. But are you going to tell me why?'

'I will,' I promised, 'if it works.'

She nodded. 'I'll do it.'


The following evening Slattery turned up at my restaurant. I made him a double espresso but I could see from his face that he did not have good news for me.

'I spoke to Matt Spicer. He's got a perfect alibi that covers the time of the murder.'

'What is it?' I asked, gloomily.

'He was on some kind of Zoom call, with an IT shindig in Dublin. It ran from eight till ten on the night of the murder. It was like a mini conference slash seminar, he was one of the speakers. There were about a hundred and fifty participants. The whole thing was date-stamped as well. He was present throughout, so we're going to have to remove him from any list of suspects.'

'Oh.' I was bitterly disappointed and I guess that it showed. First we couldn't use the laptop, now this. But at least Slattery had tried.

'I'm sorry, Charlie. It was a good call.' He was obviously trying to humour me. I felt touched. 'Cheer up Charlie, it's early days yet.'

'I know, but I'm sure she's innocent.'

'Let's hope so, Charlie,' Slattery said, but something in his voice made me doubt he believed it.

So that promising avenue looked like being a complete dead-end. Maybe Matt was innocent after all, but who had installed that spyware, if not him? Who else had a motive to kill Tris, unless there was some embittered ex around that I didn't know of?

Then, during the following week unexpectedly, a chink of light appeared in the darkness. Murdo and I had a ferociously busy Tuesday night service, which was highly unusual. But I was kind of glad of the relentless pressure as it distracted me from thinking about all my current problems.

Now it was Wednesday morning and, yawning and tired, I was up at 6 o'clock to get four hours of prep in before Murdo started at 10. The problem was the desserts which had virtually all gone. They had more or less been eaten the night before, and they are time-consuming to make.

I made a promise to myself that I wasn't even going to think about Cassandra or Matt Spicer today. I had reached the limits of what I could do. Any more thought about her would simply be counter-productive. I would just be going around in circles, re-treading the same old paths of thought and getting nowhere. I made a mental note to find out which prison she was being held in and see if she wanted a visit from me.

I didn't bring Matt Spicer up, DI Slattery did. Later that night, at closing time again, he materialised like a very corporeal ghost at my door. As I let him in I could see he was smiling for a change. At least someone's happy, I thought. I still hadn't heard from Bryony and I was beginning to get very antsy.

'Brandy?'

'A large one. Would you care to join me?' His good humour was palpable.

'Okay.' I poured a large drink for him and a much smaller one for myself. As the aromatic, comforting fumes rose around us I asked, 'Are we celebrating something?'

'Maybe.' He settled back in his chair. 'I called round to speak to Matt Spicer again about his alibi, the night of Tris Smith's murder. It seems ok.'

'So he couldn't have killed Tris?' I was disappointed to discover that. More than disappointed obviously. I had been so sure.

'Unfortunately not. But...'

'There's a but?'

He smiled. 'There is indeed a but. So, it was lunchtime as I drove back to Wycombe, and I called in at the school where his wife works.'

'Abigail Spicer?' I remembered her name from when Jess had told me.

Slattery's grin broadened. 'Yes and no. I asked for her at reception and for a moment the woman looked puzzled then she went, "Oh, you mean, Abigail Manzoni, yeah, sure I'll get her for you."'

'What's that, her maiden name?'

'Yeah. Manzoni before she became Spicer. Now, here's the thing. When John Mayhew was murdered and I checked on possible suspects, as I told you I looked at people who'd lost money in his Ponzi scheme. The biggest loser from round here was a guy in his sixties called John Manzoni.'

'Abigail's dad?' I felt suddenly excited.

'Exactly!' He drank some brandy and continued. 'I did some further digging. It seems he was like a broken man after he lost his money to Mayhew. It wasn't a huge amount of money, but it was for him. He wasn't rich, he was a bus driver for Carousel. He never recovered from the loss and the betrayal, and the guilt that he felt from being stupid enough, as he saw it, to be conned. I remember I spoke to his widow at the time.'

'His widow!'

'Yeah, John Manzoni killed himself in January this year. Mrs Manzoni blames one man for it.'

'John Mayhew.'

'Exactly, Charlie, John Mayhew.'

This was certainly great news. It also raised the intriguing possibility that maybe Abi, Matt's wife was involved. Well, at least I had finally managed to get Slattery to shed doubt on the guilt of Cassandra. If I hadn't found about the Spicers, husband and wife, this would never have come to light. I felt a welcome glow of achievement for once.

I went to bed happy that night. Now we had a motive for Matt killing Mayhew, as well as the attack on Tris. I appreciated that Matt had what seemed an unbreakable alibi; was it possible that Abi's previous love for Tris had turned to hate and she had done it? Had Matt confronted her with Tris's revolting log of female conquests and her eyes had been opened to what kind of a man she'd given herself to? I remembered there was a word for that, love turning to hate, a complete reversal of feelings. Edward Hamilton had taught me it. Enantiodromia. Is that what had happened?

I felt that maybe the net was closing in on the true killers at long last.

# Chapter Thirty-Two

Bryony arrived at my restaurant at my kitchen door the following morning. I was alone in the kitchen, baking this time. I had already made two Victoria sponges for the café side of things and was now making a white chocolate parfait for the restaurant menu, which I would present with some plum compote I had in my freezer that I wanted to get rid of. When I served it, I would send it out on a small, dark plate so the whiteness of the parfait would stand out, and place a small sprig of mint on top for a tiny splash of vivid colour. I made a mental note to keep a hawkish eye on Francis. If he was doing desserts, he'd be quite capable of sending it out with a sprig of basil or parsley on top, which would obviously ruin things. Or possibly, beef jus instead of plum compote. There was no end really to what he might achieve, given the chance.

There was a tap on the glass panel of the door and I opened it. Bryony was there, wearing an above the knee white mini-dress with a dark floral print and biker boots, emerald earrings gracing her earlobes Her cornflower-blue eyes were bright and I remember thinking that she looked crazily pretty.

'Come in,' I said. She did so and I closed the door. 'Coffee? Tea?'

She shook her head, emerald earrings sparkling as she did so. 'No thanks, I can't stay.'

'Bryony, did you get my text?'

Earlier that morning, I'd woken up at about 3 o'clock and lain awake, unable to get back to sleep. I couldn't stop thinking about Cass, locked in some horrible jail cell for a crime I was convinced she had nothing to do with. She'd be in her sixties by the time she came out. I rolled from side to side and then got up, opened my curtains and gazed over the common. The lights of a car washed over the grass as it drove up the incline from the road at the bottom, past my restaurant, heading towards Potter's Hill. I noted as it passed that it wasn't a car, but a pick-up truck. Probably, I thought gloomily, one of the fly-tippers. That made me think of the Earl and his spy cameras. He owned the fields between here and the next village; maybe, I wondered, maybe there would be footage of Matt up to no good. I couldn't imagine what that might look like, but I felt it was worth asking anyway. The cameras might have spotted something that had been overlooked. The Earl would only have been looking for the fly-tippers. So at 3.10 I'd sent the text and got back into bed. Sleep was, thank God, immediate.

'What, that one about the cameras? Yeah, I showed James.'

'What did he say?'

'He said he'd ask the estate manager to have another look at the footage. The trouble is the cameras are motion-activated and the Muntjac deer, foxes and the occasional badger often trigger them at night, so there's a lot of activity to look through.'

'Oh, well, if you wouldn't mind…'

''S'okay. But we're pretty busy at the moment. We've got some Peruvian ecologists coming over for a working breakfast. The Spectacled bear's habitat is increasingly threatened, James is raising money for them to help protect them… Anyway, changing the subject,' she handed me a small plastic bag, 'ta da!'

I opened it and took out a black lacy bra. I looked at the label, Ysé, Paris.

'My God, Bryony, this is perfect!' And it was so obviously Pascale's!

It was the kind of garment that would set Chris's pulse racing. Actually, it would have raced so much it would have induced some sort of terrible stroke. More importantly, it was just the kind of thing Sandra envisaged the non-existent lovers in her husband's life wearing as they lured him into acts of unspeakable depravity and lust in some den of vice somewhere. Like a bedroom in Prestwood overlooking a cul de sac with numbered parking bays.

We studied the bra. 'It's very nice,' Bryony said thoughtfully. 'I'm glad it will do.'

I put it on the prep table and took a photo, then I put it in another plastic bag and then in a drawer.

'What are you going to do with it?'

'Set a trap,' I said smugly. 'And this is the perfect bait.'

So, Friday, Saturday and Sunday came and went. The day of rest was spent with a ferociously busy lunch service and then a leisurely evening spent watching an old Matrix film with Murdo. We were interrupted halfway through by Lucy calling him. He disappeared into his room and emerged half an hour later. I remembered when I was his age, the way you could see your boyfriend at some point during the day and then still find things to talk about on the phone later that night. It also reminded me that I hadn't spoken to my boyfriend for a while. I made a mental note to call Andrea in the morning. If he was at his parents' house it might be seen as bad form to interrupt a Sunday get-together with the adored son whom they didn't get to see very much, although they were seeing quite a bit of him at the moment. They probably wondered why he couldn't find a nice Italian girl closer to home. But right now he was home quite a bit. And for once he was spending a lot more time with them than me, that was for sure. I felt a twinge of jealousy.

We watched Neo and Trinity battle the attack of the machines and then sadly, Neo died. I went to bed feeling slightly depressed, but as Murdo pointed out optimistically, he couldn't really be dead as they made a new Matrix film with Neo, much older now, only a couple of years ago.

Monday morning found me knocking on the door of Esther's house. The solstice was just three days away now, we were really going down to the wire. I could see the other witches had arrived. There was Chris's Twingo and Pascale's pumped up Volvo 4x4.

Esther let me in. 'They're both here,' she said, rolling her eyes. Then she looked at me hopefully. I could see the anguish and the pain in her expression, the dark bags under her eyes that make-up hadn't concealed. The theft had taken a terrible toll on her; it wasn't just the theft of an object, her identity as a leader, her soul, had been stolen as well.

'It's okay, Esther, it's all under control. We should have the diadem back soon,' I reassured her.

'Charlie, there are only three days to go!' she wailed, but quietly, maybe more of an agonised moan.

'It's all in hand, Esther, fear not.' I hoped to God I was right.

'Thank you, Charlie,' she breathed.

In the living room I found the three witches: the vet and the leisure facility director for Milton Keynes, and a rat-faced woman with yellowy teeth, the former finance director, now the witches' treasurer. Also present was Sandra, glowering at Pascale, like Mount Etna threatening to explode. She was there to stamp her authority, to let the love rivals know if they were thinking of trying to take her husband away they would have to go through her first. I had forgotten how intimidating she could be. I don't think Pascale had met her, I was willing to bet she had never seen anything like her before.

Sandra had dressed for the occasion, dressed to impress. No girly dress this time. She was wearing jeans and a T-shirt. Her huge arms were the size of Esther's but unlike hers they were predominately muscle, a weightlifter gone to seed. As well as the tattoos that Bryony had noticed, there were a couple of broad-looking scars on her forearms, relics of her Hells Angel past. She was wearing steel-toed work boots, not dissimilar to the ones I wear in the kitchen, but not nearly so attractive.

To say there was an atmosphere in the room would be a wild understatement. You could have cut it with a knife and served it with a sprig of mint on top like the parfait. Pascale was looking downcast at her feet while Sandra was obviously halfway through an illustrative anecdote. 'So I says to the screw, look, officer, you'd better move her otherwise I'll smash her teeth so far down her throat she'll have to clean them through her bumhole.' Probably, I thought to myself, a witty vignette from her recent time on remand before she was found not guilty of murder.

'Hello, Sandra,' I said cheerily. 'Pascale… Chris.' I nodded politely at the treasurer whose name I had forgotten. At this point I abandoned the idea of a food discussion and thought I'd just remove Sandra. They'd all be grateful for that.

'Sandra,' I said with a winning smile, 'Esther said you'd be dropping by. Would you like to come over to my place for a coffee and some cake?'

Sandra considered this momentarily. She obviously decided that her mission was accomplished, her job here was done. 'Love to, Charlie,' she said and stood up. Her scowl raked the four seated figures and as she left the room with me, she turned and growled, 'Be seeing you.'

That sounded much more of a threat than a promise.

We got to the front door. I heard the noise of relieved chatter from behind the closed door, that need to talk you get when you've been under intolerable stress.

'Sandra,' I asked, 'could you do me a favour and drive us over to my place. I walked here but I've got a foot injury from running and it's still niggling. You can come back later for Chris.'

'Yeah, of course.' She put her hand in her jeans pocket and took out the car keys. I found it totally predictable that she was the driver when there were the two of them in the Twingo.

Five minutes later I settled her at a table in my restaurant with a nice view of the common.

'Now, we've got lemon drizzle cake that I made yesterday,' I said encouragingly as if talking to a small child, 'or a Victoria sponge with cream. It's got Esther's homemade blackcurrant jam in it.'

She decided on the Victoria and I brought her an Americano to go with it. She thanked me and looked out of the window and then around the restaurant appreciatively.

'This is lovely. I'll have to get Chris to bring me here for our anniversary. It's in a week's time, thirty years.'

'That'd be nice,' I said. It wouldn't. She would almost certainly imagine that Jess or Katie were flirting with Chris. God knows why she thought women found her husband irresistible, but she did. Her mission in life seemed to be to ward off the predators, and the fact that they were illusory did not deter her at all.

I patted my pockets. 'Oh bother,' I said, dramatically. I winced internally. I sounded like the total liar that I was, surely she would suspect. 'Something's fallen out of my pocket, it must be in your car… can I borrow your keys a sec.'

'Sure,' she bit into her cake, 'delicious…' and handed them to me.

'Thank you,' I said, flashing a winning smile. I hardly dared to breathe, my heart was thumping uncontrollably.

I went out into the car park, unlocked the car, opened the passenger door and leaned in. I took Pascale's bra out of my pocket and stuffed it under the passenger seat. I leaned forward so my ear was pressed against the footwell and peered underneath the metal frame of the car seat. The black material was practically invisible and none of it poked out. Unless you put your hand under the seat you would never know it was there. Satisfied, I went back inside. I thought about the ethics of what I was doing. Yes, it was wrong, and if it failed, it could have dreadful consequences but they would only affect Chris and Pascale, so nobody innocent would be hurt. Or at least that's what I told myself, that and desperate needs require desperate means.

I sat down with Sandra and she told me about her church and Jesus. How He had saved her from a life of crime and violence (although seemingly not the threat of implied violence as I had witnessed at Esther's, Jesus was obviously on board with that.) I listened politely as she spoke of the need for forgiveness in life and various other moral messages. Fortunately for my plan, Sandra did not look remotely like a woman prepared to turn the other cheek, whatever she might say.

She thanked me for the coffee and cake and I watched her get into the car. It sank on its axles under her weight as she clambered in behind the wheel. She put the car in gear and drove off out of my car park to go and pick Chris up. Blissfully unaware of the hand grenade lurking under the seat next to her.

# Chapter Thirty-Three

'Hi, who is this please?'

'It's Charlie Hunter.'

'Oh, hi Charlie... Everything okay?'

'Um, I'm afraid not Pascale. There's a terrible crisis that's affecting the catering. I need to discuss it with you, asap... like... now.'

'My God, what's gone wrong?' I could hear the alarm in her voice and I smiled to myself in satisfaction.

'I can't talk about it over the phone.' I did my best to sound extremely worried, conveying the urgency of the situation. 'Can I come round?'

'Errm... okay...' It was obviously not okay, but she had no choice. 'Please do, if you think it's necessary.'

'It is or I wouldn't be calling you. I'll see you in about twenty minutes.'

It was 7 o'clock on Tuesday night. Unlike the week before we had hardly anyone booked in, and I'd asked Murdo if he was happy to look after things for a while on his own. 'I've got to go out for an hour, I'll be back by eight.'

I turned to Francis by the sink. 'Francis, can you cover

for me for an hour?' I was entrusting the starters and desserts to him. I mentally crossed my fingers.

'Yes, Chef.' He beamed, delighted at my trust in him.

'You'll be okay with the desserts?'

'I'll be fine, Chef, they'll be as safe as sardines in my hands,' he assured me.

'Err, great.' As I walked to my car I thought 'What!'

Francis's way with the English language was getting stranger.

I drove the twenty minutes or so to Prestwood and Pascale's house. The 4x4 was neatly parked in the designated bay outside. I knocked on her door.

'Charlie!' She smiled as she opened it. 'Please come in.' You won't be smiling in a minute, I thought to myself.

I walked in and she motioned me to a seat then sat down opposite me.

'So Charlie, what's the problem?' Her face looked concerned.

'You,' I said calmly. 'You're the problem.'

The smile froze on her face. 'What... what are you implying?' She was understandably confused, this was not what she had anticipated.

'I'm not implying anything, Pascale,' I said levelly. 'You stole the diadem from Esther, and now I want it back.'

'I don't know what you're talking about!' She was angry now, angry and defiant.

'Don't waste my time, Pascale.' My voice was calm, conversational even.

She got to her feet. 'Please leave now!' She pointed at

the door, in case I hadn't got the message. 'I haven't got time to listen to this rubbish.'

'Before I go, I'm going to show you a photo I took.' She had no option but to glare impotently at me as, taking my time, I took my phone out of my pocket and brought up an image on the screen. I stood up and showed it to her.

'What is this?' She looked at me angrily. 'Some sort of pervy joke?'

'Don't you recognise it?' I asked innocently. 'It's yours.'

She looked more closely. 'But how... Why?' Anger, confusion, uncertainty, all of these emotions flitted across her pretty face. You couldn't blame Chris for being besotted. She was remarkably attractive.

'I stole it from you.' I said, matter-of-factly.

'Where is it?' she demanded, puzzled and annoyed. 'Give it back!'

'Maybe I will, maybe I won't.' I smiled sweetly. 'Currently it's hidden in very close proximity to Chris.' I looked at her levelly and said, 'Do you know what Sandra's reaction would be, when she finds it?' I rested a beat, 'And she will find it, Pascale, believe me, she will.'

She froze at the thought. She blurted out, 'She wouldn't know it was mine.' But she sounded far from certain. I could see the doubt in her eyes and a dawning fear as to what this could mean.

'Really? Are you certain?' I dropped my voice menacingly. 'Sandra is already fairly sure Chris is having an affair with you. When she finds this, she'll be one hundred per cent sure of it. Cherchez la femme, Pascale...'

I was proud of deploying this snippet of French, about the only French I know.

'She'll come gunning for you, Pascale, you saw her yesterday. You know what she's capable of. The law won't stop her, appealing for mercy won't stop her and she certainly is not going to listen to reason. And you, Pascale,' I paused to let this sink in, 'will be very much in her sights. Now,' I added briskly, 'that bra is obviously not mine and certainly not Esther's or Isabella's.' Too small and too big respectively. My eyes narrowed threateningly. 'Whose do you think she'll think it is? Who among us is that size and owns lingerie made in Paris?' As the label had helpfully proclaimed.

'You wouldn't….' her voice quavered, whereas mine was brutal as I countered, 'I would Pascale.' I stared into her beautiful brown eyes, 'And you know it.'

Pascale was looking very worried now, doubtless thinking of what Sandra might do. I decided to give her some indication of the range of possibilities facing her.

'She beat one of my chefs up over a drug debt once,' I said, conversationally. 'He was incredibly badly bruised. Luckily no bones broken, but there was sheer fluke. And when she thought I was seeing Chris, well, you know what happened. I was lucky, somebody stopped her. You never know, you might get lucky too.'

I pointed at the photo. 'That bra belongs to you, Pascale.' I smiled triumphantly. 'The slipper fits, Cinderella, you may as well own it.'

She sat down heavily on the sofa. I think her knees had gone weak.

I paused to let this sink in. 'Of course, now she's gone religious, things may be different... maybe crucifixion, I wouldn't be surprised. But, Pascale, I can make sure she doesn't find the bra, if...'

'I'll give you the sodding diadem,' she muttered angrily. 'I get the picture, there's no need to go on.' She stood up and I could hear her feet stamping on the stairs, once on the way up, and once on the way down.

She handed me a small cardboard box. I opened it, inside was the diadem. It looked beautiful and its semi-precious stones glowed in the lights of Pascale's flat. I closed the lid.

'Merci beaucoup, Pascale.' That was now my French exhausted. 'You'll get the bra tomorrow, I'll send someone round with it.'

And Esther will get her crown back.

As she saw me out she said, 'You're an evil bitch aren't you, Charlie Hunter.'

I smiled winningly. 'I try, Pascale, I try.'

The evening's excitement did not end there. 11 o'clock brought DI Slattery. I was beginning to be in two minds about these continual updates on the progress of the investigation into Tris's murder. On the one hand I appreciated it. Cass was my friend, I was sure she was innocent or, even if she had killed Tris, it would have been justified. And I liked the frisson of being privy to classified information. On the downside I had reluctantly come to agree with Jess that Slattery wanted more than just friendship. He wasn't creepy, frightening, persistent or anything like that. Far from it. I was not unflattered. He was an attractive man and if I'd got drunk with him in some far flung place like the Davaar View Hotel, well… But, did I want to go out with him, no. I like Slattery the same way I like marzipan, in small doses. Anyway, I was spoken for. He knew that, but I suspected it didn't stop him pining for me.

Anyway, here he was again. Jess had gone and we were alone in my empty restaurant sitting by the bar, with Slattery doubtless hoping for the day when I would say, 'Shall we go upstairs to my flat? It's cosier up there.' And one thing would lead to another. A day that sadly for him was never going to come.

'So how did things go today?' I asked.

'Interesting. I've been going over the forensics from the cottage where Tris Smith died. When you were running with him did you ever notice what kind of shoes he wore?'

'Umm,' I cast my mind back. Mine were New Balance trail shoes. I conjured up an image of Tris in my mind. The trouble was, it was conjuring – how much was real and how much was imagination was hard to say. 'Nike. I would say I was pretty certain they were Nike. But they'll still be at his house, you could check.'

'Oh, I will, don't worry. How about Cassandra?'

'Lululemon.' I knew that, they were very attractive.

'Good,' said Slattery with approval. What was this? Footwear fetish night?

'And Matt Spicer?'

'Well, that's easy. He had those weird shoes with individual toes. Green, to be precise. Why are you asking me all this?'

'There's a flowerbed outside the living room window of

272

Tris and Lizzie's cottage,' Slattery said. He looked very serious now. 'There hadn't been any rain for a while so the ground was bone-dry, but the flowerbed had been watered by the gardener the day before Tris was murdered. I was looking at the photos, there are indentation marks in the soil that are from Five Finger Shoes as I believe those trainers are called.'

'So Matt was peering through his window?' I said excitedly. Motive, sexual jealousy. Presence at the crime scene, it seemed to be all coming together, at least in my fevered mind. 'Are you going to arrest him?'

Slattery smiled indulgently. 'All in good time, Charlie. You know that I told you he had an alibi?'

'Yeah, he was participating in that conference in Dublin.'

Slattery's smile broadened. 'Yes he was. He was indeed. Tris's phone records show he had texted Lizzie at ten to nine, so he was alive then. Cassandra called you just before ten o'clock, that gives us a one-hour window when the murder was committed. Now, Charlie, Matt claims to have been at that conference all the time.'

'Yeah, it was eight until ten wasn't it? Didn't he show you the date stamp on his recording of it?'

'He did indeed, Charlie. I called his colleague back again, it was a one hour conference but the time was not nine till ten but eight till nine.' He paused while I let the significance of this sink in. He had no alibi. Slattery continued, 'he must have doctored the display on his screen to read an hour later and I stupidly believed it.' He sighed, 'I guess I'm getting old and I'm too easily taken in by technology. If it hadn't been for old fashioned footprint evidence I would never have checked. Matt has no alibi at all.'

'So…'

He nodded. 'So not only could he have killed Tris, but his footprints show that he was there.'

'So he did do it!' I was jubilant. 'Cass is innocent!'

He shook his head. 'No, you really are jumping the gun, Charlie. There is no evidence at all to show that he did do it. But I am going to question him again, at least I will when he gets back from Dubai, he's with clients out there right now. He's due back tomorrow morning. I think I'll be taking him in for another interview. At the very least, I just thought you would like to know that the case is still being investigated. I'll call in tomorrow evening and let you know how things are going.'

'Thank you,' I said. I looked at Slattery's tough, tanned face with great affection. 'Thank you so much for letting me know.'

# Chapter Thirty-Four

'Oh, thank you, thank you, thank you…' It was Wednesday morning and I had just returned the diadem to Esther. She threw her arms around me and crushed me to her huge chest. It was like being enveloped by a very soft, fleshy mattress smelling strongly of some intensely floral perfume. She let me go and I took a step back to recover.

Esther looked radiantly happy. 'Was it Pascale?' she asked.

'Pascale.' I nodded.

Esther's face darkened. 'I knew it. Bitch.'

'Are you going to do anything about it?'

'I'm not quite sure what I could do. She might do the decent thing and apologise, or she might move out of the area, which is what I would prefer, quite frankly. But I'm not a confrontational person. After all, I guess I'll be seeing her tomorrow for the Litha celebration. I don't really want to cause a scene and I'm assuming that she doesn't either. I shall pray to the goddess to give me a solution.'

'That seems like a very sensible idea,' I said. We had won; I didn't see any need to make a big thing of it. My mind was so fixated on seeing Slattery to find out what was happening with Matt Spicer that it was hard to think about anything else.

'I'll be over in the early afternoon to set up for the Feast,' I said. 'Jess will be helping me.'

'Thank you so much, Charlie, you're a real friend.' She opened the box again and stared at the jewelled head-dress. 'Boy, this one went down to the wire.'

'Better late than never,' I remarked.

Later that day, after service, I called Esther. Now my plan to blackmail Pascale had worked, it was time to retrieve the bait.

'Could you do me a favour?'

'Yes, of course I can Charlie.'

'Could you invite Chris over on some kind of pretext, I need to speak to him. Ask him to call in at my place when he comes.'

'I'll do that, Charlie. When would be convenient?'

'Early this evening.'

'Will do. He's coming over today anyway, just to go over yet again the order of proceedings for the ritual tomorrow. It's the same every year, but better to make sure everyone knows their role… oh, I have to go, I'll call you back.'

She was as good as her word. Ten minutes later she was on the phone to me. 'He'll be over at your place at half five this evening. Are you going to tell me what this is about, Charlie?'

'It's just a question of house-keeping, Esther, I left something in his car.'

*

Chris was as good as his word, he came round at 5.20 and I made him a coffee.

'What's all this about, Charlie?' he asked. I had toyed with the idea of telling him the truth, but I didn't.

'It's your wedding anniversary soon isn't it?' I asked. 'The twenty-fourth of June.'

He looked surprised. 'Yes, how did you know?'

'Sandra told me.'

'Oh.' He was puzzled, he obviously wasn't sure where this was leading.

'I've made you both a cake,' I said. It was true. I had earlier that morning covered a chocolate gateau with rolled out fondant and piped 'Happy 30th Anniversary Chris and Sandra' and made little fondant pink and red roses. It looked very pretty. I was pleased with my handiwork. I love cake decoration.

'Thank you!' He looked genuinely touched.

'Can you unlock your car? Murdo will put it in the rear footwell so it won't slide around when you drive. It's in a cake box so it should be safe, but try not to brake suddenly, okay?'

'The car's unlocked.'

'Fine.' I stood up, went into the kitchen. Murdo looked at me expectantly.

'Go and put the cake in the car and get the other thing, where I told you to look.'

'Yes Chef. Under the passenger seat.'

'That's correct.'

I went back to Chris in the dining room and sat down opposite him.

'Did you get the diadem back?' he asked.

I nodded. 'Yeah, but I'm not going to talk about it, Chris. That chapter's closed.'

'I see. Well, I'm so relieved. It could have had catastrophic psychic repercussions. You've saved us all, Charlie, not just Esther.'

I mentally shook my head. I would have thought that the diadem, which was after all manmade from reset family jewellery belonging to a wealthy home counties woman, not mysteriously conjured up from the depths by the Lady of the Lake, like Excalibur, or created by dwarves like Odin's spear Gungnir, but by some jeweller in Gerrards Cross, would have approximately zero magic power. But they all believed, and that was kind of the point, I guess.

'I'll do an active visualisation with the goddess to ask her to visit her protection and benefaction on you.' He nodded to himself. 'That's the best way to repay you.' I was touched, he was obviously sincere. 'Thank you Charlie, and thank you for the cake.'

'You're welcome,' I said. 'Give my love to Esther.'

I watched through the window as he walked over to his Twingo and drove off.

That night, at 11 o'clock, Slattery was over, as promised. It was a short and to the point meeting. Matt Spicer had indeed visited the cottage that night, at 7.30.

'His lawyer was in attendance. Matt said he had wanted to speak to Tris about a "personal matter"' – Slattery allowed himself a humourless laugh – 'probably related to settling scores. Spicer said he had heard voices and music from the living room, and looked through the curtains which were drawn but not completely. There was a bottle on the table and Tris and Cassandra were in an embrace on the sofa. So he had left.'

'And you believed him?' I was incredulous. It all seemed to be working out so perfectly, and now this! To me it was obvious that he had bided his time until nearer the start of the Zoom call and then pounced.

'Yes, I did,' Slattery said. I scowled at him. He shook his head wearily. 'Charlie, you can glare at me all you like, there is simply no evidence whatsoever that Matt Spicer killed Tris Smith. While he did lie at first, we can't disprove this account. Just a few pieces of circumstantial evidence that do not add up to a coherent case. CPS would never authorise a charge on it. I'm sorry.'

And with that, I had to be content.

# Chapter Thirty-Five

The Thursday was taken up with the Midsummer Solstice feast of Litha. Esther had been resplendent in her robes and diadem, Pascale mysteriously absent. I had been too busy to think or draw breath and had finally crawled into bed about 2.00.

I was still feeling gloomy the following morning. It was a Friday and it was another busy day ahead. I woke early and felt too exhausted to go running, I'd only had about four hours' sleep. It was 6 o'clock and I hauled myself out of bed and blearily washed and dressed. I also felt flat and depressed now the adrenaline of the night before had worn off. It seemed so obvious to me that Cassandra hadn't killed Tris but everyone was happy to pin the blame on her when she had simply been cruelly used. Tris had got her so drunk she had passed out so he could have his evil way with her and someone else had framed her. End of. Simple as.

I didn't think for one moment she had killed him in blackout. Maybe if she had a history of violence. I could well imagine a totally sloshed Cliff Yeats killing someone, or obviously Matt Spicer come to that, but not Cass.

I tried to stop thinking about her by losing myself in work, yawning and rubbing my eyes. On autopilot, I made a couple of carrot cakes and while they were cooking in the oven, I started cracking eggs and separating them for the meringues when there was a knock on the kitchen door. It was more of a demanding rap than a knock. There was nothing hesitant or nuanced about it, it was one of those insistent knocks that means, let me in, now.

I sighed with irritation and glanced up at the kitchen clock, it was 7.50. I rinsed my hands and opened the door. There, framed in the doorway, partially obscured by the long silver fly chains, stood the Earl.

The Earl, James Rupert Harrington Winslow, the Earl of Hampden Green, to give him his full name, although obviously most people referred to him as either simply the Earl or Earl Hampden, was an imposing figure. Six foot four, with silver-grey hair and matching moustache, piercing, grey eyes and a steel-hard demeanour, he was borderline frightening. His clothes, as ever, looked expensive and tailored to fit, probably because they were. Today he was wearing tweed trousers and a linen shirt. He was terrifically popular in the village because although he was crazily aristocratic and rich as Croesus, he somehow had the common touch. And he was certainly larger than life.

'Good morning, Charlie,' he said, icily, his gaze traversing me in my whites, 'you look terrible.'

I gave him a withering look and a kind of half sneer by way of reply. It bounced off him. His eyes swept around my kitchen with a look of, at best indifferent curiosity, but more, in my opinion, with a kind of contempt, as if to say, so this how the peasants live. He was very misanthropic. The Earl favoured animals over people, he was a zealous eco-activist. For all his faults, I kind of liked him. Maybe because I was a pleb and centuries of downtrodden servitude was encoded in my genes.

'And what can I do for you?' I replied. I never really knew what to call him. 'James' sounded, to my ears anyway, slightly ridiculous. I believe the correct way to address an Earl is to call them, 'my Lord', but that would have sounded equally stupid. So I settled with not using anything when I was talking to him.

'Can we talk?' It wasn't really a question, I wasn't going to say no, how could I? Besides, I was overcome with curiosity as to what this could be about.

'Yeah, sure, come in. We'll go through to the restaurant.'

I ushered him in and he sat down in a chair and stared at me opposite him.

'What did you want to talk about?' I asked.

'Cassandra Jenkins.'

'Sure.' I looked at him in surprise. It had been several days since I'd made the request via Bryony as to whether or not he could find anything on those spy cameras of his. I'd assumed nothing had come of it. I looked at him through narrowed eyes. You never knew where you stood with the Earl, he could be a real bastard at times. If you weren't an animal, preferably endangered, you were of little concern to him.

I wondered what he might have to tell me that would be of any use to her case.

'I gather that there is a lack of credible alternatives to Cassandra as the killer,' he said.

'Unfortunately that's correct. Everyone seems to have an alibi or lacks sufficient evidence against them for the police to proceed.'

'Well,' he raised an eyebrow, 'we'll see about that.' He uncrossed his long legs and leaned forward. 'Well, there are five of them, surveillance cameras that is. One of them is deployed to monitor the passing place by the entrance to Monksland's Field on the road between here and Potter's Hill.'

'That's presumably the place where they keep dumping the mattresses and stuff like that.' I knew the lay-by well. There was a long, metal-barred gate between a gap in the hawthorn hedgerow. I'd run past it just the other day, sure enough some bastard had dumped yet another mattress, this one green coloured, the other side of the gate.

'Yes, that's the place.' He took his phone out of his pocket and showed me an image. It was of a car that seemed familiar, a VW of some make or other, I only knew that because of the logo, but it rang a bell. It was obviously night-time but the number plate was clearly visible. It was labelled with the date and time at the bottom, 21:30 on May 30.

'That's the night Tris was killed.' I said with surprise.

'Exactly,' he leaned back in his chair and said with quiet triumph, 'and this car belongs to Lizzie Summers.'

I blinked at him rather stupidly as the implications of what he was saying sank in. Slattery had told me that David Summers had said that Lizzie was down in Chichester over that weekend, and here was definitive proof that she wasn't. The chances of some third party using her car and killing her fiancé would be practically zero. Lizzie had killed him. I closed my eyes for a moment and repeated that thought to myself. Lizzie had killed Tris. Not Matt Spicer as I had thought. Oh my God, I thought, Lizzie of all people. I still couldn't quite believe it.

'Do the police know this?' I asked.

'I'm on my way to Wycombe police station now,' he said. 'I know that Cassandra was a good friend of yours so I thought I would call in and put you out of your misery. I imagine it will take some time to investigate this, but I suspect that by the end of the week Cassandra should be free. I take it you have her lawyer's contact details?'

I nodded. 'I do.'

'Well, forward them to me and after I have spoken to Slattery, I will get in touch with them.'

He stood up.

'Thank you for coming.' I led him to the door and let him out into the car park. 'It's a huge weight off my mind.'

'As it will be for Cassandra, I'm sure,' he said drily.

I watched as he walked over to his dark blue Mercedes saloon and the expensive-looking vehicle glided silently out of my car park. I punched the air with savage joy. She didn't do it and it could be proved!

For some reason I thought of Chris and his promise to invoke the Triple Aspected Goddess on my behalf. Thank you Gaia, I breathed in grateful relief.

# Chapter Thirty-Six

The following morning I was savouring my double espresso at 9 o'clock while the soup for the Saturday lunch service, a chicken consommé. was simmering on the stove. I was also waiting for two large pans of water to boil so I could cook off some carrots and green beans for vegetable sides, when my phone rang.

It was Hamilton to say that he had just been informed that David Summers had been taken into custody and charged with the murder of Tris Smith.

'Seriously!' I hadn't expected this. 'Not Lizzie?'

'No, apparently not.' His voice was as dry and dispassionate as ever. 'I had a call from the police as a courtesy to inform me that a suspect had been arrested and that charges against my client, and your friend, Cassandra Jenkins, were going to be dropped. A notice of discontinuance will be issued by the CPS and she should be released very soon, almost certainly by the end of the day.'

'That is fantastic news.' I had no idea things would happen so fast. 'Thank you so much for telling me.'

He laughed. 'I knew that you would want to know. It was a pleasure seeing you again, Charlie Hunter.'

'And you.'

We said our goodbyes and I finished my coffee and went back into the kitchen. It was ironic really that Summers had hired me, and it was a result of my idea, that the Earl's cameras might have recorded something, that he was now in a cell for murder. Everything was going smoothly. Cassandra was as good as free and I had managed to get the diadem back in time. Then at lunchtime things got even better. I had a text from Andrea apologising for not being in touch, but there were family issues and work was very pressured. He was going to be in London for a couple of days for discussions with lawyers, would I be free to meet up at Heathrow on Wednesday, Terminal 3 before he flew back to Bologna at 5.00 for meetings. My heart leaped, my cup runneth over as Sandra would say. Or I was happy as a sandboy as Francis would put it.

Then I looked at the date for my rendezvous with Andrea, that would be the 26th. I had a birthday party booked that night; it would be a stretch but I wanted to see him so much that I texted back immediately. 'Can do coffee and cake, meet you at Caffè Nero, Terminal 3 in the Arrivals area.'

'3pm?'

I sent him a thumbs-up message and a heart. It was far from perfect, but it was a lot better than nothing. I turned my attention to the prep for the rest of the day.

At closing time that night, Slattery visited me. I had been kind of expecting him. I got the Armagnac out and I joined him in a glass, I was celebrating Cass's release. She was home with her mother, she had messaged me earlier. She said that normal service would be resumed in the coming week.

'So,' I said, 'David Summers.'

'David Summers indeed,' Slattery confirmed. 'After the Earl brought us that camera footage of Lizzie's car,' thanks to me, I thought proudly, 'we went round to his house in Chichester to interview the two of them. He said he had something he wanted to get off his chest and basically, when we took him down the police station he asked for a lawyer to be present. He had a word with him, and then confessed to Tris Smith's murder. In addition to that, we're still waiting for confirmation, but there are traces of dried blood in the car which I think we can safely assume will have come from Tris Smith. Summers must have been quite blood-stained by the stabbing, not least when he smeared the blood over Cassandra to make it look like she was the guilty party. Not that we need corroborative evidence but it's there, should we do.'

'That was surprising,' I said. 'I don't mean that there was blood in the car, but that he did it.'

'How do you mean?'

'Well, I thought he was trying to get her to break it off… that seemed to be his plan. Not direct action.' I explained to Slattery how and why he had hired me.

He shrugged. 'Well, now you've told me all that it makes it not surprising at all. If Lizzie had married Tris, the chances are that she would have come to a sticky end sooner rather than later. He'd have taken her for everything he could while she was alive. I take it she was paying for that cottage and the lifestyle. David Summers was obviously footing the bill.'

'Yeah, almost certainly. Industry wages aren't high. Tris would have been earning a good salary for restaurants, but nowhere near as much as say a train driver or a very junior civil servant.'

'And no' – Slattery's fingers sketched quotation marks in the air – '"working from home".'

I laughed. 'No, none of that. Ten in the morning until half eleven or midnight, five days a week. Six or seven if they were short-staffed.'

'Presumably he thought even if he told Lizzie everything you had found out, it would have made no difference.'

'That's exactly what I think. I reckon Summers had turned up maybe hoping to buy Tris out, tell him he was putting his money where Lizzie couldn't touch it, maybe a trust fund, and in the event of her death it would all go elsewhere. Then when he saw Tris assaulting an unconscious woman, something snapped.'

'Well, it didn't stop him doing a very good job of framing Cassandra Jenkins who could well be doing thirty years no parole for his murder.'

'Well,' I gestured vaguely, 'I never said he was a nice man. He's certainly stiffed me over payment.'

Slattery smiled. 'You don't get rich by being nice.'

I laughed. 'Are you turning socialist in your old age?'

He grinned. 'Yeah. Older, stiffer and more left-wing.' He proffered his empty glass to me. 'Any chance of some more?'

'Sure.' I got up, went behind the bar and topped him

up. I glanced at the clock, 11.30. I had to be up at 7 o'clock. I yawned. 'Well, that's one murder solved. How about the crossbow killer?'

Slattery drummed his fingers on the table. 'I don't know. We've just drawn a complete blank. John Mayhew was not a popular man. He was deeply disliked by most people – "cantankerous old git" – was the majority opinion, and he was certainly hated by those he had wronged... It's odd that we should have two killers in the same area, but Summers is adamant he had nothing to do with Mayhew's death and I can't see he has any reason to lie. I suppose that we still have a killer on the loose.'

'Matt Spicer,' I said hopefully.

'Quite possibly, but there is absolutely no evidence that he killed him. Then there was the attack on Tris Smith himself...'

'Spicer again, I would suggest.' My mind went back to when I had seen him in the wood, that same day I had discovered Tris and Cass together.

'Once again, who knows?' Slattery was not going to be drawn.

'Well, anyway... Cass's out now, cheers!'

We clinked glasses, downed our drinks and he left.

# Chapter Thirty-Seven

After service on Sunday at 3 o'clock, when the last customers had left the restaurant, I sat wearily down with Jess and we opened the last bottle of the Washington State Cabernet.

'Cassandra is coming round on Tuesday, first thing,' I said as I poured us each a large glass of wine.

'Good job too,' Jess said. 'I was wondering what we were going to do when that nice wine ran out.'

I smiled. 'Cheers!' We clinked glasses. I was feeling exhausted. The business with Tris Smith had left me emotionally drained, as well as out of pocket. You bastard, David Summers, I thought. Why couldn't you have just killed him outright without me having to waste your money and my time and energy going to Oxford and Scotland and trying to teach Lizzie to cook. Then the emotional wear and tear of the Cassandra business, not to mention having to find out who had stolen the diadem and getting it back.

When I saw Andrea on Wednesday I would tell him I was free for a week's holiday. I didn't care where, just him and me. We'd drink, eat and have sex nightly. And I wouldn't do any cooking, nor would I think about anyone else's troubles; there would just be the two of us. Probably at the Davaar View. It would be nice and quiet. Just us and the midges in the rain.

'What are you smiling about?' Jess asked curiously.

'Oh, nothing,' I replied innocently, my thoughts far from innocent.

'I see you've still got Tris's laptop,' Jess said.

I groaned. Slattery had returned it. Thanks for reminding me, I thought. It was one of those jobs that you really should do, but you are continually putting it off. I kept seeing the slim silver computer every time I went into my office and I kept meaning to take it back to Lizzie's. So far I hadn't. I couldn't imagine she would want it for one moment. What would there be in there for her? Only pain if she ever got to read his womanising notes, or maybe, I suddenly thought, closure. If she did ever read that horrible log of women remorselessly stalked then seduced and rated out of ten for sexual performance and gratification (his, not theirs), then she would realise she was much better off without him and lobby for her father's early release. It wasn't like he was a threat to anyone else.

Later that afternoon, after Jess was gone, I wandered around my empty restaurant and flat feeling restless and strangely dissatisfied. Maybe it was because everything was sorted, more or less. I would have gone for a drink with Murdo, but he was in Oxford with Lucy. 'Sod it,' I said. Time to grasp the nettle. I went into my office and picked up the laptop and, resisting the temptation to just chuck it into the wheelie bin with the rest of my general rubbish, got into my car and drove the short distance to Potter's Hill.

It was a lovely summer's late afternoon. I guess we were maybe technically still in Spring, I only have a hazy idea of when these things begin and end. The hawthorn hedge-rows, recently clipped, framed the narrow, single-track road with a brilliant green border. The verges though hadn't been trimmed and long, feathery grasses and nettles swayed in the gentle breeze, occasionally brushing the wing mirror of my car. I glanced down at the silver laptop sitting on the passenger seat. It looked so innocuous yet contained the sordid details of Tris's sex life. Life was the right word. Chasing, hunting women, seemed to have dominated his every waking hour. Maybe, I thought, he was just as addicted to sex as Cassandra was to booze. Would I be as censorious of her if Jess hacked her laptop and it was full of details of how many men she had slept with, complete with details of penis length and girth and staying power? I smiled at the thought. Strickland, innately competitive, would want to know where he stood in the rankings – that was for sure.

Anyway, my responsibility was to return someone else's property, that was all. And I was not going to speak to Lizzie, that was definite. I would drop the laptop off in the shed by the side of the cottage.

I pulled up in the small parking space near the duck pond, and, carrying the laptop, walked back down the road to the cottage. There was no sign of anyone, good, she was out. I let myself in the gate, walked along by the side of the house and down to the shed. The shed door was unlocked and I went in. I stood for a moment breathing in the cool air of the shed, which smelled strongly of shed. That strange musty generic smell of wood shavings, chemicals, a tang of metal, the earthy, woolly scent of sacking. A shed is like a church or a school or a hospital, you would be able to guess where you were if someone brought you in blind-folded.

I looked around for a place to prominently display the computer so Lizzie wouldn't miss it. It wasn't a big space. There was an electric lawnmower, a strimmer, and a leaf-blower occupying one corner. A large, full wine rack, Tris's legacy. A couple of rakes and a fork and spade. There was an old chest of drawers with various items like watering cans and plant pots on top, and at the end, under the window, so dirty it was opaque, the light dimly filtering through, a hefty workbench and an old Windsor-style chair. I walked over to the bench. There was something wrapped in canvas cloth lying there. I put my hand out to move it to make space for the computer and I felt what appeared to be a rifle butt. I was intrigued. I lifted the canvas. My mouth gaped and my eyes widened in astonishment. I was looking down at a crossbow.

It was sinister to look at, jet-black and metallic, with a telescopic sight on top and a trigger underneath. I thought to myself, so it was Tris who was behind the shooting after all, I knew it, and suddenly I felt an explosion in my head and darkness closed around me.

Light returned to my vision. Sensations of constriction; I swallowed painfully. Unconsciousness had come like a light switch being pressed or when you get an anaesthetic in a hospital. But whereas you snap out of an anaesthetic like you've just blinked, this was like groggily swimming upwards into consciousness, and I was aware that I had a splitting headache.

I opened my eyes. I was bound to the Windsor chair that I had noticed earlier. About four circles of nylon rope wound their way across my chest. And standing in front of me was Lizzie.

'What the hell are you doing?' I said, bewildered.

'I'm sorry, Charlie. I came back the other day.' Her voice was level, reasonable, as if we were having a nice chat, 'but you saw the crossbow. And now you know I killed that man, I can't let you go now.'

I then realised the stupidity of my earlier mistake. It hadn't been Tris at all then who had killed John Mayhew.

I blinked stupidly. 'But why?'

'Well, two birds with one stone, Charlie. Mayhew had stolen money from us, and I couldn't let that pass. Tris was too sweet-natured to do anything about it. He thought that if he were nice to Mayhew, he would return the money, or at least do what he promised to do.' Well, she'd obviously never read his emails, I thought, but of course, Tris wouldn't allow her anywhere near his laptop. 'He had it all worked out, but I knew it was a waste of time. Then I found out something that really upset me.'

'What was that?' Like I cared, but I couldn't say that. Please let me go, I willed.

'Tris was having an affair with that slut Suzi,' she explained. 'She obviously seduced him, my poor Tris was easily swayed, he was weak in that way.' She shook her head and sighed. 'But if I'd killed her, well, he might have suspected it was me, or the police might have. So I decided to kill another of the running group so people would think that they were being targeted.'

'And you also fired at Tris!'

'Well, duh, yes.' She opened her mouth and shook her head in a parody of my stupidity. 'But I wasn't going to hit him. That was a red herring to draw attention away from us… I'm a bloody good shot. Look, I'll show you.'

She picked up the crossbow and put a bolt or an arrow or whatever it's called into the groove that ran along the top and pulled the metal cord back. There's no need to show me, Lizzie, I thought, I'm happy to take your word for it.

'I've always been interested in crossbows, Charlie,' she said, almost dreamily. 'You know it's part of my heritage…' What was she on about? Then came a left of field question: 'What was your favourite book as a kid?'

'I don't know!' I almost wailed. I didn't read much. I've never been a book person.

She frowned. 'Think!'

'Mog the Cat,' I gasped, 'I loved Mog.'

'Mine was William Tell. My mum was Swiss, you never knew that did you.'

'No.' I also hadn't got a clue who William Tell was.

'Yeah, she died when I was young, it was a bond I shared with Tris. Didn't Daddy tell you?'

'No, I just assumed she'd left.' Like mine had done. But Lizzie had lost interest in her dead mother.

'You do know who William Tell was, don't you?' she asked. 'Tris knew, bless him, he was very well-educated, but he told me a lot of British people haven't heard of him. Have you?'

I just knew that in Tris's meticulous notes there was bound to be a reference to William Tell. He would have stalked Lizzie as painstakingly as all the others, utilising his IEA principles, maybe more so since money was what he was after. He would have boned up on all things Swiss.

'No, I haven't heard of William Tell.' No point in lying. I could see that Lizzie was enjoying playing with me like a cat with a mouse. I suppose normally she was down-trodden, by her father, by Tris, by the world because she was fat and dumpy, and, I realised, by me – who had patronised her because she had no idea about cooking. Here was payback time. The revenge of the weak on the strong. I was only just beginning to realise how much she probably hated me. It was not a happy feeling.

'Well, Tris was brainy, he'd been to uni' – she shook her head pityingly –'not like you.' The tone in her voice was one of utter contempt. 'One of the things I can't stand about you, Charlie, is that you're a thicko, a stupid woman who works in a kitchen and gives herself airs and graces that she's not entitled to.' There was real venom in her voice now. There was no probably about it, she did hate me. If it were possible, my heart sank a little more. 'He was a Swiss hero,' she informed me. 'He assassinated a tyrant and fought for Switzerland's freedom against the Austrians.' She frowned. 'Are you sure you've never heard of him and his son?'

'No,' I muttered.

'You're in for a treat. I've just got to go and get something. Hang on.' She grinned and I realised I had never seen her so happy. 'Don't run away now.'

The door closed behind her and I struggled to get free, without any success. I was certainly seeing a new side to Lizzie. An hour or so ago I didn't think that she was good at anything, now I learned, she was good at shooting, good at killing people, good at tying knots and good at getting away with stuff. Also that she loathed me. And so what if I hadn't been to university, neither had she. But the difference was of course, she was rich. And, quite probably, insane.

I toyed with the idea of toppling the chair over on its side, maybe that would help, but I didn't see how. All it would do would hurt me, make a loud crash and anger Lizzie. I was still looking around the shed for inspiration when the door opened and she entered.

'Found what I needed,' she said and produced an apple, of all things. Why? I had a terrible feeling of apprehension about what I was about to find out. I had a sudden vision of a medieval roast pig with an apple in its mouth. I shuddered.

She picked up the crossbow with one hand and balanced the apple on my head.

'Don't move!' she said warningly, 'or I'll shoot you in the face.'

There was something peculiarly horrible about the thought of this. I did not want to be shot in the face. I sat bolt upright, totally still. I wanted to do everything in my power to appease her. I wanted to put off the inevitable as long as possible. There was always the chance that someone might rescue me. While there was life there was hope.

Lizzie took up a position at the end of the shed opposite me. I sat stock-still, hardly daring to breathe, the apple precariously balanced on my crown.

'William Tell did this.' She smiled at me. 'The tyrant had heard that he was a crack shot, so he had Tell's son tied to a tree and he balanced an apple on the child's head and ordered Tell to shoot the apple. He did, perfectly. So, I'm recreating it for your benefit.'

She raised the crossbow, pointed it at my head. I thought, it's only a distance of a couple of metres, she can't miss.

I heard the sound of the bow as she pulled the trigger, a momentary sensation of something flying towards me and then the thud as the arrow buried itself in the wall of the shed next to the window.

'Hurrah!' She looked childishly delighted with her shooting, then she looked at me and an expression of cold evaluation immediately replaced it. My turn, I thought. I felt bile rise in my throat. Keep her talking, I thought.

'So what happened the night Tris died?' I asked.

'I knew he was upset after what he thought was a near-death experience,' she said. 'He never suspected for a moment that it was me behind that crossbow. So I thought I would pay him a surprise visit and cheer him up. You know' – she looked coy – 'in a womanly way. But when I walked up the garden path I could see the curtains were drawn and that made me suspicious.'

'Why?'

'Tris was claustrophobic, he didn't like drawing the curtains, said it made him anxious, so when I saw them closed I knew something was wrong.'

Her face hardened. 'There was a gap in the middle and I looked through.' Just like Matt Spicer, I thought. I had a vision of a queue of Peeping Toms lining up to gawp through Lizzie's curtains. I had a crazy desire to laugh, hysteria I suppose. I clamped my teeth together and swallowed the urge. She carried on. 'I could see he was playing with her breasts, well, not that she has any worth speaking of, and I could see her eyes were closed and she was kind of slumped there. That's when I knew what I had to do.'

'How do you mean?'

'Well, it was obvious' – she shook her head pityingly – 'you really don't understand men, do you? Can't you see Charlie, he was weak and he couldn't help himself, not with all those women throwing themselves at him.'

I marvelled at this, then I found some courage to speak up for Cassandra. I think by now I thought I had very little to lose. I was sick of listening to her. Besides, I realised I hated her guts. 'But she was unconscious and drunk,' I protested.

'Exactly my point!' Lizzie said triumphantly.

I think she was enjoying our conversation, it was giving her an unparalleled opportunity to justify her actions to an audience, admittedly a captive audience, but you can't have everything.

'I'm afraid you've lost me.'

'She got drunk deliberately to lead him on and then to deliberately make herself helpless so he would have no option but to molest her. She knew his weakness, she knew he couldn't resist, and she played on it, with virtuoso skill.'

'Oh.' So it was her fault he was trying to assault her. Not his.

'And her plan worked. He was busy unbuttoning her blouse, one hand inside when I walked in with that knife of mine you so admired the other day. I'd gone in the back door and picked it up as I went through to them.'

'The Sabatier?'

She nodded. 'That's the one. I thought about how she had wronged me and I thought the best punishment would be for her to take the blame for his death, because, after all, if she hadn't led him on he would still be alive. Prison is the best place for that home-wrecker.'

'But why kill Tris?'

'Like I said Charlie, he was a nice man, but he was weak.' She shook her head sadly. 'I decided that enough was enough.' She shook her head again. 'He didn't suffer, it was quick. I'm sure you would agree it was for the best.' She said, almost sadly, 'sometimes you have to do these things.'

She really is crazy, I thought. Then, I still hate her.

'And your dad is taking the blame for all of this?' I was incredulous.

She shrugged. 'He's old and ill. He won't end up doing thirty years, maybe five, ten tops, before he kicks the bucket... maybe he'll lose his marbles and won't even know he's in prison. Anyway,' she added sotto voce, 'it's not like it's the first time he's covered up for me...' Oh my God, how many more times have you done this, I wondered. 'Okay then Charlie, I'll make this quick too.' She pulled the cord of the crossbow back and fitted an arrow into the long groove on the top. 'It'll be painless.' She walked over to me and stood looking down into my eyes, holding the crossbow in her left hand.

I felt sick and faint with fear. I screwed my eyes shut. Then I heard a series of raps that must have come from the knocker on the backdoor. I opened my mouth to scream for help but Lizzie moved incredibly fast. There was an old tea towel lying on the bench and she seized it with her free hand and shoved it into my open mouth, pushing so hard I thought my neck might snap. I tasted dust, sawdust and old paint. She dropped the crossbow and grabbed a reel of gaffer tape which she tugged at with her teeth, all the while jamming the cloth into my mouth while I retched and gurgled. Then when she had a couple of centimetres free of the tape she wound it round my head a few times, securing the gag. I made inaudible, muffled sounds, my eyes bulging out of their sockets.

More rapping on the back door. Then a hoarse, loud voice.

'Hello, I know there's someone in. I'm here on the Lord's business and His mission will be heeded.'

It was Sandra. Help me God, I prayed, you have sent your emissary…

'Oh for God's sake,' Lizzie muttered. She checked the ropes binding me then went to the shed door, opened it, went out and closed it firmly behind her. I carried on praying; if Sandra was here, maybe Jesus was too. Smite her God like you did the priests of Baal. I remembered the story from my C of E primary school and my copy of the Children's Bible.

'What do you want?' she said irritably to Sandra. They were obviously both in the side passage just a couple of metres away from me.

'I am a voice crying in the wilderness,' Sandra replied. She made it sound quite menacing.

I took a deep breath, it was now or never. Gritting my teeth, I hurled the weight of my bound body to the left and the chair crashed over on its side. The noise was considerable, to me it was an ear-splitting crash, I only hoped it was audible.

'What was that?' Sandra asked sharply. I could hear suspicion in her voice.

'Nothing,' Lizzie said in that obviously guilty tone which meant, I don't want you to ask what's going on.

I was lying on the floor, looking up at the garden implements propped against the wall. Two rakes, one for leaves and the other, T-shaped, for soil. A spade, a garden fork and a hoe. All made of metal. I jerked my body and my knees attached to the chair, moved forward enough to knock into them. They toppled around me in a metallic cacophony.

'What's going on in there?' Sandra demanded to know. She sounded quite bellicose now, as did Lizzie.

'Mice.'

'Bollocks,' Sandra said. 'Mice my arse.' Bet Elijah never said that, I thought hysterically.

'None of your business, anyway,' Lizzie snapped. 'Now leave, please.'

'Not before I've seen what's going on.' Sandra sounded adamant. I prayed, prayed fervently that she would open the door.

'Well, you can't.'

Sandra had never been one to take no for an answer.

'You try and stop me!' she growled.

I couldn't see what was going on, but judging by the sudden, loud groan, I guessed that Lizzie had tried and that

Sandra had hit her. Lizzie would be no match for her in a fight.

I made frantic loud moaning noises as I couldn't open my mouth, well as loud as possible through the fabric of the tea towel and the gaffer tape. I heard the door being flung open.

'Oh my God! Charlie!' Then she spun round. I heard her say, 'Oh no you don't… you fat bitch,' followed by a loud thud and a crash. I guessed Sandra had felled Lizzie properly. Then she was in the shed, hauling the chair with me attached to it effortlessly upwards. She cut the ropes at the back with a pair of secateurs from the bench and I gently pulled the tape off my face and spat out the foul-tasting towel.

'Sandra!'

I threw my arms around her and burst into tears. I have never in my life been so pleased to see a doorstepping evangelist. Or an ex-Hells Angel.

'Jesus saves!' I gasped into her ear.

'Of course He does, Charlie,' she said, patting me on the back, 'of course He does! He never lets you down.'

# Chapter Thirty-Eight

I was having my second double espresso on the Wednesday at 3.05 at Caffè Nero in Terminal 3 at Heathrow when I saw Andrea walking towards me. He must have checked in his suitcase already, he only had a small bag that I guessed by its shape contained his laptop.

I waved at him, he saw me and came over. He was handsomer than ever, wearing a light-grey two-piece suit and a serious expression. The meeting with the lawyers can't have gone well.

'Hi, darling,' I jumped up and called out as he approached. If anything, his serious expression deepened. Oh, God, I was feeling thoroughly alarmed now, someone must be ill in his family, or worse.

'Hello, Charlie,' he said, no trace of a smile. I began to get a cold, sinking feeling in the pit of my stomach. No, no, no, this can't be happening. My legs felt unaccountably weak. The welcoming grin on my face froze, then slowly disappeared.

'Er, is everything okay, Andrea?' My mouth suddenly dry, my heart beating too fast, this isn't happening. 'Can I get you a coffee?'

He shook his head. 'This is difficult, Charlie.' I knew then what he was going to say, and it wasn't that he'd given up coffee.

I waited for the axe to fall. For the guillotine blade to crash down on my outstretched neck.

'I wanted to say this in person, not in a message or a text.' He breathed deeply. 'I've met someone else. I'm afraid it's over.'

'Oh.' It was all I could manage. He'd obviously rehearsed his little speech. Eight words or so. What could I say? He looked at me, I stared at him. Idiotically I came out with, 'Who is she?'

He frowned in a kind of exasperated way. It was an expression I knew very well. He'd done a lot of exasperated frowning over the years. 'She's a doctor, an Italian doctor... does it matter?'

'No, I'm sorry.' I don't know why I was apologising.

'Goodbye, Charlie.'

And that was that.

I watched him turn away and walk to where the Departures were. I took a deep breath and closed my eyes momentarily. I wasn't going to cry, but when I opened them they were wet. But I wasn't crying.

I could still see him in the distance.

'Bon voyage, baby,' I whispered.

I left the café and headed for the car park. I had a party that night to cater for. Another birthday party. Thank God I'd already done the icing.

*

Eight hours later, I was sitting in my now empty restaurant with Jess after a busy service. I was exhausted. Jess was heart-broken. She had been convinced that Andrea was the one for me and she felt personally betrayed as well as sad for me.

The party had gone well. My chef's whites were still damp with sweat from the heat of the kitchen but the adrenaline high was still pumping round my body from having executed not only the party for ten but about thirty other flawless main courses in three hours. I thought, and tomorrow I'll be doing it all over again. Like Sisyphus in Greek mythology endlessly pushing his boulder up the mountain. But I was feeling tough and indestructible. Besides, I loved my boulder.

I had survived Lizzie's attack and I had survived being dumped by Andrea. What does not kill me makes me stronger, well, that was how I felt anyway. I had been in two major battles, one physical and one emotional, and I was still standing.

After Andrea's bombshell news I had driven home in a kind of numb shock. I'd broken my vow to myself not to cry, but that had been between the M25 exit for the M40 and the Beaconsfield services cut-off, so only about six or seven minutes of waterworks. That was enough grieving, I decided. Rather than grieve, brooding about my broken heart, I had worked like I was possessed, in a kind of trance. The food was stupendous.

'Another drink?' Jess asked me, breaking into my thoughts.

'Yeah, one more and then bed for me. There's quite a lot of prep to do tomorrow morning.'

'I searched online for the death of Kirsten Summers,' Jess said. 'When you told me that Lizzie had said her mother was Swiss I looked her up, doing the search in German.'

'I didn't know you spoke German.'

'I don't, a friend of mine helped.' When she said the word 'friend' I noticed a faint blush in Jess's cheeks. Maybe more than just a friend, I thought to myself. 'Anyway, he found an article in the *Tages-Anzeiger*, which is a Zurich-based newspaper. Dominik.'

Dominik, I thought to myself. So that's his name, is it.

'Translated it for me. Ten years ago there was a terrible mishap. Kirsten Summers died in a tragic accident in the garden of her house in the country. Frau Summers was the vice president of the Bogensport Club. Bogen is the German for bow.'

'So her mother was a competitive archer.'

'Yeah. According to the article, she was killed by a crossbow bolt accidentally discharged by her husband, David. An inquiry ruled it was indeed accidental death.'

I thought back to what Lizzie had muttered as an aside '… it's not like it's the first time he's covered up for me…'

'Oh my God, she killed her own mother,' I murmured.

'It certainly looks that way, and David Summers covered up for her, like he tried to when he took the rap for Tris.' She looked at me critically. 'How are you feeling, Charlie?'

'Oh, don't worry about me, I'm over it.'

'I didn't mean Lizzie, I meant Andrea.'

'So did I,' I said. 'Strickland sent me a WhatsApp message, do you want to see?' I got my phone and found what I was looking for.

'Sorry to hear your news. People come, people go, it's the food that's important, and you're a good chef, Charlie. Respect.' I looked up at Jess. 'Smiley face.'

Jess looked genuinely baffled. 'I don't know what to make of that,' she confessed.

'It's the greatest compliment he could possibly pay me,' I said seriously. It had cheered me up enormously. Strickland felt that he'd been put on this earth to cook and I kind of shared that feeling. I'd been working in kitchens all my adult life. But unlike Strickland I had another string to my bow. I had a talent for crime-solving. I clinked glasses with her. 'We've got thirty booked in for lunch tomorrow, I haven't got time to waste thinking about him.'

That wasn't true at all. I couldn't stop thinking about him. But it would pass.

In the immortal words of Gloria Gaynor, I would survive.

# ABOUT THE AUTHOR

Photo credit © Alex Coombs

Alex Coombs was born in Lambeth in South London and studied Arabic at Oxford and Edinburgh Universities, and is a qualified chef. Alex lives in the Chilterns.

**www.alexcoombs.co.uk**

# NO EXIT PRESS
More than just the usual suspects

'A very smart, independent publisher delivering the finest literary crime fiction' *Big Issue*

MEET NO EXIT PRESS, an award-winning crime imprint bringing you the best in crime and suspense fiction. From classic detective novels, to page-turning spy thrillers and literary writing that grabs the attention. Our books are carefully crafted by some of the world's finest writers and delivered to you by a small, but passionate, team.

In over 30 years of business, we have published award-winning fiction and non-fiction including the work of a Pulitzer Prize winner, the British Crime Book of the Year, numerous CWA Dagger Awards, a British million-copy bestselling author, the winner of the Canadian Governor General's Award for Fiction and the Scotiabank Giller Prize, to name but a few. We are the home of many crime and noir legends from the USA whose work includes iconic film adaptations and TV sensations. We pride ourselves in uncovering the most exciting new or undiscovered talents. New and not so new – you know who you are!

We are a proactive team committed to delivering the very best, both for our authors and our readers.

Want to join the conversation and find out more about what we do?

Catch us on social media or sign up to our newsletter for all the latest news from No Exit Press.

**f** fb.me/noexitpress     **X** @noexitpress

**noexit.co.uk**